PENGUIN SCIENCE FICTION

THE BLACK CLOUD

Fred Hoyle, F.R.S., well known as an astronomer, writer, broadcaster, and television personality, was born at Bingley, Yorkshire, in 1915 and educated at Bingley Grammar School and Emmanuel College, Cambridge. A Fellow of St John's College, Cambridge, he was a university lecturer in mathematics from 1945 to 1958, when he was appointed to his present post as Plumian Professor of Astronomy and Experimental Philosophy. Since 1956 he has been a staff member at the Mount Wilson and Palomar Observatories, where he is able to use the world's largest reflector telescopes. He is visiting Professor of Astrophysics at the California Institute of Technology, and Director of the Institute of Theoretical Astronomy, Cambridge.

His other publications include *The Nature of the Universe* (1950; a Pelican), *A Decade of Decision* (1953), *Frontiers of Astronomy* (1956), *Of Men and Galaxies* (1965), and *Man in the Universe* (1966). His other novels are *Ossian's Ride* (1959), *Fifth Planet* (1963; with G. Hoyle) and *October the First is Too Late* (1966). Fred Hoyle, who expresses himself at one and the same time with the precision of a scientist and the bluntness of a Yorkshireman, has also published a play, *Rockets in Ursa Major* (1962), and is the joint author of *A for Andromeda* (1962).

FRED HOYLE

THE BLACK CLOUD

Leslie Swan,
St George's Cathedral House,
Westminster Bridge Rd,
SOUTHWARK, S.E.P.

PENGUIN BOOKS

April 1973

Penguin Books Ltd, Harmondsworth, Middlesex, England
Penguin Books Australia Ltd, Ringwood, Victoria, Australia

—

First published by William Heinemann Ltd 1957
Published in Penguin Books 1960
Reprinted 1961, 1963, 1964, 1965, 1967, 1968, 1971 (twice)

—

Copyright © Fred Hoyle, 1957

—

Made and printed in Great Britain
by Richard Clay (The Chaucer Press) Ltd, Bungay, Suffolk
Set in Monotype Times

PREFACE

I hope that my scientific colleagues will enjoy this frolic. After all, there is very little here that could not conceivably happen.

Since institutional posts that actually exist are mentioned in the story, I have been at particular pains to ensure that the associated characters have no reference to actual holders of these posts.

It is commonplace to identify opinions forcibly expressed by a character with the author's own. At the risk of triviality, I would add that this association may be unwarranted.

F. H.

CONTENTS

PROLOGUE

THE episode of the Black Cloud has always had a great fascination for me. The thesis that won me my Fellowship at Queens' College, Cambridge, was concerned with some aspects of this epic event. This work was later published, after suitable modifications, as a chapter in Sir Henry Clayton's History of the Black Cloud, *much to my gratification.*

It was not altogether surprising therefore that Sir John McNeil, our late Senior Fellow and well-known physician, should have willed to me on his death a voluminous collection of papers dealing with his own personal experiences of the Cloud. More surprising, however, was the letter that accompanied the papers. It read:

> Queens' College, 19 August 2020

My dear Blythe,

I trust you will forgive an old man for chuckling occasionally to himself over some of your speculations concerning the Black Cloud. As it happened, I was so placed during the crisis that I learned of the real nature of the Cloud. This information for various cogent reasons has never been made public and seems unknown to the writers of official histories (*sic!*). It has caused me much anxiety of mind to decide whether my knowledge should pass away with me or not. In the event I have decided to hand on my difficulties and uncertainties to you. These will I believe become clearer to you when you have read my MS., which, incidentally, I have written in the third person so that I myself do not obtrude too much on the story!

In addition to the MS., I am leaving you an envelope containing a roll of punched paper tape. I beg you to guard this tape with the greatest care until you come to understand its significance.

> Sincerely,
>
> JOHN MCNEIL

Chapter One

OPENING SCENES

It was eight o'clock along the Greenwich meridian. In England the wintry sun of 7 January 1964 was just rising. Throughout the length and breadth of the land people were shivering in ill-heated houses as they read the morning papers, ate their breakfasts, and grumbled about the weather, which, truth to tell, had been appalling of late.

The Greenwich meridian southward passes through western France over the snow-covered Pyrenees, and through the eastern corner of Spain. The line then sweeps to the west of the Balearic Islands, where wise people from the north were spending winter holidays – on a beach in Minorca a laughing party might have been seen returning from an early morning bathe. And so to North Africa and the Sahara.

The primary meridian then swings towards the equator through French Sudan, Ashanti, and the Gold Coast, where new aluminium plants were going up along the Volta River. Thence into a vast stretch of ocean, unbroken until Antarctica is reached. Expeditions from a dozen nations were rubbing elbows with each other there.

All the land to the east of this line, as far as New Zealand, was turned towards the Sun. In Australia, evening was approaching. Long shadows were cast across the cricket ground at Sydney. The last overs of the day were being bowled in a match between New South Wales and Queensland. In Java, fishermen were busying themselves in preparation for the coming night's work.

Over much of the huge expanse of the Pacific, over America, and over the Atlantic it was night. It was three a.m. in New York. The city was blazing with light, and there was still a good deal of traffic in spite of recent snow and a cold wind from the northwest. And nowhere on the Earth at that moment was there more activity than in Los Angeles. The evening was well along there, midnight: the boulevards were crowded, cars raced along the freeways, restaurants were still pretty full.

A hundred and twenty miles to the south the astronomers on Palomar Mountain had already begun their night's work. But although the night was clear and stars were sparkling from horizon to zenith, conditions from the point of view of the professional astronomer were poor, the 'seeing' was bad – there was too much wind at high levels. So nobody was sorry to down tools for the midnight snack. Earlier in the evening, when the outlook for the night already looked pretty dubious, they had agreed to meet in the dome of the 48-inch Schmidt.

Paul Rogers walked the four hundred yards or so from the 200-inch telescope to the Schmidt, only to find Bert Emerson was already at work on a bowl of soup. Andy and Jim, the night assistants, were busy at the cooking stove.

'Sorry I got started,' said Emerson, 'but it looks as though tonight's going to be a complete write-off.'

Emerson was working on a special survey of the sky, and only good observing conditions were suitable for his work.

'Bert, you're a lucky fellow. It looks as though you're going to get another early night.'

'I'll keep on for another hour or so. Then if there's no improvement I'll turn in.'

'Soup, bread and jam, sardines, and coffee,' said Andy. 'What'll you have?'

'A bowl of soup and cup of coffee, thanks,' said Rogers.

'What're you going to do on the 200-inch? Use the jiggle camera?'

'Yes, I can get along tonight pretty well. There's several transfers that I want to get done.'

They were interrupted by Knut Jensen, who had walked the somewhat greater distance from the 18-inch Schmidt.

He was greeted by Emerson.

'Hello, Knut, there's soup, bread and jam, sardines, and Andy's coffee.'

'I think I'll start with soup and sardines, please.'

The young Norwegian, who was a bit of a leg-puller, took a bowl of cream of tomato, and proceeded to empty half a dozen sardines into it. The others looked on in astonishment.

'Judas, the boy must be hungry,' said Jim.

Knut looked up, apparently in some surprise.

'You don't eat sardines like this? Ah, then you don't know the real way to eat sardines. Try it, you'll like it.'

Then having created something of an effect, he added:

'I thought I smelled a skunk around just before I came in.'

'Should go well with that concoction you're eating, Knut,' said Rogers.

When the laugh had died away, Jim asked:

'Did you hear about the skunk we had a fortnight ago? He degassed himself near the 200-inch air intake. Before anybody could stop the pump the place was full of the stuff. It sure was some hundred per cent stink. There must have been the best part of two hundred visitors inside the dome at the time.'

'Lucky we don't charge for admission,' chuckled Emerson, 'otherwise the Observatory'd be sunk in for compensation.'

'But unlucky for the clothes cleaners,' added Rogers.

On the way back to the 18-inch Schmidt, Jensen stood listening to the wind in the trees on the north side of the mountain. Similarities to his native hills set off an irrepressible wave of homesickness, longing to be with his family again, longing to be with Greta. At twenty-four, he was in the United States on a two-year studentship. He walked on, trying to kick himself out of what he felt to be a ridiculous mood. Rationally he had no cause whatsoever to be dispirited. Everyone treated him with great kindness, and he had a job ideally suited to a beginner.

Astronomy is kind in its treatment of the beginner. There are many jobs to be done, jobs that can lead to important results but which do not require great experience. Jensen's was one of these. He was searching for novae, stars that explode with uncanny violence. Within the next year he might reasonably hope to find one or two. Since there was no telling when an outburst might occur, nor where in the sky the exploding star might be situated, the only thing to do was to keep on photographing the whole sky, night after night, month after month. Some day he would strike lucky. It was true that, should he find a nova located not too far away in the depths of space, then more experienced hands than his would take over the work. Instead of the 18-inch Schmidt, the full power of the great 200-inch would then be directed to revealing the spectacular secrets of these strange stars. But at all events he would have the honour of first discovery. And the experience he was gaining in the world's greatest observatory would stand well in his favour when he returned home – there were good hopes of a job. Then he and Greta could get married. So what on earth was he worried about? He cursed himself for a fool to be unnerved by a wind on the mountainside.

By this time he had reached the hut where the little Schmidt was housed. Letting himself in, he first consulted his notebook to find the next section of the sky due to be photographed. Then he set the appropriate direction, south of the constellation of Orion: mid-winter was the only time of the year when this particular region could be reached. The next step was to start the exposure. All that remained was to wait until the alarm clock should signal its end. There was nothing to do except sit waiting in the dark, to let his mind wander where it listed.

Jensen worked through to dawn, following one exposure with another. Even so his work was not at an end. He had still to develop the plates that had accumulated during the night. This needed careful attention. A slip at this stage would lose much hard work, and was not to be thought of.

Normally he would have been spared this last exacting task. Normally he would have retired to the dormitory, slept for five or six hours, breakfasted at noon, and only then would he have tackled the developing job. But this was the end of his 'run'. The moon was now rising in the evening, and this meant the end of observing for a fortnight, since the nova search could not be carried on during the half of the month when the moon was in the night sky – it was simply that the moon gave so much light that the sensitive plates he was using would have been hopelessly fogged.

So on this particular day he would be returning to the Observatory offices in Pasadena, 125 miles away. The transport to Pasadena left at half past eleven, and the developing must be done before then. Jensen decided that it would be best done immediately. Then he would have four hours' sleep, a quick breakfast, and be ready for the trip back to town.

It worked out as he had planned, but it was a very tired young man who travelled north that day in the Observatory transport.

There were three of them: the driver, Rogers, and Jensen. Emerson's run had still another two nights to go. Jensen's friends in wind-blown, snow-wrapped Norway would have been surprised to learn that he slept as the car sped through the miles of orange groves that flanked the road.

*

Jensen slept late the following morning and it wasn't until eleven that he reached the Observatory offices. He had about a week's work in front of him, examining the plates taken during the last fortnight. What he had to do was to compare his latest observations with the other plate that he had taken in the previous month. And this he had to do separately for each bit of the sky.

So, late on this morning of 8 January 1964, Jensen was down in the basement of the Observatory buildings setting up an instrument known as the 'blinker'. As its name implies, the 'blinker' was a device that enabled him to look first at one plate, then at the other, then back to the first one again, and so on in fairly rapid succession. When this was done, any star that had changed appreciably during the time interval between the taking of the two plates stood out as an oscillating or 'blinking' point of light, while on the other hand the vast majority of stars that had not changed remained quite steady. In this way it was possible to pick out with comparative ease the one star in ten thousand or so that had changed. Enormous labour was therefore saved because every single star did not have to be examined separately.

Great care was needed in preparing plates for use in the 'blinker'. They must not only be taken with the same instrument, but so far as possible must be shot under identical conditions. They must have the same exposure times and their development must be as similar as the observing astronomer can contrive. This explains why Jensen had been so careful about his exposures and development.

His difficulty now was that exploding stars are not the only sort to show changes. Although the great majority of stars do not change, there are a number of brands of oscillating stars, all of which 'blink' in the manner just described. Such ordinary oscillators had to be checked separately and eliminated from the search.

Jensen had estimated that he would probably have to check and eliminate the best part of ten thousand ordinary oscillators before he found one nova. Mostly he would reject a 'blinker' after a short examination, but sometimes there were doubtful cases. Then he would have to resort to a star catalogue, and this meant measuring up the exact position of the star in question. So all in all there was quite a bit of work to do before he got through his pile of plates – work that was not a little tedious.

By 14 January he had nearly finished the whole pile. In the evening he decided to go back to the Observatory. The afternoon he had spent at the California Institute of Technology, where there had been an interesting seminar on the subject of the spiral arms of the galaxies. There had been quite a discussion after the seminar. Indeed he and his friends had argued throughout dinner about it and during the drive back to the Observatory. He reckoned he would just about get through the last batch of plates, the ones he had taken on the night of 7 January.

He finished the first of the batch. It turned out a finicking job. Once again, every one of the 'possibilities' resolved into an ordinary, known oscillator. He would be glad when the job was done. Better to be on the mountain at the end of a telescope than straining his eyes with this damned instrument, he thought, as he bent down to the eye-piece. He pressed the switch and the second pair flashed up in the field of view. An instant later Jensen was fumbling at the plates, pulling them out of their holders. He took them over to the light, examined them for a long time, then replaced them in the 'blinker' and switched on again. In a rich star field was a large, almost exactly circular, dark patch. But it was the ring of stars surrounding the patch that he found so astonishing. There they were, oscillating, blinking, all of them. Why? He could think of no satisfactory answer to the question, for he had never seen or heard of anything like this before.

Jensen found himself unable to continue with the job. He was too excited about this singular discovery. He felt he simply must talk to someone about it. The obvious man of course was Dr Marlowe, one of the senior staff members. Most astronomers specialize on one or other of the many facets of their subject. Marlowe had his specialities too, but he was above all a man of immense general knowledge. Perhaps because of this he made fewer mistakes than most people. He was ready to talk astronomy at all hours of the day and night, and he would talk with intense enthusiasm to anyone, whether a distinguished scientist like himself or a young man at the threshold of his career. It was natural therefore that Jensen should wish to tell Marlowe about his curious find.

He carefully put the two plates in question in a box, switched off the electrical equipment and the lights in the basement, and made his way to the notice board outside the library. The next step was to consult the observing list. He found to his satisfaction that Marlowe was not away either at Palomar or Mount Wilson. But, of course, he might have gone out for the evening. Jensen's luck was in, however, for a phone call soon elicited that Marlowe was at home. When he explained that he wanted to talk to him about something queer that had turned up, Marlowe said:

'Come right over, Knut, I'll be expecting you. No, it's all right. I wasn't doing anything particular.'

It says much for Jensen's state of mind that he rang for a taxi to take him to Marlowe's house. A student with an annual emolument of two thousand dollars does not normally travel by taxi. This was particularly so in Jensen's case. Economy was important to him because he wished to travel around the different observatories in the United States before he returned to Norway, and he had presents to buy, too. But on this occasion the matter of money never entered his head. He rode up to Altadena, clutching his box of plates, and wondered whether in some way he'd made a fool of himself. Had he made some stupid mistake?

Marlowe was waiting.

'Come right in,' he said. 'Have a drink. You take it strong in Norway, don't you?'

Knut smiled.

'Not so strong as you take it, Dr Marlowe.'

Marlowe motioned Jensen to an easy chair by the log fire (so beloved by many who live in centrally heated houses), and after moving a large cat from a second chair, sat down himself.

'Lucky you rang, Knut. My wife's out for the evening, and I was wondering what to do with myself.'

Then, typically, he plunged straight to the issue – diplomacy and political finesse were unknown to him.

'Well, what've you got there?' he said, nodding at the yellow box that Jensen had brought.

Somewhat sheepishly, Knut took out the first of his two pictures, one taken on 9 December 1963, and handed it over without comment. He was soon gratified by the reaction.

'My God!' exclaimed Marlowe. 'Taken with the 18-inch, I expect. Yes, I see you've got it marked on the side of the plate.'

'Is there anything wrong, do you think?'

'Nothing so far as I can see.' Marlowe took a magnifying glass out of his pocket and scanned carefully over the plate.

'Looks perfectly all right. No plate defects.'

'Tell me why you're so surprised, Dr Marlowe.'

'Well, isn't this what you wanted me to look at?'

'Not by itself. It's the comparison with a second plate that I took a month later that looks so odd.'

'But this first one is singular enough,' said Marlowe. 'You've had it lying in your drawer for a month! Pity you didn't show it to me right away. But of course, you weren't to know.'

'I don't see why you're so surprised by this one plate, though.'

'Well, look at this dark circular patch. It's obviously a dark cloud obscuring the light from the stars that lie beyond it. Such globules are not uncommon in the Milky Way, but usually they're tiny things. My God, look at this! It's huge, it must be the best part of two and a half degrees across!'

'But, Dr Marlowe, there are lots of clouds bigger than this, especially in the region of Sagittarius.'

'If you look carefully at what seem like very big clouds, you'll find them to be built up of lots of much smaller clouds. This thing you've got here seems, on the other hand, to be just one single spherical cloud. What really surprises me is how I could have missed anything as big as this.'

Marlowe looked again at the markings on the plate.

'It is true that it's in the south, and we're not so concerned with the winter sky. Even so, I don't see how I could have missed it when I was working on the Trapezium in Orion. That was only three or four years ago and I wouldn't have forgotten anything like this.'

Marlowe's failure to identify the cloud – for this is undoubtedly what it was – came as a surprise to Jensen. Marlowe knew the sky and all the strange objects to be found in it as well as he knew the streets and avenues of Pasadena.

Marlowe went over to the sideboard to renew the drinks. When he came back, Jensen said:

'It was this second plate that puzzled me.'

Marlowe had not looked at it for ten seconds before he was back to the first plate. His experienced eye needed no 'blinker' to see that in the first plate the cloud was surrounded by a ring of stars that were either absent or nearly absent in the second plate. He continued to gaze thoughtfully at the two plates.

'There was nothing unusual about the way you took these pictures?'

'Not so far as I know.'

'They certainly look all right, but you can never be quite sure.'

Marlowe broke off abruptly and stood up. Now, as always when he was excited or agitated, he blew out enormous clouds of aniseed-scented tobacco smoke, a South African variety. Jensen marvelled that the bowl of his pipe did not burst into flames.

'Something crazy may have happened. The best thing we can do is to get another plate shot straight away. I wonder who is on the mountain tonight.'

'You mean Mount Wilson or Palomar?'

'Mount Wilson. Palomar's too far.'

'Well, as far as I remember, one of the visiting astronomers is using the 100-inch. I think Harvey Smith is on the 60-inch.'

'Look, it would probably be best if I went up myself. Harvey won't mind letting me have a few moments. I won't be able to get the whole nebulosity of course, but I can get some of the star fields at the edge. Do you know the exact co-ordinates?'

'No. I phoned as soon as I'd tried the plates in the "blink". I didn't stop to measure them.'

'Well, never mind, we can do that on the way. But there's no real need to keep you out of bed, Knut. Why don't I drop you at

your apartment? I'll leave a note for Mary saying I won't be back
until sometime tomorrow.'

Jensen was excited when Marlowe dropped him at his lodging.
Before he turned in that night he wrote letters home, one to his
parents telling them very briefly of the unusual discovery, and
another to Greta saying that he believed he'd stumbled on something important.

Marlowe drove to the Observatory offices. His first step was to
get Mount Wilson on the phone and to talk to Harvey Smith.
When he heard Smith's soft southern accent, he said:

'This is Geoff Marlowe. Look, Harvey, something pretty queer
has turned up, so queer that I'm wondering if you'd let me have
the 60-inch for tonight. What is it? I don't know what it is. That's
just what I want to find out. It's to do with young Jensen's work.
Come down here at ten o'clock tomorrow and I'll be able to tell
you more about it. If you're bored I'll stand you a bottle of
Scotch. That's good enough for you? Fine! Tell the night assistant that I'll be up at about one o'clock, will you?'

Marlowe next put through a call to Bill Barnett of Caltech.

'Bill, this is Geoff Marlowe ringing from the offices. I wanted to
tell you that there'll be a pretty important meeting here tomorrow
morning at ten o'clock. I'd like you to come along and bring a
few theoreticians along. They don't need to be astronomers. Bring
several bright boys ... No, I can't explain now. I'll know more tomorrow. I'm going on the 60-inch tonight. But I'll tell you what,
if you think by lunch-time tomorrow that I've got you out on a
wild-goose chase, I'll stand you a crate of Scotch ... Fine!'

He hummed with excitement as he hurried down to the basement where Jensen had been working earlier in the evening. He
spent some three-quarters of an hour measuring Jensen's plates.
When at last he was satisfied that he would know exactly where
to point the telescope, he went out, climbed into his car, and
drove off towards Mount Wilson.

*

Dr Herrick, the Director of the Observatory, was astonished to
find Marlowe waiting for him when he reached his office at seven-
thirty the following morning. It was the Director's habit to start

his day some two hours before the main body of his staff, 'in order to get some work done', as he used to say. At the other extreme, Marlowe usually did not put in an appearance until ten-thirty, and sometimes later still. This day, however, Marlowe was sitting at his desk, carefully examining a pile of about a dozen positive prints. Herrick's surprise was not lessened when he heard what Marlowe had to say. The two men spent the next hour and a half in earnest conversation. At about nine o'clock they slipped out for a quick breakfast, and returned in time to make preparations for a meeting to be held in the library at ten o'clock.

When Bill Barnett's party of five arrived they found some dozen members of the Observatory already assembled, including Jensen, Rogers, Emerson, and Harvey Smith. A blackboard had been fitted up and a screen and lantern for showing slides. The only member of Barnett's party who had to be introduced round was Dave Weichart. Marlowe, who had heard a number of reports of the abilities of this brilliant twenty-seven-year-old physicist, noted that Barnett had evidently done his best to bring a bright boy along.

'The best thing I can do,' began Marlowe, 'is to explain things in a chronological way, starting with the plates that Knut Jensen brought to my house last night. When I've shown them you'll see why this emergency meeting was called.'

Emerson, who was working the lantern, put in a slide that Marlowe had made up from Jensen's first plate, the one taken on the night of 9 December 1963.

'The centre of the dark blob,' went on Marlowe, 'is in Right Ascension 5 hours 49 minutes, Declination minus 30 degrees 16 minutes, as near as I can judge.'

'A fine example of a Bok globule,' said Barnett.

'How big is it?'

'About two and a half degrees across.'

There were gasps from several of the astronomers.

'Geoff, you can keep your bottle of whisky,' said Harvey Smith.

'And my crate, too,' added Bill Barnett amidst the general laughter.

'I reckon you'll be needing the whisky when you see the next plate. Bert, keep rocking the two backwards and forwards, so that we can get some idea of a comparison,' went on Marlowe.

'It's fantastic,' burst out Rogers, 'it looks as if there's a whole ring of oscillating stars surrounding the cloud. But how could that be?'

'It can't,' answered Marlowe. 'That's what I saw straight away. Even if we admit the unlikely hypothesis that this cloud is surrounded by a halo of variable stars, it is surely quite inconceivable that they'd all oscillate in phase with each other, all up together as in the first slide, and all down together as in the second.'

'No, that's preposterous,' broke in Barnett. 'If we're to take it that there's been no slip-up in the photography, then surely there's only one possible explanation. The cloud is moving towards us. In the second slide it's nearer to us, and therefore it's obscuring more of the distant stars. At what interval apart were the two plates taken?'

'Rather less than a month.'

'Then there must be something wrong with the photography.'

'That's exactly the way I reasoned last night. But as I couldn't see anything wrong with the plates, the obvious thing was to take some new pictures. If a month made all that difference between Jensen's first plate and his second, then the effect should have been easily detectable in a week – Jensen's last plate was taken on 7 January. Yesterday was 14 January. So I rushed up to Mount Wilson, bullied Harvey off the 60-inch, and spent the night photographing the edges of the cloud. I've got a whole collection of new slides here. They're not of course on the same scale as Jensen's plates, but you'll be able to see pretty well what's happening. Put them through one by one, Bert, and keep referring back to Jensen's plate of 7 January.'

There was almost dead silence for the next quarter of an hour, as the star fields on the edge of the cloud were carefully compared by the assembled astronomers. At the end Barnett said:

'I give up. As far as I'm concerned there isn't a shadow of a doubt but that this cloud is travelling towards us.'

And it was clear that he had expressed the conviction of the meeting. The stars at the edge of the cloud were being steadily blacked out as it advanced towards the solar system.

'Actually there's no doubt at all about it,' went on Marlowe. 'When I discussed things with Dr Herrick earlier this morning he pointed out that we have a photograph taken twenty years ago of this part of the sky.'

Herrick produced the photograph.

'We haven't had time to make up a slide,' said he, 'so you will have to hand it round. You can see the black cloud, but it's small on this picture, no more than a tiny globule. I've marked it with an arrow.'

He handed the picture to Emerson who, after passing it to Harvey Smith, said:

'It's certainly grown enormously over the twenty years. I'm a bit apprehensive about what's going to happen in the next twenty. It seems as if it might cover the whole constellation of Orion. Pretty soon astronomers will be out of business.'

It was then that Dave Weichart spoke up for the first time.

'I've two questions that I'd like to ask. The first is about the position of the cloud. As I understand what you've said, the cloud is growing in its apparent size because it's getting nearer to us. That's clear enough. But what I'd like to know is whether the centre of the cloud is staying in the same position, or does it seem to be moving against the background of the stars?'

'A very good question. The centre seems, over the last twenty years, to have moved very little relative to the star field,' answered Herrick.

'Then that means the cloud is coming dead at the solar system.'

Weichart was used to thinking more quickly than other people, so when he saw hesitation to accept his conclusion, he went to the blackboard.

'I can make it clear with a picture. Here's the Earth. Let's suppose first that the cloud is moving dead towards us, like this, from

Earth   B   A

A to *B*. Then at *B* the cloud will look bigger but its centre will be in the same direction. This is the case that apparently corresponds pretty well to the observed situation.'

There was a general murmur of assent, so Weichart went on:

'Now let's suppose that the cloud is moving sideways, as well as towards us, and let's suppose that the motion sideways is about as fast as the motion towards us. Then the cloud will move about like this. Now if you consider the motion from *A* to *B* you'll see that there are two effects – the cloud will seem bigger at *B* than it was at *A*, exactly as in the previous case, but now the centre will have moved. And it will move through the angle *AEB* which must be something of the order of thirty degrees.'

'I don't think the centre has moved through an angle of more than a quarter of a degree,' remarked Marlowe.

'Then the sideways motion can't be more than about one per cent of the motion towards us. It looks as though the cloud is heading towards the solar system like a bullet at a target.'

'You mean, Dave, that there's no chance of the cloud missing the solar system, of it being a near-miss, let us say?'

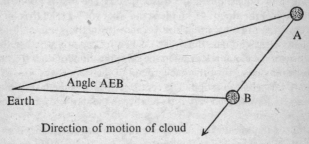

'On the facts as they've been given to us that cloud is going to score a bull's eye, plumb in the middle of the target. Remember that it's already two and a half degrees in diameter. The transverse velocity would have to be as much as ten per cent or so of the radial velocity if it were to miss us. And that would imply a far greater angular motion of the centre than Dr Marlowe says has taken place. The other question I'd like to ask is, why wasn't the cloud detected sooner? I don't want to be rude about it, but it seems very surprising that it wasn't picked up quite a while ago, say ten years ago.'

'That of course was the first thing that sprang to my mind,' answered Marlowe. 'It seemed so astonishing that I could scarcely credit the validity of Jensen's work. But then I saw a number of reasons. If a bright nova or a supernova were to flash out in the sky it would immediately be detected by thousands of ordinary people, let alone by astronomers. But this is not something bright, it's something dark, and that's not so easy to pick up – a dark patch is pretty well camouflaged against the sky. Of course if one of the stars that has been hidden by the cloud had happened to be a bright fellow it would have been spotted. The disappearance of a bright star is not so easy to detect as the appearance of a new bright star, but it would nevertheless have been noticed by thousands of professional and amateur astronomers. It happened, however, that all the stars near the cloud are telescopic, none brighter than eighth magnitude. That's the first mischance. Then you must know that in order to get good seeing conditions we prefer to work on objects near the zenith, whereas this cloud lies rather low in our sky. So we would naturally tend to avoid that part of the sky unless it happened to contain some particularly interesting material, which by a second mischance (if we exclude the case of the cloud) it does not. It is true that to observatories in the southern hemisphere the cloud would be high in the sky, but observatories in the southern hemisphere are hard put to it with their small staffs to get through a host of important problems connected with the Magellanic Clouds and the nucleus of the Galaxy. The cloud had to be detected sooner or later. It turned out to be later, but it might have been sooner. That's all I can say.'

'It's too late to worry about that now,' said the Director. 'Our next step must be to measure the speed with which the cloud is moving towards us. Marlowe and I have had a long talk about it, and we think it should be possible. Stars on the fringe of the cloud are partially obscured, as the plates taken by Marlowe last night show. Their spectrum should show absorption lines due to the cloud, and the Doppler shift will give us the speed.'

'Then it should be possible to calculate how long the cloud will be before it reaches us,' joined in Barnett. 'I must say I don't like the look of things. The way the cloud has increased its angular diameter during the last twenty years makes it look as if it'll be on top of us within fifty or sixty years. How long do you think it'll take to get a Doppler shift?'

'Perhaps about a week. It shouldn't be a difficult job.'

'Sorry I don't understand all this,' broke in Weichart. 'I don't see why you need the speed of the cloud. You can calculate straight away how long the cloud is going to take to reach us. Here, let me do it. My guess is that the answer will turn out at much less than fifty years.'

For the second time Weichart left his seat, went to the blackboard, and cleaned off his previous drawings.

'Could we have Jensen's two slides again please?'

When Emerson had flashed them up, first one and then the other, Weichart asked: 'Could you estimate how much larger the cloud is in the second slide?'

'I would say about five per cent larger. It may be a little more or a little less, but certainly not very far away from that,' answered Marlowe.

'Right,' Weichart continued, 'let's begin by defining a few symbols.'

Then followed a somewhat lengthy calculation at the end of which Weichart announced:

'And so you see that the black cloud will be here by August 1965, or possibly sooner if some of the present estimates have to be corrected.'

Then he stood back from the blackboard, checking through his mathematical argument.

'It certainly looks all right – very straightforward in fact,' said Marlowe, putting out great volumes of smoke.*

---

* The details of Weichart's remarks and work while at the blackboard were as follows:

Write α for the present angular diameter of the cloud, measured in radians,

> d for the linear diameter of the cloud,
> D for its distance away from us,
> V for its velocity of approach,
> T for the time required for it to reach the solar system.

To make a start, evidently we have $\alpha = d/D$

Differentiate this equation with respect to time t and we get $\dfrac{d\alpha}{dt} = \dfrac{-d}{D^2}\dfrac{dD}{dt}$.

'Yes, it seems unimpeachably correct,' answered Weichart.

At the end of Weichart's astonishing calculation, the Director had thought it wise to caution the whole meeting to secrecy. Whether they were right or wrong, no good could come of talking outside the Observatory, not even at home. Once the spark was struck the story would spread like wildfire, and would be in the papers in next to no time. The Director had never had any cause to think highly of newspaper reporters, particularly of their scientific accuracy.

From midday to two o'clock he sat alone in his office, wrestling with the most difficult situation he had ever experienced. It was utterly antipathetic to his nature to announce any result or to take steps on the basis of a result until it had been repeatedly checked and cross-checked. Yet would it be right for him to maintain silence for a fortnight or more? It would be two or three weeks at least before every facet of the matter were fully investigated. Could he afford the time? For perhaps the tenth time he worked through Weichart's argument. He could see no flaw in it.

At length he called in his secretary.

'Please will you ask Caltech to fix me a seat on the night plane to Washington, the one that leaves about nine o'clock? Then get Dr Ferguson on the phone.'

*

James Ferguson was a big noise in the National Science Foundation, controlling all the activities of the Foundation in physics, astronomy, and mathematics. He had been much surprised at Herrick's phone call of the previous day. It was quite unlike Herrick to fix appointments at one day's notice.

But $V = -\dfrac{dD}{dt}$, so that we can write $\dfrac{d\alpha}{dt} = \dfrac{d}{D^2} V$.

Also we have $\dfrac{D}{V} = T$. Hence we can get rid of V, arriving at $\dfrac{d\alpha}{dt} = \dfrac{d}{DT}$.

This is turning out easier than I thought. Here's the answer already $T = \alpha \dfrac{dt}{d\alpha}$.

The last step is to approximate $\dfrac{dt}{d\alpha}$ by finite intervals, $\dfrac{\Delta t}{\Delta \alpha}$, where $\Delta t = 1$ month corresponding to the time difference between Dr Jensen's two plates; and from what Dr Marlowe has estimated $\Delta \alpha$ is about 5 per cent of α, i.e. $\dfrac{\alpha}{\Delta \alpha} = 20$. Therefore $T = 20\Delta t = 20$ months.

'I can't imagine what can have bitten Herrick,' he told his wife at breakfast, 'to come chasing over to Washington like this. He was quite insistent about it. Sounded agitated, so I said I'd pick him up at the airport.'

'Well, an occasional mystery is good for the system,' said his wife. 'You'll know soon enough.'

On the way from the airport to the city, Herrick would commit himself to nothing but conventional trivialities. It was not until he was in Ferguson's office that he came to the issue.

'There's no danger of us being overheard, I suppose?'

'Goodness, man, is it as serious as that? Wait a minute.'

Ferguson lifted the phone.

'Amy, will you please see that I'm not interrupted – no, no phone calls – well, perhaps for an hour, perhaps two, I don't know.'

Quietly and logically Herrick then explained the situation. When Ferguson had spent some time looking at the photographs, Herrick said:

'You see the predicament. If we announce the business and we turn out to be wrong, then we shall look awful fools. If we spend a month testing all the details and it turns out that we are right, then we should be blamed for procrastination and delay.'

'You certainly would, like an old hen sitting on a bad egg.'

'Well, James, I thought you have had a great deal of experience in dealing with people. I felt you were someone I could turn to for advice. What do you suggest I should do?'

Ferguson was silent for a little while. Then he said:

'I can see that this may turn out to be a grave matter. And I don't like taking grave decisions any more than you do, Dick, certainly not on the spur of the moment. What I suggest is this. Go back to your hotel and sleep through the afternoon – I don't expect you had much sleep last night. We can meet again for an early dinner, and by then I'll have had an opportunity to think things over. I'll try to reach some conclusion.'

Ferguson was as good as his word. When he and Herrick had started their evening meal, in a quiet restaurant of his choice, Ferguson began:

'I think I've got things sorted out fairly well. It doesn't seem to me to make sense wasting another month in making sure of your position. The case seems to be very sound as it is, and you can never be quite certain – it would be a matter of converting a ninety-nine per cent certainty into a ninety-nine point nine per cent certainty. And that isn't worth the loss of time. On the other hand you are ill-prepared to go to the White House just at the moment. According to your own account you and your men have spent less than a day on the job so far. Surely there are a good many other things you might get ideas about. More exactly, how long is it going to take the cloud to get here? What will its effects be when it does get here? That sort of question.

'My advice is to go straight back to Pasadena, get your team together, and aim to write a report within a week, setting out the situation as you see it. Get all your men to sign it – so that there's no question of the tale getting around of a mad Director. And then come back to Washington.

'In the meantime I'll get things moving at this end. It isn't a bit of good in a case like this starting at the bottom by whispering into the ear of some Congressman. The only thing to do is to go straight to the President. I'll try to smooth your path there.'

Chapter Two

A MEETING IN LONDON

FOUR days earlier in London a remarkable meeting had been held in the rooms of the Royal Astronomical Society. The meeting had been called, not by the Royal Astronomical Society itself, but by the British Astronomical Association, an association essentially of amateur astronomers.

Chris Kingsley, Professor of Astronomy in the University of Cambridge, travelled by train in the early afternoon to London for the meeting. It was unusual for him, the most theoretical of theoreticians, to be attending a meeting of amateur observers. But there had been rumours of unaccounted discrepancies in the positions of the planets Jupiter and Saturn. Kingsley didn't believe it, but he felt that scepticism should rest on solid ground, so he ought to hear what the chaps had to say about it.

When he arrived at Burlington House in time for the four o'clock tea, he was surprised to see that quite a number of other professionals had already arrived, including the Astronomer Royal. 'Never heard of anything like this before at the B.A.A. The rumours must have been put around by some new publicity agent,' he thought to himself.

When Kingsley went in to the meeting room some half hour later he saw a vacant place on the front row by the Astronomer Royal. No sooner had he sat down than a Dr Oldroyd who was in the chair began the meeting in the following terms:

'Ladies and gentlemen, we meet here today to discuss some new and exciting results. But before I call on the first speaker I would like to say how pleased we are to see so many distinguished visitors. I am confident they will find that the time they have consented to spend with us will not have been wasted, and I feel that the important role of the amateur in astronomy will be demonstrated yet once again.'

At this Kingsley grinned inwardly to himself, and several of the other professionals squirmed in their seats. Dr Oldroyd went on:

'I have great pleasure in asking Mr George Green to address us.'

Mr George Green jumped up from his seat half-way down the room. He then bustled forward to the rostrum, clutching a large pile of papers in his right hand.

For the first ten minutes Kingsley listened with polite attention as Mr Green showed slides of his private telescopic equipment. But when the ten minutes lengthened to a quarter of an hour he began to fidget, and for the next half hour he lived in torment, first crossing his legs one way, then the other, then squirming round every minute or so to look at the clock on the wall. It was all in vain, for Mr George Green went right ahead with the bit firmly between his teeth. The Astronomer Royal kept glancing at Kingsley, a quiet smile on his face. The other professionals hugged themselves with delight. Their eyes never left Kingsley. They were calculating when the outburst would come.

The outburst never came, for Mr Green suddenly seemed to remember the purpose of his talk. Quitting the description of his beloved equipment, he began to throw off his results, rather like a dog shaking itself after a bath. He had observed Jupiter and Saturn, measuring their positions with care, and he had found discrepancies from the Nautical Almanac. Running to the black-board he wrote down the following figures, and then sat down:

	Discrepancy in Longitude	Discrepancy in Declination
JUPITER	+ 1 minute 29 seconds	− 49 seconds
SATURN	+ 42 seconds	− 17 seconds

Kingsley never heard the loud applause offered to Mr Green as a reward for his address, for Kingsley was choking with rage. He had come up to the meeting expecting to be told of discrepancies amounting to no more than a few tenths of a second at most. These he could have attributed to inaccurate, incompetent measurement. Or there might have been a subtle mistake of a statistical nature. But the figures that Mr Green had written up on the board were preposterous, fantastic, so large that a blind man could have seen them, so large that Mr George Green must have made some quite outrageous blunder.

It must not be thought that Kingsley was an intellectual snob, that he objected to an amateur on principle. Less than two years previously he had listened in the very same room to a paper presented by an entirely unknown author. Kingsley had immediately perceived the quality and competence of the work and was the first person to give public praise to it. Incompetence was Kingsley's *bête noire*, not incompetence performed in private but incompetence paraded in public. His irritation in this respect could be aroused in art and music as much as in science.

On this occasion he was a seething cauldron of wrath. So many ideas flashed through his head that he was unable to decide on any one particular comment, it seemed such a pity to waste the others. Before he could reach a decision, Dr Oldroyd sprang a surprise:

'I have great pleasure,' said he, 'in calling on the next speaker, the Astronomer Royal.'

It had been the Astronomer Royal's first intention to speak shortly and to the point. Now he was unable to resist the temptation to expatiate at length, just for the pleasure of watching Kingsley's face. Nothing could have been calculated to torment Kingsley more than a repetition of Mr George Green's performance, and this is just what the Astronomer Royal produced. He first showed slides of the equipment at the Royal Observatory, slides of observers operating the equipment, slides of the equipment taken to pieces; and he then went on to explain the detailed operation of the equipment in terms that might have been chosen for the benefit of a backward child. But all this he did in measured confident tones, unlike the rather hesitant manner of Mr Green. After some thirty-five minutes of this he began to feel that Kingsley might be in real medical danger, so he decided to cut the cackle.

'Our results in broad outline confirm what Mr Green has already told you. Jupiter and Saturn are out of position and to amounts that are of the general order given by Mr Green. There are some small discrepancies between his results and ours but the main features are the same.

'At the Royal Observatory we have also observed that the planets Uranus and Neptune are out of their positions, not it is true to the same extent as Jupiter and Saturn, but nevertheless in very appreciable amounts.

'Finally I may add that I have received a letter from Grottwald in Heidelberg, in which he says that the Heidelberg Observatory has obtained results that accord closely with those of the Royal Observatory.'

Whereon the Astronomer Royal returned to his seat. Dr Oldroyd immediately addressed the meeting:

'Gentlemen, you have heard presented to you this afternoon results that I venture to suggest are of the very first importance. Today's meeting may well become a landmark in the history of astronomy. It is not my wish to take up any more of your time as I expect you will have much to say. In particular I expect our theoreticians will have much to say. I should like to begin the discussion by asking Professor Kingsley whether he has any comment he would like to make.'

'Not while the law of slander is still operative,' whispered one professional to another.

'Mr Chairman,' began Kingsley, 'while the two previous speakers were addressing us I had ample opportunity to perform a fairly lengthy calculation.'

The two professionals grinned at each other, the Astronomer Royal grinned to himself.

'The conclusion I have arrived at may be of interest to the meeting. I find that if the results that have been presented to us this afternoon are correct, I say if they are correct, then a hitherto unknown body must exist in the vicinity of the solar system. And the mass of this unknown body must be comparable with or even greater than the mass of Jupiter itself. While it must be granted implausible to suppose that the results given to us arise from mere observational errors, I say mere observational errors, it may also be thought implausible that a body of such large mass existing within the solar system, or on the periphery of the solar system, could so far have remained undetected.'

Kingsley sat down. The professionals who understood the general trend of his argument, and what lay under it, felt that he had made his point.

*

Kingsley glowered at the railwayman who asked to see his ticket as he boarded the 8.56 p.m. train from Liverpool Street to Cambridge. The man fell back a pace or two, as well he might, for Kingsley's rage had not been assuaged by the meal he had just eaten, a meal consisting of poor food badly cooked, condescendingly served in pretentious but slovenly conditions. Only its price had been ample. Kingsley stamped through the train looking for a compartment where he could bite the carpet in solitary splendour. Moving quickly through a first-class carriage he caught a glimpse of the back of a head that he thought he recognized. Slipping into the compartment, he dropped down by the Astronomer Royal.

'First-class, nice and comfortable. Nothing like working for the government, eh?'

'Quite wrong, Kingsley. I'm going up to Cambridge for a Trinity Feast.'

Kingsley, still acutely conscious of the execrable dinner he had just consumed, pulled a wry face.

'Always amazes me the way those Trinity beggars feed themselves,' he said. 'Feasts on Mondays, Wednesdays, and Fridays, and four square meals on each of the other days of the week.'

'Surely it's not quite as bad as that. You seem quite put out today, Kingsley. In trouble of any sort?'

Metaphorically the Astronomer Royal was hugging himself with delight.

'Put out! Who wouldn't be put out, I'd like to know. Come on, A.R.! What was the idea of that vaudeville stunt this afternoon?'

'Everything that was said this afternoon was plain sober fact.'

'Sober fact, my eye! It would have been much more sober if you'd got up on the table and done a clog dance. Planets a degree and a half out of position! Rubbish!'

The Astronomer Royal lifted down his brief case from the rack and took out a large file of papers on which a veritable multitude of observations was entered.

'Those are the facts,' he said. 'In the first fifty or so pages you'll find the raw observations of all the planets, day-by-day figures over the last few months. In the second table you'll find the observations reduced to heliocentric co-ordinates.'

Kingsley studied the papers silently for the best part of an hour, until the train reached Bishop's Stortford. Then he said:

'You realize, A.R., that there isn't the slightest chance of getting away with this hoax? There's so much stuff here that I can easily tell whether it's genuine. Can I borrow these tables for a couple of days?'

'Kingsley, if you imagine that I would go to the trouble of staging an elaborate – hoax as you call it, primarily with the object of deceiving you, of taking a rise out of you, then all I can say is that you flatter yourself unduly.'

'Let's put it this way,' answered Kingsley. 'There are two hypotheses that I can make. Both at first sight seem incredible, but one of them must be right. One hypothesis is that a hitherto unknown body with a mass of the same order as Jupiter has invaded the solar system. The second hypothesis is that the Astronomer Royal has taken leave of his senses. I don't want to give offence, but quite frankly the second alternative seems to me less incredible than the first.'

'What I admire about you, Kingsley, is the way you refuse to mince matters – curious phrase that.' The Astronomer Royal reflected thoughtfully for a moment. 'You should go in for politics one day.'

Kingsley grinned. 'Can I have these tables for a couple of days?'

'What do you propose to do?'

'Well, two things. I can check the consistency of the whole business and then I'll find out just where the intruding body is located.'

'And you'll do this how?'

'First I'll work backwards from the observations of one of the planets – Saturn might be the best one to choose. This'll determine the distribution of the intruding body, or intruding material if it isn't in the form of a discrete body. This'll be much the same thing as the J. C. Adams–Le Verrier determination of the position of Neptune. Then once I've got the intruding material pinned down, I'll work the calculation forwards. I'll work out the disturbances of the other planets Jupiter, Uranus, Neptune, Mars, etcetera. And when I've done that, I'll compare my results with

your observations of these other planets. If my results agree with
the observations then I'll know there's no hoax. But if they don't
agree – well!'

'That's all very fine,' said the Astronomer Royal, 'but how do
you propose to do all this in a couple of days?'

'Oh, by using an electronic computer. Fortunately I've got a
programme already written for the Cambridge computer. It'll
take me all tomorrow modifying it slightly, and to write a few
subsidiary routines to deal with this problem. But I ought to be
ready to start calculating by tomorrow night. Look here, A.R.,
why don't you come to the lab. after your Feast? If we work
through tomorrow night, we ought to get the matter settled very
quickly.'

*

The following day was most unpleasant; it was cold, rainy, and a
thin mist covered the town of Cambridge. Kingsley worked all
through the morning and into mid-afternoon before a blazing
fire in his College rooms. He worked steadily, writing an astonishing scrawl of symbols of which the following is a short sample,
a sample of the code by which the computer was instructed as to
how it should perform its calculations and operations:

	T		Z
0	A	23	$\ominus$
1	U	11	$\ominus$
2	A	2	F
3	U	13	$\ominus$

At about three-thirty he went out of College, thoroughly
muffled up and sheltering under his umbrella a voluminous sheaf
of papers. He worked his way by the shortest route to Corn Ex-
change Street, and so into the building where the computing
machine was housed, the machine that could do five years of
calculation in one night. The building had once been the old
Anatomy School and was rumoured by some to be haunted, but
this was far from his mind as he turned from the narrow street
into the side door.

His first move was not to the machine itself, which in any case
was being operated by others just at that moment. He still had to

convert the letters and figures he had written into a form that the machine could interpret. This he did with a special kind of typewriter, a typewriter that delivered a strip of paper in which holes were punched, the pattern of the holes corresponding to the symbols that were being typed. It was the holes in the paper that constituted the final instructions to the computer. Not one single hole among many thousands must be out of its proper place, otherwise the machine would compute incorrectly. The typing had to be done with meticulous accuracy, with literally one hundred per cent accuracy.

It was not until nearly six o'clock that Kingsley was satisfied that everything was satisfactorily in order, checked and double-checked. He made his way to the top floor of the building where the machine was housed. The heat of many thousands of valves made the machine-room pleasantly warm and dry on this cold damp January day. There was the familiar hum of electric motors and the rattle of the teleprinter.

The Astronomer Royal had spent a pleasant day visiting old friends, and a delightful evening at the Trinity Feast. Now at about midnight he felt much more like sleeping than sitting up at the Mathematical Laboratory. Still, perhaps he'd better go along and see what the crazy fellow was up to. A friend offered to take him by car to the lab., so there he was standing in the rain, waiting for the door to be opened. At length Kingsley appeared.

'Oh hello, A.R.,' he said. 'You've come at just the right moment.'

They walked up several flights of stairs to the computer.

'Have you got some results already?'

'No, but I think I've got everything working now. There were several mistakes in the routines I wrote this morning and I've spent the last few hours in tracking 'em down. I hope I've got them all. I think so. Provided nothing goes wrong with the machine, we should get some decent results in an hour or two. Good feast?'

*

It was about two o'clock in the morning when Kingsley said:

'Well, we're nearly there. We should have some results in a minute or two.'

Sure enough five minutes later there was a new sound in the room, the chatter of the high-speed punch. Out of the punch came a thin strip of paper about ten yards long. The holes in the paper gave the results of a calculation that it would have taken an unaided human a year to perform.

'Let's have a look at it,' said Kingsley as he fed the paper tape into the teleprinter. Both men watched as row after row of figures were typed out.

'The lay-out isn't very good, I'm afraid. Perhaps I'd better interpret. The first three rows give the values of the set of parameters I put into the calculations to take account of your observations.'

'And how about the position of the intruder?' asked the Astronomer Royal.

'Its position and mass are given in the next four rows. But they're not in a very convenient form – I said the lay-out isn't very good. I want to use these results to calculate next what influence the intruder should have on Jupiter. This tape is in the right form for that.'

Kingsley indicated the paper strip that had just come out of the machine.

'But I shall have to do a little calculation myself before I can reduce the tabulated numbers to a really convenient form. Before I do that, let's start the machine finding out about Jupiter.'

Kingsley pressed a number of switches. Then he put a large roll of paper tape into the 'reader' of the machine. After pressing another switch the reader began to unroll the tape.

'You see what happens,' said Kingsley. 'As the tape is unrolled a light shines through the holes in it. The light then goes into this box here, where it falls on a photo-sensitive tube. This causes a series of pulses to go into the machine. This tape I'm just putting in gives instructions to the machine as to how it is to calculate the disturbance in the position of Jupiter, but the machine hasn't had all its instructions yet. It still doesn't know where the intruder is, or how massive it is, or how fast it's moving. So the machine won't start working yet.'

Kingsley was right. The machine stopped as soon as it had

reached the end of the long roll of paper tape. Kingsley pointed to a small red light.

'This shows that the machine has stopped because the instructions aren't complete yet. Now where's that piece of tape we got out last time? That's it on the table by you.'

The Astronomer Royal handed over the long strip of paper.

'And this supplies the missing piece of information. When this has gone in, the machine will know all about the intruder as well.'

Kingsley pressed a switch and in went the second piece of tape. As soon as it had run through the reader, just as the first tape had done before it, lights began to flash on a series of cathode-ray tubes.

'Off she goes. From now on for the next hour the machine will be multiplying a hundred thousand ten-figure numbers every minute. And while it does that, let's make some coffee. I'm peckish, I haven't had anything to eat since four o'clock yesterday afternoon.'

So the two men worked on through the night. It was greying dawn on a miserable January morning when Kingsley said:

'Well, that's about it. We've got all the results here, but they need a bit of conversion before we can get to work on a comparison with your observations. I'll get one of the girls to do that today. Look, A.R., I suggest you have dinner with me tonight, and then we'll go over things with a tooth comb. Perhaps you'd like to slip along now and get a bit of sleep. I'll stay on until the lab. staff comes in.'

*

After dinner that night, the Astronomer Royal and Kingsley were again together in the latter's rooms at Erasmus College. The dinner had been a particularly good one and they were both much at their ease as they drew up to the blazing fire.

'Lot of nonsense we hear nowadays about these closed stoves,' said the Astronomer Royal, nodding towards the fire. 'They're supposed to be very scientific, but there's nothing scientific about 'em. The best form of heat is in the form of radiation from an open fire. Closed stoves only produce a lot of hot air that's extremely unpleasant to breathe. They stifle you without warming you.'

'A lot of sense in that,' added Kingsley. 'Never had any use for such devices myself. Now how about a spot of port before we get down to business? Or madeira, claret, or burgundy?'

'Very nice, I think I'd like the burgundy, please.'

'Good, I've got a quite nice Pommard '57.'

Kingsley poured out two largish glasses, returned to his seat, and went on:

'Well, it's all here. I've got my calculated values for Mars, Jupiter, Uranus, and Neptune. The agreement with your observations is fantastically good. I've made up a sort of synopsis of the main results here on these four sheets, one for each planet. You can see for yourself.'

The Astronomer Royal spent several minutes looking over the several sheets.

'This is most impressive, Kingsley. That computer of yours is certainly a quite fantastic instrument. Well, are you satisfied now? Everything fits into line. Everything fits the hypothesis of an external body invading the solar system. By the way, do you have the details of its mass, position, and motion? They're not given here.'

'Yes, I've got those too,' answered Kingsley, picking another sheet out of a large file.

'And that's just where the trouble arises. The mass comes out at nearly two-thirds of that of Jupiter.'

The Astronomer Royal grinned.

'I thought you estimated at the B.A.A. meeting that it would be *equal* to Jupiter at least.'

Kingsley grunted.

'Considering the distractions, that wasn't a bad estimate, A.R. But look at the heliocentric distance, 21·3 astronomical units, only 21·3 times the Earth's distance from the Sun. It's impossible.'

'I don't see why.'

'At that distance it must be easily visible to the naked eye. Thousands of people would have seen it.'

The Astronomer Royal shook his head.

'It doesn't follow that the thing must be a planet like Jupiter and Saturn. It may have a much higher density and a lower albedo. That might make it a very difficult naked-eye object.'

'Even so, A.R., some telescopic sky survey would have picked it up. You see it's in the night sky, somewhere south of Orion. Here are the co-ordinates; Right Ascension 5 hours 46 minutes, Declination minus 30 degrees 12 minutes. I don't know the details of the sky very well, but that is somewhere south of Orion, isn't it?'

The Astronomer Royal grinned again.

'When did you last look through a telescope, Kingsley?'

'Oh, about fifteen years ago, I suppose.'

'What happened then?'

'I had to show a party of visitors over the Observatory.'

'Well, don't you think we ought to go up to the Observatory now and see what we can see, instead of arguing about it? It seems to me that this intruder, as we keep calling it, may not be a solid body at all.'

'You mean it might be a cloud of gas? Well, in some ways that would be better. It wouldn't be so easily seen as a condensed body. But the cloud would have to be pretty localized, with a diameter not much greater than that of the Earth's orbit. A pretty dense sort of cloud it would have to be too, about 10^{-10} gm. per cm^3. A minute star in the process of formation perhaps?'

The Astronomer Royal nodded.

'We know that the very big gas clouds like the Orion nebula have average densities of perhaps 10^{-21} gm. per cm^3. On the other hand, stars like the Sun with densities of 1 gm. per cm^3 are constantly forming within the big gas clouds. This surely means that there must be patches of gas at all densities varying from say 10^{-21} gm. per cm^3 at one extreme up to stellar densities at the other extreme. Your 10^{-10} gm. per cm^3 is bang in the middle of this range, and looks quite plausible to me.'

'There is a great deal of truth in that, A.R. Clouds with that sort of density must exist, I suppose. But I think you were quite right about going up to the Observatory. I'll give Adams a ring while you finish your wine, and I'll get a taxi.'

When the two men reached the University Observatory the sky was overcast, and although they waited through the cold damp hours there was no sight of the stars that night. And so it was the following night, and the night after that. Thus did Cambridge lose the honour of the first detection of the Black Cloud, as it had lost the honour of the first detection of the planet Neptune more than a century before.

On 17 January, the day after Herrick's visit to Washington, Kingsley and the Astronomer Royal again dined together in Erasmus. Again they made their way to Kingsley's rooms after dinner. Again they sat before the fire, drinking Pommard '57.

'Thank goodness we don't have to sit up all night again. I think Adams can be trusted to ring through if the sky clears.'

'I really ought to be getting back to Herstmonceux tomorrow,' said the Astronomer Royal. 'After all, we've got telescopes there too.'

'Evidently this damn weather has got you down the same as me. Look here, A.R., I'm in favour of throwing our hand in. I've drafted a cable to send to Marlowe in Pasadena. Here it is. They won't be troubled by cloudy skies over there.'

The Astronomer Royal glanced down at the sheet of paper in Kingsley's hand.

PLEASE INFORM WHETHER UNUSUAL OBJECT EXISTS AT RIGHT ASCENSION FIVE HOURS FORTY-SIX MINUTES, DECLINATION MINUS THIRTY DEGREES TWELVE MINUTES. MASS OF OBJECT TWO-THIRDS JUPITER, VELOCITY SEVENTY KILOMETRES PER SECOND DIRECTLY TOWARDS EARTH. HELIOCENTRIC DISTANCE 21.3 ASTRONOMICAL UNITS.

'Shall I send it?' asked Kingsley, anxiously.

'Send it. I'm sleepy,' said the Astronomer Royal, good-naturedly stifling a yawn.

*

Kingsley had a lecture at nine a.m. the following morning, so he bathed, dressed, and shaved before eight. His 'gyp' had laid the table for breakfast.

'A wire for you, sir,' he said.

A quick glance showed the 'wire' to be a cable. Incredible, thought Kingsley, that they should have a reply so quickly from Marlowe. He was even more astonished when he opened the cable.

IMPERATIVE YOU AND ASTRONOMER ROYAL COME IMMEDIATELY REPEAT IMMEDIATELY TO PASADENA. CATCH 15.00 PLANE TO NEW YORK. TICKETS AT PAN AMERICAN, VICTORIA AIR TERMINAL. VISA ARRANGEMENTS AT AMERICAN EMBASSY. CAR WAITING LOS ANGELES AIRPORT. HERRICK.

*

The aircraft climbed slowly, heading westwards. Kingsley and the Astronomer Royal relaxed in their seats. It was the first moment of ease since Kingsley had opened the cablegram that morning. First he had to postpone his lecture, then he had discussed the whole matter with the Secretary of the Faculties. It was not easy to leave the University at such short notice, but eventually it was arranged. By then it was eleven a.m. This left three hours to get to London, fix his visa, collect the tickets, and board the bus from Victoria to London airport. It had been something of a rush. Things were a little easier for the Astronomer Royal, who travelled abroad so much that he always had passports and visas ready for just such an emergency.

Both men pulled out books to read on the journey. Kingsley glanced at the Astronomer Royal's book and saw a vivid cover featuring a gun fight among desperados.

'Heaven knows what he'll be reading next,' thought Kingsley.

The Astronomer Royal looked at Kingsley's book and saw it was Herodotus' *Histories*.

'My God, he'll be reading Thucydides next,' thought the Astronomer Royal.

Chapter Three

CALIFORNIAN SCENE

It is necessary now to describe the consternation that Kingsley's cablegram produced in Pasadena. A meeting was held in Herrick's office the morning after his return from Washington. Marlowe, Weichart, and Barnett were there. Herrick explained the importance of arriving quickly at a balanced view of the effects that the arrival of the Black Cloud would have.

'The position we've arrived at is this: our observations show that the cloud will take about eighteen months to reach us, or at any rate this seems rather likely. Now, what can we say about the cloud itself? Will there be any significant absorption of the Sun's radiation when it comes between us and the Sun?'

'That's very difficult to say without more information,' said Marlowe, puffing smoke. 'At the moment we don't know whether the cloud is just a tiny fellow quite close to us or whether it's a biggish cloud farther away. And we've got no idea at all of the density of the material inside it.'

'If we could get the velocity of the cloud, then we should know how big it is and how far away,' remarked Weichart.

'Yes, I've been thinking about that,' went on Marlowe. 'The Australian radio boys could get the information for us. It's very likely that the cloud consists mainly of hydrogen, and it should be possible to get a Doppler shift on the 21 cm line.'

'That's a very good point,' said Barnett. 'The obvious man is Leicester in Sydney. We ought to get a cable off to him right away.'

'I don't think that's quite our job, Bill,' Herrick explained. 'Let's stick to what we can do ourselves. When we've sent in our report, it'll be Washington's job to contact the Australians about radio measurements.'

'But surely we ought to make a recommendation about getting Leicester's group on to the problem?'

'Certainly we can do that, and I think we ought to. What I

meant was that we ought not to initiate action of this sort. The whole business is likely to have serious political implications, and I feel that we ought to keep away from such things.'

'Right enough,' broke in Marlowe; 'politics is the last thing I want to get involved in. But obviously we need the radio boys to get the velocity. The mass of the cloud is more difficult. As far as I can see the best way, perhaps the only way, would be from planetary perturbations.'

'That's pretty archaic stuff, isn't it?' asked Barnett. 'Who do it? The British, I suppose.'

'Yes, h'm,' murmured Herrick, 'perhaps we'd better not emphasize that aspect of the matter. But the Astronomer Royal probably would be the best person to approach. I'll make a point of it in the report, which I ought to start on as soon as possible. I think we're agreed on the main points. Does anyone want to bring up anything further?'

'No, we've gone over the ground pretty thoroughly, as far as we can go, that's to say,' answered Marlowe. 'I think I'll be getting back to one or two jobs that I've rather neglected during the last few days. I expect you'll want to get that report finished. Glad I don't have to write it.'

And so they filed out of Herrick's office, leaving him to get down to his writing, which he did forthwith. Barnett and Weichart drove back to Caltech. Marlowe went to his own office. But he found it impossible to work, so he strolled along to the library where there were several of his colleagues. A lively conversation of the colour-magnitude diagram of the stars of the galactic nucleus contrived to pass the time until it was generally agreed that the lunch hour had arrived.

When Marlowe returned from lunch the Secretary sought him out. 'Cablegram for you, Dr Marlowe.'

The words on the piece of paper seemed to swell to a gigantic size:

PLEASE INFORM WHETHER UNUSUAL OBJECT EXISTS AT RIGHT ASCENSION FIVE HOURS FORTY-SIX MINUTES, DECLINATION MINUS THIRTY DEGREES TWELVE MINUTES. MASS OF OBJECT TWO-THIRDS JUPITER, VELOCITY SEVENTY KILOMETRES PER SECOND DIRECTLY TOWARDS EARTH. HELIOCENTRIC DISTANCE 21.3 ASTRONOMICAL UNITS.

With a startled cry Marlowe raced along to Herrick's office, and burst in without the formality of a knock.

'I've got it here,' he shouted. 'All the things we wanted to know.'

Herrick studied the cablegram. Then he smiled somewhat wryly and said:

'This alters things quite a bit. It looks as though we shall have to consult with Kingsley and the Astronomer Royal.'

Marlowe was still excited.

'It's easy to diagnose the situation. The Astronomer Royal has supplied observational material on the planetary motions and Kingsley has done the calculations. If I know those two fellows there isn't much chance of a mistake there.'

'Well, it's easy enough to do a quick check. If the object is 21·3 astronomical units distant and it's moving towards us at seventy kilometres per second, then we can soon work out how long it should take to reach us, and we can compare the answer with Weichart's estimate of about eighteen months.'

'Right you are,' said Marlowe. He then jotted the following remarks and figures on a sheet of paper:

Distance 21·3 astr. units $= 3 \times 10^{14}$ cm approximately.
Time required to travel this distance at a speed of 70 km per sec.

$$= \frac{3 \times 10^{14}}{7 \times 10^6} = 4\cdot3 \times 10^7 \text{ seconds} = 1\cdot4 \text{ years} = 17 \text{ months approx.}$$

'Perfect agreement,' exclaimed Marlowe. 'And what's more, the position they give is almost dead on our position. It all fits together.'

'This makes my report a much more difficult matter,' Herrick said with a frown. 'It really should be written in consultation with the Astronomer Royal. I think we ought to get both him and Kingsley over here as soon as possible.'

'Absolutely right,' agreed Marlowe. 'Get the Secretary on to it right away. It should be possible to get 'em over in about thirty-six hours, the morning after tomorrow. Better still, let your friends in Washington make the arrangements. And about the report, wouldn't it be a good idea to write it in three parts? Part one could deal with our discoveries here at the Observatory. Part two would be contributed by Kingsley and the Astronomer Royal. And part three would be an account of our conclusions, especially the conclusions we reach when the British get here.'

'There's a great deal in what you say, Geoff. I can get part one finished by the time our friends arrive. We can leave part two to them, and lastly we can thrash out our conclusions.'

'Excellent. I reckon you'll probably get through by tomorrow. How about bringing Alison over for dinner tomorrow night?'

'I'd be glad to, delighted to, if I can get through by tomorrow afternoon. Can I leave it until then?'

'Sure, that's fine. Just let me know tomorrow,' said Marlowe getting up.

As Marlowe was leaving, Herrick said:

'It's pretty serious, isn't it?'

'It certainly is. I had a sort of premonition when I first saw Knut Jensen's pictures. I didn't realize how bad it was until this cable arrived. The density works out in the region of 10^{-9} to 10^{-10} gm. per cm^3. That means it'll block out the Sun's light entirely.'

*

Kingsley and the Astronomer Royal arrived in Los Angeles early on the morning of 20 January. Marlowe was waiting to meet them at the airport. After a quick breakfast in a drug store they hit the freeway system to Pasadena.

'Goodness me, what a difference from Cambridge,' grunted Kingsley. 'Sixty miles an hour instead of fifteen, blue skies instead of endless rain and drizzle, temperature in the sixties even as early in the day as this.'

He was very weary after the long flight, first across the Atlantic, then a few hours' waiting in New York – too short to be able to do anything interesting, yet long enough to be tiresome, the epitome of air travel, and lastly the trip across the U.S.A. during the night. Still it was a great deal better than a year at sea getting round the Horn, which is what men had to do a century ago. He would have liked a long sleep, but if the Astronomer Royal was willing to go straight to the Observatory, he supposed he ought to go along too.

After Kingsley and the Astronomer Royal had been introduced

to those members of the Observatory that they had not previously met, and after greetings with old friends, the meeting started in the library. With the addition of the British visitors it was the same company that had met to discuss Jensen's discovery the previous week.

Marlowe gave a succinct account of this discovery, of his own observations, and of Weichart's argument and startling conclusion.

'And so you see,' he concluded, 'why we were so interested to receive your cablegram.'

'We do indeed,' answered the Astronomer Royal. 'These photographs are most remarkable. You give the position of the centre of the cloud as Right Ascension 5 hours 49 minutes, Declination minus 30 degrees 16 minutes. That seems to be in excellent agreement with Kingsley's calculations.'

'Now would you two care to give us a short account of your investigations?' said Herrick. 'Perhaps the Astronomer Royal could tell us about the observational side and then Dr Kingsley could say a little about his calculations.'

The Astronomer Royal gave a description of the displacements that had been discovered in the positions of the planets, particularly of the outer planets. He discussed how the observations had been carefully checked to make sure that they contained no errors. He did not fail to give credit to the work of Mr George Green.

'Heavens, he's at it again,' thought Kingsley.

The rest of the company heard the Astronomer Royal out with interest, however.

'And so,' he concluded, 'I'll hand over to Dr Kingsley, and let him outline the basis of his calculations.'

'There is not a great deal to be said,' began Kingsley. 'Granting the accuracy of the observations that the Astronomer Royal has just told us about – and I must admit to having been somewhat reluctant at first to concede this – it was clear that the planets were being disturbed by the gravitational influence of some body, or material, intruding into the solar system. The problem was to use the observed disturbances to calculate the position, mass, and velocity of the intruding material.'

'Did you work on the basis that the material acted as a point mass?' asked Weichart.

'Yes, that seemed to be the best thing to do, at any rate to begin with. The Astronomer Royal did mention the possibility of an extended cloud. But I must confess that psychologically I've been thinking in terms of a condensed body of comparatively small size. I've only just begun to assimilate the cloud idea, now that I've seen these photographs.'

'How far do you think your wrong assumption affected the calculations?' Kingsley was asked.

'Hardly at all. So far as producing planetary disturbances is concerned, the difference between your cloud and a much more condensed body would be quite small. Perhaps the slight differences between my results and your observations arise from this cause.'

'Yes, that's quite clear,' broke in Marlowe amid aniseed smoke. 'How much information did you need to get your results? Did you use the disturbances of all the planets?'

'One planet was enough. I used the observations of Saturn to make the calculations about the Cloud – if I may call it that. Then having determined the position, mass, etc., of the Cloud, I inverted the calculation for the other planets and so worked out what the disturbances of Jupiter, Mars, Uranus, and Neptune ought to be.'

'Then you could compare your results with the observations?'

'Exactly so. The comparison is given in these tables that I've got here. I'll hand them round. You can see that the agreement is pretty good. That's why we felt reasonably confident about our deductions, and why we felt justified in sending our cable.'

'Now I'd like just to know how your estimates compare with mine,' asked Weichart. 'It seemed to me that the Cloud would take about eighteen months to reach the Earth. What answer do you get?'

'I've already checked that, Dave,' remarked Marlowe. 'It agrees very well. Dr Kingsley's values give about seventeen months.'

'Perhaps a little less than that,' observed Kingsley. 'You get seventeen months if you don't allow for the acceleration of the Cloud as it approaches the Sun. It's moving at about seventy kilometres per second at the moment, but by the time it reaches the Earth it'll have speeded to about eighty. The time required for the Cloud to reach the Earth works out at nearly sixteen months.'

Herrick quietly took charge of the discussion.

'Well, now that we understand each other's point of view, what conclusions can we reach? It seems to me that we have both been under some misapprehension. For our part we thought of a much larger cloud lying considerably outside the solar system, while, as Dr Kingsley says, he thought of a condensed body within the solar system. The truth lies somewhere between these views. We have to do with a rather small cloud that is already within the solar system. What can we say about it?'

'Quite a bit,' answered Marlowe. 'Our measurement of the angular diameter of the Cloud as about two and a half degrees, combined with Dr Kingsley's distance of about 21 astronomical units, shows that the Cloud has a diameter about equal to the distance from the Sun to the Earth.'

'Yes, and with this size we can immediately get an estimate of the density of the material in the Cloud,' went on Kingsley. 'It looks to me as though the volume of the cloud is roughly 10^{40} c.c. Its mass is about $1 \cdot 3 \times 10^{30}$ gm., which gives a density of $1 \cdot 3 \times 10^{-10}$ gm. per cm^3.'

A silence fell on the little company. It was broken by Emerson.

'That's an awful high density. If the gas comes between us and the Sun it'll block out the Sun's light completely. It looks to me as if it's going to get almighty cold here on Earth!'

'That doesn't necessarily follow,' broke in Barnett. 'The gas itself may get hot, and heat may flow through it.'

'That depends on how much energy is required to heat the Cloud,' remarked Weichart.

'And on its opacity, and a hundred and one other factors,' added Kingsley. 'I must say it seems very unlikely to me that much heat will get through the gas. Let's work out the energy required to heat it to an ordinary sort of temperature.'

He went out to the blackboard, and wrote:

Mass of Cloud $1 \cdot 3 \times 10^{30}$ grams.
Composition of Cloud probably hydrogen gas, for the most part in neutral form.
Energy required to lift temperature of gas by T degrees is
$$1 \cdot 5 \times 1 \cdot 3 \times 10^{30} \, RT \text{ ergs}$$
where R is the gas constant. Writing L for the total energy emitted by the Sun, the time required to raise the temperature is
$$1 \cdot 5 \times 1 \cdot 3 \times 10^{30} \, RT/L \text{ seconds}$$
Put $R = 8 \cdot 3 \times 10^7$, $T = 300$, $L = 4 \times 10^{33}$ ergs per second gives a time of about $1 \cdot 2 \times 10^7$ seconds, i.e. about 5 months.

'That looks sound enough,' commented Weichart. 'And I'd say that what you've got is very much a minimum estimate.'

'That's so,' nodded Kingsley. 'And my minimum is already very much longer than it will take the Cloud to pass us by. At a speed of 80 kilometres per second it'll sweep across the Earth's orbit in about a month. So it looks to me pretty certain that if the Cloud does come between us and the Sun it'll cut out the heat from the Sun quite completely.'

'You say *if* the Cloud comes between us and the Sun. Do you think there's a chance it may miss us?' asked Herrick.

'There's certainly a chance, quite a chance I'd say. Look here.' Kingsley moved again to the blackboard.

'Here's the Earth's orbit round the Sun. We're here at the moment. And the Cloud, to draw it to scale, is over here. If it's

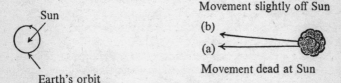

Kingsley's drawing of present situation

moving like this, dead set for the Sun, then it'll certainly block the Sun. But if it's moving this second way, then it could well miss us altogether.'

'It looks to me as if we're rather lucky,' Barnett laughed uneasily. 'Because of the Earth's motion round the Sun, the Earth will be on the far side of the Sun sixteen months hence when the Cloud arrives.'

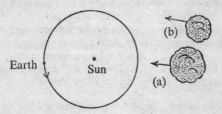

Kingsley's drawing of situation in sixteen months' time

'That only means that the Cloud will reach the Sun before it reaches the Earth. It won't stop the sunlight being blocked out if the Sun gets covered, as in Kingsley's case (a),' Marlowe remarked.

'The point about your cases (a) and (b),' said Weichart, 'is that you only get case (a) if the Cloud has almost exactly zero angular momentum about the Sun. It only needs a very slight angular momentum and we have case (b).'

'That's exactly it. Of course my case (b) was only one example. The Cloud could equally well sweep past the Sun and the Earth on the other side, like this:'

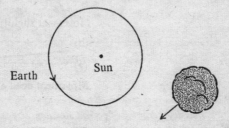

'Do we have anything to say about whether the Cloud is coming dead at the Sun or not?' asked Herrick.

'Not on the observational side,' answered Marlowe. 'Look at

Kingsley's drawing of the present situation. Only a very slight difference of velocity makes a big difference, all the difference between the Cloud hitting and missing. We can't say yet which it's to be, but we can find out as the Cloud comes in nearer.'

'So that's one of the important things to be done,' concluded Herrick.

'Can you say anything more from the theory?'

'No, I don't think we can; the calculations aren't accurate enough.'

'Astonishing to hear you distrusting calculations, Kingsley,' remarked the Astronomer Royal.

'My calculations were based on your observations, A.R.! Anyway I agree with Marlowe. The thing to do is to keep a close watch on the Cloud. It should be possible to see whether we're going to have a hit or a miss without too much trouble. A month or two should settle it, I suppose.'

'Right!' answered Marlowe. 'You can rely on us to watch this fellow from now on as carefully as if it was made of gold.'

After lunch Marlowe, Kingsley, and the Astronomer Royal were sitting in Herrick's office. Herrick had explained the plan of writing a joint report.

'And I think our conclusions are very clear. May I just outline them for you?

1. A cloud of gas has invaded the solar system from outer space.

2. It is moving more or less directly towards us.

3. It will arrive in the vicinity of the Earth about sixteen months from now.

4. It will remain in our vicinity for a time of about a month.

'So if the material of the Cloud interposes itself between the Sun and the Earth, the Earth will be plunged into darkness. Observations are not yet sufficiently definitive to decide whether or not this will occur, but further observations should be capable of deciding this question.'

'And I think we can go a little further concerning future observations,' Herrick went on. 'Optical observations will be prosecuted here with all energy. And we feel that work by the Australian radio astronomers will be complementary to ours, particularly with regard to keeping a watch on the line of sight motion of the Cloud.'

'That seems to sum up the situation admirably,' agreed the Astronomer Royal.

'I propose that we proceed with the report at full speed, that we four sign it, and that it be communicated to our respective Governments forthwith. I hardly need say that the whole matter is highly secret, or at least that we should treat it as so. It is rather unfortunate that so many are aware of the position, but I believe that we can rely on everybody proceeding with great discretion.'

Kingsley did not agree with Herrick on this point. Also he was feeling very tired, which no doubt made him express his views rather more forcibly than he would otherwise have done.

'I'm sorry, Dr Herrick, but I don't follow you there. I see no reason why we scientists should go to the politicians like a lot of dogs thumping our tails, saying "Please, sir, here's our report. Please give us a pat on the back and perhaps even a biscuit if you feel so disposed." I can't see the slightest point in having to do with a crowd of people that can't even run society properly during normal times when there's no serious stress. Will the politicians pass statutes to stop the Cloud coming? Will they be able to prevent it cutting off the light of the Sun? If they can, then consult them by all means, but if they can't, let's leave them out of the picture altogether.'

Dr Herrick was quietly firm.

'I'm sorry, Kingsley, but as I see it the United States Government and the British Government are the democratically elected representatives of our respective peoples. I regard it as our obvious duty to make this report, and to maintain silence until our Governments have made a pronouncement on it.'

Kingsley stood up.

'I'm sorry if I seem brusque. I'm tired. I want to go and get some sleep. Send your report if you wish, but please understand that if I decide to say nothing publicly for the time being, it will be because I wish to say nothing, not because I feel under any form of compulsion or duty. And now if you'll excuse me, I'd like to get round to my hotel.'

When Kingsley had gone, Herrick looked at the Astronomer Royal.

'Dr Kingsley seems a trifle … er …'

'A trifle unstable?' said the Astronomer Royal. He smiled and went on:

'That's not very easy to say. Whenever you can follow his reasoning, Kingsley is always very sound and often brilliantly deductive. And I am inclined to think this is always so. I think he seemed rather odd just now because he was arguing from unusual premises, rather than because his logic was faulty. Kingsley probably thinks about society in quite a different way from us.'

'Anyway I think that while we work on this report it would be a good idea if Marlowe were to look after him,' remarked Herrick.

'That's fine,' Marlowe agreed, still struggling with his pipe, 'we've got a lot of astronomy to talk about.'

*

When Kingsley came down to breakfast the following morning he found Marlowe waiting.

'Thought you might like to drive out for the day into the desert.'

'Spendid, there's nothing I'd like better. I'll be ready in a few minutes.'

They drove out of Pasadena, turned sharply right off Highway 118 at La Canada, then cut through the hills, past the side road to Mount Wilson, and so on to the Mohave Desert. Three more hours' driving brought them under the wall of the Sierra Nevada, and at last they could see Mount Whitney plastered with snow. The far desert stretching towards Death Valley was veiled in a blue haze.

'There are a hundred and one tales,' said Kingsley, 'of what a man feels like when he's told that he's only got a year to live – incurable diseases, and so on. Well, it's odd to think that every one of us probably only has a little more than a year to live. A couple of years hence, the mountains and the desert will be much the same as they are now, but there'll be no you and me, no people at all to drive along through it.'

'Oh my God, you're much too pessimistic,' grunted Marlowe. 'As you said yourself, there's every chance that the Cloud will sweep to one side or the other of the sun, and give us a complete miss.'

'Look, Marlowe, I didn't want to press you too much yesterday, but if you've got a photograph going back a number of years you must have a pretty good idea of whether or not there's any proper motion. Did you find any?'

'None that I could swear to.'

'Then surely that's pretty good evidence that the Cloud is coming dead towards us, or at any rate dead towards the Sun.'

'You might say so, but I can't be certain.'

'So what you mean is that the Cloud is probably going to hit us, but there's still a chance that it might not.'

'I still think you're being unduly pessimistic. We'll just have to see what we can learn during the next month or two. And anyway, even if the Sun *is* blotted out, don't you think we can see it through? After all it'll only be for about a month.'

'Well, let's go into it from scratch,' began Kingsley. 'After a normal sunset the temperature goes down. But the decline is limited by two effects. One is the heat stored in the atmosphere, which acts as a reservoir that keeps us warm. But I reckon that this reservoir would soon become exhausted, I calculate, in less than a week. You've only got to think how cold it gets at night out here in the desert.'

'How do you square that with the arctic night, when the Sun may be invisible for a month or more? I suppose the point is that the Arctic is constantly receiving air from lower latitudes, and that this air has been heated by the Sun.'

'Of course. The Arctic is constantly warmed by air that flows up from tropical and temperate regions.'

'What was your other point?'

'Well, the water vapour in the atmosphere tends to hold in the heat of the Earth. In the desert, where there's very little water vapour, the temperature goes down a long way at night. But in places where there's lots of humidity, like New York in summer, there's very little cooling at night.'

'And what does that lead you to?'

'You can see what will happen,' continued Kingsley. 'For the first day or two after the Sun is hidden – if it *is* shut out, that's to say – there won't be a great deal of cooling, partly because the air will be still warm and partly because of the water vapour. But as the air cools the water will gradually turn, first into rain, then into snow, which will fall to the ground. So the water vapour will be removed from the air. It may take four or five days for that to happen, perhaps even a week or ten days. But then the temperature will go racing down. Within a fortnight we shall have a hundred degrees of frost, and within a month there'll be two hundred and fifty or more.'

'You mean it'll be as bad here as it is on the Moon?'

'Yes, we know that at sunset on the Moon the temperature declines by over three hundred degrees in a single hour. Well, it'll be much the same here except that it'll take longer because of our atmosphere. But it'll come to the same thing in the end. No, Marlowe, I don't think we can last out a month, even though it doesn't seem very long.'

'You reject the possibility that we might keep warm the same way as they keep warm in winter in the Canadian prairies, by efficient central heating?'

'It's just possible I suppose that some buildings are sufficiently well insulated to stand the tremendous temperature gradients that'll be set up. They'll have to be very exceptional, because when we build offices and houses, and so on, we don't build with these temperature conditions in mind. Still I'll grant you that a few people may survive, people that have specially well designed buildings in cold climates. But I think there's no chance at all for anyone else. The tropical peoples with their ramshackle houses will be in a very poor case.'

'Sounds very grim, doesn't it?'

'I suppose the best thing will be to find a cave where we can get deep underground.'

'But we need air to breathe. What should we do when that gets very cold?'

'Have a heating plant. That wouldn't be too difficult. Heat the air going into a deep cave. That's what all the Governments that Herrick and the A.R. are so keen on will do. They'll have nice warm caves, while you and me, Marlowe my boy, will get the icicle treatment.'

'I don't believe they're quite as bad as that,' Marlowe laughed.

Kingsley went on quite seriously:

'Oh, I agree they won't be blatant about it. There'll be good reasons for everything they do. When it becomes clear that only a tiny nucleus of people can be saved, then it'll be argued that the lucky fellows must be those who are most important to society; and that, when it's boiled down and distilled, will turn out to mean the political fraternity, field-marshals, kings, archbishops, and so on. Who are more important than these?'

Marlowe saw that he had better change the subject slightly.

'Let's forget about humans for the time being. How about other animals and plants?'

'All growing plants will be killed, of course. But plant seeds will probably be all right. They can stand intense cold and still be capable of germination as soon as normal temperatures return. There'll probably be sufficient seeds around to ensure that the flora of the planet remains essentially undamaged. The case is very different with the animals. I don't see any large land animal surviving at all, except a small number of men, and perhaps a few animals that men take into shelter with them. Small furry burrowing animals may be able to get deep enough into the ground to withstand the cold, and by hibernating they may save themselves from dying for lack of food.

'Sea animals will be very much better off. Just as the atmosphere is a reservoir of heat, the sea is a vastly greater reservoir. The temperature of the seas won't fall very much at all, so the fish will probably be all right.'

'Now isn't there a fallacy in your whole argument?' exclaimed Marlowe with considerable excitement. 'If the seas stay warm, then the air over the seas will stay warm. So that there'll always be a supply of warm air to replenish the cold air over the land!'

'I don't agree there,' answered Kingsley. 'It isn't even certain that the air over the seas will stay warm. The seas will cool enough for them to freeze up at the surface although the water lower down will stay quite warm. And once the seas freeze over, there won't be much difference between the air over the land and the sea. It'll all get extremely cold.'

'Unfortunately what you say sounds right. So it looks as if a submarine might be the right place to be!'

'Well, a sub wouldn't be able to surface because of the ice, so a complete air supply would be needed and that wouldn't be easy. Ships wouldn't be any good either because of the ice. And there's another objection to your argument. Even if the air over the sea did stay comparatively warm, it would not supply heat to the air over the land, which being cold and dense would form tremendous stable anticyclones. The cold air would stay on the land and the warm air on the sea.'

'Look here, Kingsley,' laughed Marlowe, 'I'm not going to have my optimism damped by your pessimism. Have you thought of this point? There may be quite an appreciable radiation temperature inside the Cloud itself. The Cloud may have an appreciable heat of its own, and this might compensate us for the loss of sunlight, always supposing – as I keep saying – that we do find ourselves inside the Cloud!'

'But I thought the temperature inside the interstellar clouds was always very low indeed?'

'That's the usual sort of cloud, but this one is so much denser and smaller that its temperature may be anything at all, so far as we know. Of course it can't be extremely high, otherwise the Cloud would be shining bright, but it can be high enough to give us all the heat we want.'

'Optimist, did you say? Then what's to stop the Cloud being so hot that it boils us up? I didn't realize there was so much uncertainty about the temperature. Frankly, I like this possibility even less. It'll be completely disastrous if the Cloud is too hot.'

'Then we shall have to go into caves and refrigerate our air supply!'

'But that isn't so good. Plant seeds can stand cold but they can't stand excessive heat. It wouldn't be much good for Man to survive if the whole flora was destroyed.'

'Seeds could be stored in the caves, along with men, animals, and refrigerators. My God, it puts old Noah to shame, doesn't it?'

'Yes, maybe some future Saint-Saëns will write the music for it.'

'Well, Kingsley, even if this chat hasn't been exactly consoling, at least it's brought out one highly important point. We must find the temperature of that Cloud and without delay too. It's obviously another job for the radio boys.'

'Twenty-one centimetre?' asked Kingsley.

'Right! You have a team at Cambridge that could do it, haven't you?'

'They've started in on the twenty-one centimetre game quite recently, and I think they could give us an answer to this point pretty quickly. I'll get on to 'em as soon as I get back.'

'Yes, and let me know how it comes out as soon as you can. You know, Kingsley, while I don't necessarily go along with all you say about politics, I don't quite like the idea of everything going outside our control. But I can't do anything myself. Herrick has asked for the whole business to be put on the secret list, and he's my boss, and I can't go above him. But you're a free agent, especially after what you told him yesterday. So you can look into this business. I should get ahead with it as fast as you can.'

'Don't worry, I will.'

*

The drive was a long one, and it was evening by the time they dropped down through the Cajon Pass to San Bernardino. They stopped for an excellent dinner at a restaurant of Marlowe's choice on the western side of the township of Arcadia.

'I'm not normally keen on parties,' Marlowe said, 'but I think a party away from scientists would do us both good tonight. One of my friends, a business tycoon over San Marino way, invited me to drive over.'

'But I can't go along and gatecrash.'

'Nonsense, of course you can come – a guest from England! You'll be the lion of the party. Probably half a dozen film moguls from Hollywood will want to sign you up on the spot.'

'All the more reason for not going,' said Kingsley. But he went all the same.

The house of Mr Silas U. Crookshank, successful real estate operator, was large, spacious, well decorated. Marlowe was right about Kingsley's reception. A super-large tumbler of hard liquor, which Kingsley took to be Bourbon whisky, was thrust into his hand.

'That's great,' said Mr Crookshank. 'Now we're complete.'

Why they were complete Kingsley never discovered.

After polite talk to the vice-president of an aircraft company, to the director of a large fruit-growing company, and other worthy men, Kingsley at last fell into conversation with a pretty, dark girl. They were interrupted by a handsome fair woman who laid a hand on each of their arms.

'Come along, you two,' she said in a low, husky, much culti-vated voice. 'We're going along to Jim Halliday's place.'

When he saw that the dark girl was going to accept Husky Voice's plan, Kingsley decided he might as well go along too. No point in bothering Marlowe, he thought. He could get back to his hotel somehow.

Jim's place was a good deal smaller than the residence of Mr S. U. Crookshank, but nevertheless they managed to clear a floor space on which two or three couples began dancing to the some-what raucous strains of a gramophone. More drinks were handed round. Kingsley was glad of his, for he was no shining light of the dancing world. The dark girl was engaged by two men, to whom Kingsley, in spite of the whisky, took a hearty dislike. He decided to muse on the state of the world until he could prise the girl loose from the two bounders. But it was not to be. Husky Voice came across to him. 'Let's dance, honey,' she said.

Kingsley did his best to adjust himself to the creeping rhythm, but apparently he did not succeed in gaining his partner's approval.

'Why don't you relax, sweetheart?' the voice breathed.

No remark could have been better calculated to baffle Kings-ley, for he saw no prospect of relaxing in the overcrowded space. Was he expected to go limp, leaving Husky Voice to support his dead weight?

He decided to counter with nonsense of an equal order.

'I never feel too cold, do you?'

'Say, that's darned cute,' said the woman in a sort of amplified whisper.

In a state of acute desperation Kingsley edged her off the floor, and grabbing his glass took a deep swig. Spluttering violently, he raced for the entrance hall, where he remembered seeing a telephone. A voice behind him said:

'Hello, looking for something?'

It was the dark girl.

'I'm ringing for a taxi. In the words of the old song, "I'm tired and I want to go to bed." '

'Is that quite the right thing to say to a respectable young woman? Seriously though, I'm going myself. I've got a car, so I'll give you a lift. Forget about the taxi.'

The girl drove smartly into the outskirts of Pasadena.

'It's dangerous to drive too slowly,' she explained. 'At this time of night the cops are on the look-out for drunks and for people going home from parties. And they don't just pick up cars that are driven too fast. Slow driving makes 'em suspicious too.' She switched on the dashboard light to check the speed. Then she noticed the fuel gauge.

'Hell, I'm almost out of gas. We'd better stop at the next station.'

It was only when she came to pay the attendant at the station that she discovered that her handbag was not in the car. Kingsley settled for the petrol.

'I can't think where I can have left it,' she said. 'I thought it was in the back of the car.'

'Was there much in it?'

'Not a great deal. But the trouble is I don't see how I'm going to get into my apartment. The door key was in it.'

'That's distinctly awkward. Unfortunately I'm not a great hand at picking locks. Is it possible to climb in somehow?'

'Well, I think it might be, if I had some help. There's a highish window that I always leave open. I couldn't reach it alone, but I might if you gave me a lift. Would you mind? It's not very far from here.'

'Not in the least,' said Kingsley. 'I rather fancy myself as a burglar.'

The girl was right about the window being high. It could only be reached by one person standing on another's shoulder. The manoeuvre wouldn't be altogether easy.

'I'd better do the climbing,' said the girl. 'I'm lighter than you.'

'So instead of the dashing cracksman, I'm to be cast in the role of a carpet?'

'That's right,' said the girl as she pulled off her shoes. 'Now get down, so I can climb on your shoulders. Not so far down, or you'll never get up again.'

Once the girl nearly slipped, but she recovered balance by knotting her hand in Kingsley's hair.

'Stop pulling my head off,' he grunted.

'Sorry, I knew I shouldn't have drunk so much gin.'

Eventually it was done. The window was pushed open, and the girl disappeared inside, head and shoulders first, feet last. Kingsley picked up the shoes and walked over to the door. The girl opened it. 'Come in,' she said. 'I've laddered my nylons. I hope you're not shy about coming in?'

'I'm not in the least shy. I want my scalp back please if you've finished with it.'

*

It was nearly lunch time when Kingsley arrived at the Observatory the following day. He went straight to the Director's office, where he found Herrick, Marlowe, and the Astronomer Royal.

'My God, he looks shockingly dissipated,' thought the Astronomer Royal.

'My God, the whisky treatment seems to have fixed him,' thought Marlowe.

'He looks even more unstable,' thought Herrick.

'Well, well, are all those reports finished?' said Kingsley.

'All finished and waiting for your signature,' answered the Astronomer Royal. 'We were wondering where you'd got to. Our plane is booked back for tonight.'

'Plane booked back? Nonsense. First we race over half the world through all those damned airports, and now that we're here, enjoying the sunshine, you want to rush back again. It's ridiculous, A.R. Why don't you relax?'

'You seem to forget that we've got very serious business to attend to.'

'The business is serious enough. I'm with you there, A.R. But I tell you in all seriousness that it's a business that neither you nor anyone else can attend to. The Black Cloud is on its way and neither you, nor all the King's horses nor all the King's men, nor the King himself, can stop it. My advice is to drop all this nonsense about a report. Get out into the sunshine while it's still with us.'

'We were already acquainted with your views, Dr Kingsley, when the Astronomer Royal and I decided to fly east tonight,' broke in Herrick in measured tones.

'Am I to understand that you are going to Washington, Dr Herrick?'

'I have already arranged an appointment with the President's secretary.'

'Then in that case I think it would be as well if the Astronomer Royal and I were to travel on to England without delay.'

'Kingsley, that is exactly what we've been trying to tell you,' growled the Astronomer Royal, thinking that in some ways Kingsley was the most obtuse person he had ever met.

'It wasn't exactly what you told me, A.R., although it may have seemed that way to you. Now about those signatures. In triplicate, I suppose?'

'No, there are only two master copies, one for me and one for the Astronomer Royal,' answered Herrick. 'Would you sign here?'

Kingsley took out his pen, scribbled his name twice, and said:

'You're quite sure, A.R., that our plane to London is booked?'

'Yes, of course.'

'Then that seems all right. Well, gentlemen, I shall be at your disposal at my hotel from five o'clock onwards. But in the meantime there are various important matters that I must attend to.'

And with that Kingsley walked out of the Observatory.

The astronomers in Herrick's room looked at each other in surprise.

'What important matters?' said Marlowe.

'Heaven knows,' answered the Astronomer Royal. 'Kingsley's ways of thinking and behaving are more than I pretend to understand.'

Herrick left the east-bound plane at Washington. Kingsley and the Astronomer Royal flew on to New York, where they had a three-hour wait before boarding the London plane. There was some doubt as to whether they could take off because of fog. Kingsley was greatly agitated until eventually they were told to proceed to gate 13 and to have their boarding cards ready. Half an hour later they were in the air.

'Thank God for that,' said Kingsley, as the plane headed steadily to the north-east.

'I would agree that there are many things for which you ought to thank God, but I don't see that this is one of them,' remarked the Astronomer Royal.

'I would be glad to explain, A.R., if I thought that the explanation would commend itself to you. But as I fear it wouldn't, let's have a drink. What'll you have?'

Chapter Four

MULTIFARIOUS ACTIVITIES

THE U.S. Government was the first official body to learn of the approach of the Black Cloud.

It took Herrick some days to get through to the higher strata of the U.S. Administration, but when he did the results were far from disappointing. On the evening of 24 January, he received instructions to present himself at nine-thirty the following morning at the President's office.

'A very queer state of affairs you've come up with, Dr Herrick, very queer,' said the President. 'But you and your team at Mount Wilson stand so high that I won't waste any time doubting what you've told us. Instead I've called these several gentlemen together so that we can get down to settling what's to be done about it.'

Two hours' discussion was aptly summed up by the Secretary of the Treasury:

'Our conclusions seem to me quite clear, Mr President. Any really serious economic dislocation is likely to be prevented by the two favourable factors in the situation. Dr Herrick assures us that this – er, visitation is not expected to be prolonged much beyond a month. This is so short a time that, even if the fuel consumption rate rises enormously, the overall quantity required to maintain ourselves against the period of extreme cold remains very moderate. There is accordingly no serious problem in building up adequate fuel stocks – it is even possible that our present stocks might be sufficient. A more serious issue is whether we can transfer supplies fast enough from stock to the domestic and industrial consumer; whether we can pump gas and oil fast enough. This is something that must be looked into, but with nearly a year and a half in which to prepare there will surely be no difficulties that cannot be overcome.

'The second favourable factor is the date of the visitation. We should have much of our harvest in by mid-July, which Dr Herrick gives as the likely beginning of the emergency. The same favourable situation applies the world over, so that food loss, which would have been really serious had the period of cold occurred in May or June, should also be quite moderate.'

'Then I think we are all agreed on what immediate steps are to be taken,' added the President. 'When we have decided on our own dispositions we shall have to consider the more awkward problem of what help we can offer to peoples throughout the world. But for the moment let us put our own house in order. Now I take it that you gentlemen will all be wishing to get back to various important matters, and there are a few questions that I would personally like to put to Dr Herrick.'

When the meeting had broken up, and they were alone together, the President went on:

'Now, Dr Herrick, you will understand that for the time being this is a matter that must be treated with the closest security. I see that, in addition to your own, there are three other names on your report. These gentlemen, I take it, are members of your staff? Can you also let me have the names of any others who may be aware of its contents?'

Herrick in reply gave the President a short account of the circumstances that led up to the discovery, pointing out that it was inevitable that the information should have become common knowledge throughout the Observatory before its importance was realized.

'Of course, that is natural enough,' remarked the President. 'We must be thankful that the matter has not gone beyond the confines of the Observatory. I trust, I earnestly trust, Dr Herrick, that you can assure me of that.'

Herrick remarked that as far as he was aware there were four men outside the Observatory with a full knowledge of the Black Cloud, Barnett and Weichart of the California Institute of Technology – but that was practically the same thing – and two English scientists, Dr Christopher Kingsley of Cambridge and the Astronomer Royal himself. The names of the last two appeared on the report. The President's manner sharpened.

'Two Englishmen!' he exclaimed. 'This is not at all good. How did it come about?'

Herrick, realizing that the President could only have read a synopsis of his report, explained how Kingsley and the Astronomer Royal had independently deduced the existence of the Cloud, how Kingsley's telegram had been received in Pasadena, and how the two Englishmen had been invited to California. The President softened.

'Ah, they're both in California, are they? You did well to send that invitation, perhaps better than you realized, Dr Herrick.'

It was then that Herrick first realized the significance of Kingsley's sudden decision to return to England.

*

Some hours later, flying back to the West Coast, Herrick was still pondering his visit to Washington. He had hardly expected to receive the President's quiet but firm censure, nor had he expected to be sent home so soon. Curiously the unmistakable censure worried him far less than he would have supposed. In his own eyes he had done his duty, and the critic that Herrick feared most was himself.

It also took the Astronomer Royal some days to reach the fountain-head of government. The route to the summit lay through the First Lord of the Admiralty. The ascent would have been made sooner had he been willing to declare his purpose. But the Astronomer Royal would say nothing but that he desired an interview with the Prime Minister. Eventually he obtained an interview with the Prime Minister's private secretary, a young man of the name of Francis Parkinson. Parkinson was frank: the Prime Minister was extremely busy. As the Astronomer Royal must know, quite apart from all the usual business of state, there was a delicate international conference in the offing, there was Mr Nehru's visit to London in the spring, and the Prime Minister's own coming visit to Washington. If the Astronomer Royal would not state his business, then quite certainly there would be no interview. Indeed the business would need to be of exceptional importance, otherwise with regret he must decline to be of any assistance whatever. The Astronomer Royal capitulated by giving Parkinson a very brief account of the affair of the Black Cloud. Two hours later he was explaining the whole matter, this time in full detail, to the Prime Minister.

The following day the Prime Minister held an emergency meeting of the inner Cabinet, to which the Home Secretary was also invited. Parkinson was there, acting as secretary. After giving a quite accurate précis of Herrick's report, the Prime Minister looked round the table and said:

'My purpose in calling this meeting was to acquaint you with the facts of a case that may possibly become serious, rather than to discuss any immediate action. Our first step must obviously be to satisfy ourselves of the correctness or otherwise of this report.'

'And how may we do that?' asked the Foreign Secretary.

'Well, my first step was to ask Parkinson to make discreet inquiries concerning the – er, scientific reputations of the gentlemen who have signed this report. Perhaps you would like to hear what he has to say?'

The meeting signified that it would. Parkinson was slightly apologetic.

'It wasn't altogether easy to get really reliable information, especially about the two Americans. But the best I could get from my friends in the Royal Society was that any report bearing the signature of the Astronomer Royal or of the Mount Wilson Observatory will be absolutely sound from an observational point of view. They were, however, far less certain about the deductive powers of the four signatories. I gather that only Kingsley of the four might claim to be an expert on that side.'

'What do you mean by "might claim to be"?' asked the Chancellor.

'Well, that Kingsley is known to be an ingenious scientist, but not everyone regards him as thoroughly sound.'

'So what it amounts to is that the deductive parts of this report depend on only one man, and at that on a man who is brilliant but unsound?' said the Prime Minister.

'What I gleaned could be construed in that way, although it would be a somewhat extreme way of putting it,' answered Parkinson.

'Possibly,' went on the Prime Minister, 'but at any rate it gives us fair grounds for a measure of scepticism. Evidently we must look further into it. What I want to discuss with you all is the means we should now adopt for gaining further information. One possibility would be to ask the Council of the Royal Society to appoint a committee who would carry out a thorough probe of the whole matter. The only other line of attack that recommends itself to me is a direct approach to the U.S. Government, who must surely also be much concerned with the veracity, or perhaps I should say the accuracy, of Professor Kingsley and others.'

After several hours' discussion it was decided to communicate immediately with the U.S. Government. This decision was reached largely through the powerful advocacy of the Foreign Secretary, who was not short of arguments to support an alternative that would place the matter in the hands of his own department.

'The decisive point,' he said, 'is that an approach to the Royal Society, however desirable from other points of view, must of necessity place quite a number of people in possession of facts that would at the present stage best be left secret. I think we can all agree on this.'

They all did. Indeed the Minister for Defence wanted to know: 'What steps can be taken to ensure that neither the Astronomer Royal nor Dr Kingsley shall be allowed to disseminate their alarmist interpretation of the presumed facts?'

'This is a delicate and important point,' answered the Prime Minister. 'It is one that I have already given some thought to. That is actually the reason why I asked the Home Secretary to attend this meeting. I had intended raising the question with him later.'

It was generally agreed that the point be left to the Prime Minister and the Home Secretary, and the meeting broke up. The Chancellor was thoughtful as he made back to his offices. Of all those at the meeting he was the only one to be very seriously perturbed, for he alone appreciated how very rickety the nation's economy was, and how very little would be needed to topple it in ruins. The Foreign Secretary on the other hand was rather pleased with himself. He felt he had shown up rather well. The Minister of Defence thought that the whole business was rather a storm in a tea cup and that in any case it was quite definitely nothing to do with his department. He wondered why he had been called to the meeting.

The Home Secretary, on the other hand, was very pleased to have been called to the meeting, and he was very pleased to be staying on to discuss further business with the Prime Minister.

'I am quite sure,' said he, 'that we can dig up some regulation that will enable us to detain the two of them, the Astronomer Royal and the man from Cambridge.'

'I am quite sure of it too,' answered the Prime Minister. 'The Statute Book doesn't go back so many centuries for nothing. But it would be much better if we can manage things tactfully. I have already had the opportunity of a conversation with the Astronomer Royal. I put the point to him and from what he said I feel we can be quite sure of his discretion. But from certain hints that he let drop I gather that it may be rather different with Dr Kingsley. At all events it is clear that Dr Kingsley must be contacted without delay.'

'I will send someone up to Cambridge immediately.'

'Not someone, you must go yourself. Dr Kingsley will be – er – shall I say flattered if you go to see him in person. Ring him up saying that you will be in Cambridge tomorrow morning and would like to consult him on an important matter. That I think should be quite effective, and it will be much simpler that way.'

*

Kingsley was extremely busy from the moment he returned to Cambridge. He made good use of the few days that elapsed before the political wheels began to turn. A number of letters, all carefully registered, were sent abroad. An observer would probably have made special note of the two addressed to Greta Johannsen of Oslo and to Mlle Yvette Hedelfort of the University of Clermont-Ferrand, these being Kingsley's only female correspondents. Nor could a letter to Alexis Ivan Alexandrov have passed notice. Kingsley hoped that it would reach its intended destination, but one could never be certain of anything sent to Russia. True, Russian and Western scientists, when they met together at international conferences, worked out ways and means whereby letters could pass between them. True, the secret of those ways and means was extremely well kept, even though it was known to many people. True, many letters did pass successfully through all censorships. But one could never be quite sure. Kingsley hoped for the best.

His main concern however was with the radio astronomy department. He chivvied John Marlborough and his colleagues into intensive observations of the approaching Cloud, south of Orion. It required a good deal of persuasion to get them started. The Cambridge equipment (for 21 cm work) had only just recently come into operation and there were many other observations that Marlborough wanted to make. But Kingsley eventually managed to get his own way without revealing his real purposes. And once the radio astronomers were fairly started on the Cloud the results that came in were so startling that Marlborough needed no persuasion to continue. Soon his team were working twenty-four hours continuously round the clock. Kingsley found himself hard put to it to keep up in reducing the results and in distilling significance out of them.

Marlborough was elated and excited when he lunched with Kingsley on the fourth day. Judging the time to be ripe, Kingsley remarked:

'It's clear that we ought to aim at publishing this new stuff pretty soon. But I think it might be desirable to get someone to confirm. I've been wondering about whether one or other of us shouldn't write to Leicester.'

Marlborough swallowed the bait.

'A good idea,' he said. 'I'll write. I owe him a letter, and there are some other things I want to tell him about.'

What Marlborough really meant, as Kingsley well knew, was that Leicester had got in first on one or two matters recently and Marlborough wanted the opportunity to show him that he, Leicester, wasn't the only fish in the sea.

Marlborough did in fact write to Leicester at the University of Sydney, Australia, and so for good measure (and unknown to Marlborough) did Kingsley. The two letters contained much the same factual material but Kingsley's also had several oblique references, references that would have meant much to anyone who knew of the threat of the Black Cloud, which of course Leicester did not.

When Kingsley returned to College after his lecture next morning an excited porter shouted after him:

'Dr Kingsley, sir, there's an important message for you.'

It was from the Home Secretary to the effect that he would be glad to be favoured by an interview with Professor Kingsley at three that afternoon. 'Too late for lunch, too early for tea, but he probably expects to make a good meal for all that,' thought Kingsley.

The Home Secretary was punctual, extremely punctual. Trinity clock was striking three when the self-same porter, still excited, showed him into Kingsley's rooms.

'The Home Secretary, sir,' he announced with a touch of grandeur.

The Home Secretary was both brusque and tactfully subtle at the same time. He came to the point straight away. The Government had naturally been surprised and perhaps a little alarmed at the report they had received from the Astronomer Royal. It was widely appreciated how much the report owed to Professor Kingsley's subtle powers of deduction. He, the Home Secretary, had come specially to Cambridge with a two-fold purpose: to compliment Professor Kingsley on the swiftness of his analysis of the strange phenomena that had been brought to his notice, and to say that the Government would much appreciate being in constant touch with Professor Kingsley so that they might have the full benefit of his advice.

Kingsley felt he could do little but demur at the eulogy and offer with the best grace he could muster to give the best help that he could.

The Home Secretary expressed his delight, and then added, almost as an afterthought, that the Prime Minister himself had given close thought to what Professor Kingsley might think a small point, but which he, the Home Secretary, felt nevertheless to be a point of some delicacy: that for the immediate present awareness of the situation should be closely confined to a very select few, in fact to Professor Kingsley, to the Astronomer Royal, the Prime Minister, and to the Inner Cabinet, of which for this purpose he, the Home Secretary, was considered a member.

'Cunning devil,' thought Kingsley, 'he's put me just where I don't want to be. I can only get out of it by being damnably rude, and in my own rooms too. I'd better try to warm things up by degrees.'

Aloud he said:

'You may take it that I understand and fully appreciate the naturalness of your wish for secrecy. But there are difficulties that I think ought to be appreciated. First, time is short: sixteen months is not a long time. Secondly, there are quite a number of things that we urgently need to know about the Cloud. Thirdly, those things will not be found out by maintaining secrecy. The Astronomer Royal and I could not possibly do everything alone. Fourthly, secrecy can in any case only be temporary. Others may follow the lines of reasoning that are contained in the Astronomer Royal's report. At most you can expect only a month or two's grace. In any case by the late autumn the situation will be plain to anyone who cares to glance up at the sky.'

'You misunderstand me, Professor Kingsley. I explicitly referred to the immediate present just now. Once our policy is formulated we intend to go ahead full steam. Everyone whom it is necessary to inform of the Cloud will be informed. There will be no unnecessary silence. All we ask for is a strict security in the interim period until our plans are ready. We naturally do not wish the matter to become public gossip before we have marshalled our forces, if I may use such a military term in this connexion.'

'I very much regret, sir, that all this does not sound to me very well considered. You speak of formulating a policy and of then pressing ahead. This is very much a matter of the cart getting before the horse. It is impossible, I assure you, to formulate any worthwhile policy until further data become available. We do not know for instance whether the Cloud will strike the Earth at all. We do not know whether the material of the Cloud is poisonous. The immediate tendency is to think that it will get very cold when the Cloud arrives, but it is just possible that the reverse may happen. It may get too hot. Until all these factors become known, policy in any social sense is meaningless. The only possible policy is to collect all relevant data with the least delay, and this, I repeat, cannot be done while a really strict secrecy is maintained.'

Kingsley wondered how long this eighteenth-century sort of conversation would continue. Should he put the kettle on for tea?

The climax was rapidly approaching, however. The two men were mentally too dissimilar for more than a half hour of conversation between them to be possible. When the Home Secretary talked, it was his aim to make those to whom he was talking react according to some pre-arranged plan. It was irrelevant to him *how* he succeeded in this, so long as he succeeded. Anything was grist to the mill: flattery, the application of common-sense psychology, social pressure, the feeding of ambition, or even plain threats. For the most part, like other administrators, he found that arguments containing some deep-rooted emotional appeal, but couched in seemingly logical terms, were usually successful. For strict logic he had no use whatever. To Kingsley on the other hand strict logic was everything, or nearly everything.

Now the Home Secretary made a mistake.

'My dear Professor Kingsley, I fear you underestimate us. You may rest assured that when we make our plans we shall prepare for the very worst that can possibly overtake us.'

Kingsley leaped.

'Then I fear you will be preparing for a situation in which every man, woman, and child will meet their death, in which not an animal, nor any plant will remain alive. May I ask just what form such a policy will take?'

The Home Secretary was not a man to offer a staunch defence to a losing argument. When an argument led him to an awkward *impasse* he simply changed the subject and never referred to the old topic again. He judged the time ripe to change his style, and in this he made a second, and bigger, mistake.

'Professor Kingsley, I have been trying to put things to you in a fair-minded way, but I feel you are making it rather awkward for me. So it becomes necessary to deal plainly. I need hardly tell you that if this story of yours becomes public there will be very grave repercussions indeed.'

Kingsley groaned.

'My dear fellow,' said he, 'how very dreadful. Grave repercussions indeed! I should think there will be grave repercussions, especially on the day that the Sun is blotted out. What is your Government's plan for stopping that?'

The Home Secretary kept his temper with difficulty.

'You are proceeding on the assumption that the Sun *will* be blotted out, as you call it. Let me tell you with frankness that the Government has made inquiries and we are not at all satisfied with the accuracy of your report.'

Kingsley was wrong-footed.

'What!'

The Home Secretary followed up his advantage.

'Perhaps that possibility had not occurred to you, Professor Kingsley. Let us suppose, I say let us *suppose*, that the whole matter comes to nothing, that it turns out to be a storm in a tea-cup, a chimera. Can you imagine what your position would be, Professor Kingsley, if you were responsible for public alarm over what turned out to be a mere mare's nest? I can assure you very solemnly that the matter could only have one ending, a very serious ending.'

Kingsley recovered slightly. He felt the explosion growing within him.

'I cannot say how grateful I am at your concern for me. I am also not a little surprised at the Government's evident penetration into our report. Indeed, to be frank, I am astonished. It seems a pity that you cannot display an equal penetration into matters with which you might more properly claim a less amateur acquaintance.'

The Home Secretary saw no reason to mince matters. He rose from his chair, took up his hat and stick, and said:

'Any revelations you make, Professor Kingsley, will be regarded by the Government as a serious contravention of the Official Secrets Act. In recent years we have had a number of cases in which scientists have set themselves above the law and above public interest. You will be aware of what happened to them. I will wish you good-day.'

For the first time Kingsley's voice became commanding and sharp. 'And may I point out, Mr Home Secretary, that any attempt by the Government to interfere with my freedom of movement will quite certainly destroy any chance you may have of maintaining secrecy? So long as this matter is not known to the general public you are in my hands.'

When the Home Secretary had gone Kingsley grinned at himself in the mirror.

'I played that part rather well, I think, but I wish it hadn't had to happen in my own rooms.'

*

Events now moved quickly. By evening a group of M.I.5 men arrived in Cambridge. Kingsley's rooms were raided while he was dining in the College Hall. A long list of his correspondents was discovered and copied. A record of letters posted by Kingsley since his return from the U.S. was obtained from the Post Office. This was easy because the letters had been registered. It was found that of these only one was still likely to be in transit, the letter to Dr H. C. Leicester of the University of Sydney. Urgent cables were sent out from London. This led within a few hours to the letter being intercepted at Darwin, Australia. Its contents were telegraphed to London, in code.

At ten o'clock sharp the following morning a meeting was held at 10 Downing Street. It was attended by the Home Secretary, by Sir Harold Standard, head of M.I.5, Francis Parkinson, and the Prime Minister.

'Well, gentlemen,' began the Prime Minister, 'you have all had ample opportunity to study the facts of the case, and I think that we can all agree that something must be done about this man Kingsley. The letter sent to the U.S.S.R. and the contents of the intercepted letter give us no alternative but to act promptly.'

The others nodded without comment.

'The question we are here to decide,' went on the Prime Minister, 'is the form that such action shall take.'

The Home Secretary was in no doubt of his own opinion. He favoured immediate incarceration.

'I do not think we should take Kingsley's threat of public exposure too seriously. We can seal up all the obvious leaks. And although we might suffer some damage, the amount of damage will be limited and will probably be far less than if we try any form of compromise.'

'I agree that we can seal up the obvious leaks,' said Parkinson.

'What I am not satisfied about is that we can seal up the leaks that are not obvious. May I speak frankly, sir?'

'Why not?' queried the Prime Minister.

'Well, I was a little uneasy at our last meeting about my report on Kingsley. I said that many scientists regard him as clever but not altogether sound, and in that I was reporting them correctly. What I didn't say was that no profession is more consumed by jealousy than the scientific profession, and jealousy will not allow that anyone can be both brilliant *and* sound. Frankly, sir, I do not think there is much chance of the Astronomer Royal's report being in error in any substantial particular.'

'And where is all this leading?'

'Well, sir, I have studied the report pretty closely and I think I have picked up some idea of the characters and abilities of the men who signed it. And I simply do not believe that anyone of Kingsley's intelligence would have the slightest difficulty in exposing the situation if he really wanted to. If we could draw a net round him very slowly over a period of several weeks, so slowly that he suspected nothing, then perhaps we might succeed. But he surely must have anticipated that we might make a grab. I'd like to ask Sir Harold about this. Would it be possible for Kingsley to spring a leak if we put him under sudden arrest?'

'I fear what Mr Parkinson says is pretty well correct,' began Sir Harold. 'We could stop all the usual things, leakages in the press, on the radio, our radio. But could we stop a leakage on Radio Luxembourg, or any one of the scores of other possibilities? Undoubtedly yes, if we had time, but not overnight, I'm afraid. And another point,' he went on, 'is that this business would spread like wildfire if it once got out even without the help of newspapers or radio. It'd go like one of these chain reactions we hear so much about nowadays. It'd be very difficult to guard against such ordinary leaks, because they could occur anywhere. Kingsley may have deposited some document in any of a thousand possible places, with an arrangement that the document be read on a certain date unless he gave instructions to the contrary. You know, the usual sort of thing. Or of course he may have done something not so usual.'

'Which seems to concur with Parkinson's view,' broke in the

Prime Minister. 'Now, Francis, I can see you have some idea up your sleeve. Let's hear it.'

Parkinson explained a scheme that he thought might work. After some discussion it was agreed to give it a trial, since if it would work at all it would work quickly. And if it did not work there was always the Home Secretary's plan to fall back on. The meeting then broke up. A telephone call to Cambridge followed immediately. Would Professor Kingsley see Mr Francis Parkinson, Secretary to the Prime Minister, at three that afternoon? Professor Kingsley would. So Parkinson travelled to Cambridge. He was punctual and was shown into Kingsley's rooms as the Trinity clock was striking three.

'Ah,' murmured Kingsley as they shook hands, 'too late for lunch and too early for tea.'

'Surely you're not going to throw me out as quickly as all that, Professor Kingsley?' countered Parkinson with a smile.

Kingsley was quite a lot younger than Parkinson had expected, perhaps thirty-seven or thirty-eight. Parkinson had visualized him as a tallish, slim man. In this he was right, but Parkinson had not expected the remarkable combination of thick dark hair with astonishingly blue eyes, astonishing enough in a woman. Kingsley was decidedly not the sort of person one would forget.

Parkinson drew a chair up to the fire, settled himself comfortably, and said:

'I have heard all about yesterday's conversation between you and the Home Secretary, and may I say that I thoroughly disapprove of you both?'

'There was no other way in which it could end,' answered Kingsley.

'That may be, but I still deplore it. I disapprove of all discussions in which both parties take up positions of no compromise.'

'It would not be difficult to divine your profession, Mr Parkinson.'

'That may well be so. But quite frankly I am amazed that a person of your position should have taken up such an intransigent attitude.'

'I should be glad to learn what compromise was open to me.'

'That is exactly what I came here to tell you. Let me compromise first, just to show how it's done. By the way, you mentioned tea a little while ago. Shall we put the kettle on? This reminds me of my Oxford days and all matters nostalgic. You fellows in the University don't know how lucky you are.'

'Are you hinting at the financial support afforded by the Government to the Universities?' grunted Kingsley as he resumed his seat.

'Far be it from me to be so indelicate, although the Home Secretary did mention it this morning as a matter of fact.'

'I'll bet he did. But I'm still waiting to hear how I should have compromised. Are you sure that "compromise" and "capitulate" are not synonymous in your vocabulary?'

'By no means. Let me prove my point by showing how we're prepared to compromise.'

'You, or the Home Secretary?'

'The Prime Minister.'

'I see.'

Kingsley busied himself with the tea things. When he had finished, Parkinson began:

'Well, in the first place I apologize for any reflections that the Home Secretary may have cast on your report. Secondly, I agree that our first step must be the accumulation of scientific data. I agree that we must go ahead as quickly as possible and that all those scientists who are required to make some contribution should be fully apprised of the situation. What I do not agree with is that any others should be taken into our confidence at the present stage. That is the compromise I ask from you.'

'Mr Parkinson, I admire your candour but not your logic. I defy you to produce one single person who has learned from me of the menacing threat of the Black Cloud. How many persons have learned from you, Mr Parkinson, and from the Prime Minister? I was always against the Astronomer Royal in his wish to inform you, because I knew you couldn't keep anything really secret. By now I am wishing most heartily that I had overridden him.'

Parkinson was wrong-footed.

'But surely you don't deny writing an extremely revealing letter to Dr Leicester of the University of Sydney?'

'Of course I don't deny it. Why should I? Leicester knows nothing about the Cloud.'

'But he would have done if the letter had reached him.'

'Ifs and buts are the stuff of politics, Mr Parkinson. As a scientist I am concerned with facts, not with motives, suspicions, and airy-fairy nothingness. The fact is, I must insist, that no one has learned anything of importance from me in this affair. The real gossip is the Prime Minister. I told the Astronomer Royal that that's the way it would be, but he wouldn't believe me.'

'You haven't very much respect for my profession, have you, Professor Kingsley?'

'Since it is you who wish for frankness, I will tell you that I have not. I regard politicians rather as I regard the instruments on the dashboard of my car. They tell me what is going on in the engine of state, but they don't control it.'

Quite suddenly it flashed on Parkinson that Kingsley was pulling his leg and pulling it hard at that. He burst out laughing. Kingsley joined in. Relations were never again difficult between the two of them.

After a second cup of tea and some more general conversation Parkinson returned to the matter in hand.

'Let me make my point, and I am not to be fobbed off this time. The way you are going about collecting scientific information is not the quickest way, nor is it the way that gives us the best security, interpreting security in a wide sense.'

'There is no better way open to me, Mr Parkinson, and time, I need not remind you, is precious.'

'There may be no better way open to you at the moment, but a better way can be found.'

'I don't understand.'

'What the Government wants to do is to bring together all the scientists who ought to be fully cognisant of the facts. I understand you have recently been working with a Mr Marlborough of the radio astronomy group here. I accept your assurance that you have given away no essential information to Mr Marlborough, but wouldn't it be far better if arrangements to give him the information could be made?'

Kingsley remembered his initial difficulties with the radio astronomy group.

'Undoubtedly.'

'Then that's agreed. Our second point is that Cambridge, or indeed any university, is hardly the right place to conduct these investigations. You are part of an integrated community here and you cannot expect to combine both secrecy and freedom of speech at the same time. You cannot form a group within a group. The correct procedure is to form an entirely new establishment, a new community specially designed to meet the emergency, and one that would be given every facility.'

'Like Los Alamos for instance.'

'Exactly so. If you will think fairly about it I think you must agree that no other way is really feasible.'

'Perhaps I should remind you that Los Alamos is situated in the desert.'

'There would be no question of your being put in a desert.'

'And where would we be put? *Put*, you know, is a charming verb.'

'I think you would have no cause for complaint. The Government is just finishing the conversion of an extremely pleasant eighteenth-century manor house at Nortonstowe.'

'Where is that?'

'Cotswolds, on high ground to the north-west of Cirencester.'

'Why and how was it being converted?'

'It was intended to be an Agricultural Research College. A mile from the house we have built an entirely new estate for housing the staff – gardeners, workpeople, typists, and so on. I said you would be given every facility and I can assure you most sincerely that I meant it.'

'Won't the Agriculture people have something to say if they're shot out and we're moved in?'

'There's no difficulty in that. Not everyone views the Government with quite the same disrespect that you do.'

'No, more's the pity. I suppose the next honours list will take care of that. But there are difficulties you haven't thought of.

Scientific instruments would be needed – a radio telescope for instance. It's taken a year to erect the one here. How long would it take you to move it?'

'How many men were employed to erect it?'

'Perhaps a couple of dozen.'

'We would use a thousand, ten thousand if need be. We would guarantee to move and re-erect any instruments you think necessary within some reasonable stated period, say within a fortnight. Are there any other large instruments?'

'We should need a good optical telescope, although not necessarily a very large one. The new Schmidt here in Cambridge would be the most suitable, although how you'd persuade Adams to give it up I can't think. It's taken him years to get.'

'I don't think there would be any real difficulty. He won't mind waiting six months for a bigger and better telescope.'

Kingsley put more logs on the fire, and settled back in his chair.

'Let's stop fencing around this proposition,' he said. 'You want me to allow myself to be fastened up in a cage, albeit a gilded cage. That's the compromise you want from me, a pretty big compromise too. Now we ought to give some thought to the compromise that I shall want from you.'

'But I thought that's just what we've been doing.'

'It was, but only in a vague sort of way. I want everything quite clear-cut. First, that I be empowered to recruit the staff to this Nortonstowe place, that I be empowered to offer what salaries seem reasonable, and to use any argument that may seem appropriate other than divulging the real state of things. Second, that there shall be no, I repeat *no*, civil servants at Nortonstowe, and that there shall be no political liaison except through yourself.'

'To what do I owe this exceptional distinction?'

'To the fact that, although we think differently and serve different masters, we do have sufficient common ground to be able to talk together. This is a rarity not likely to be repeated.'

'I am indeed flattered.'

'You mistake me then. I am being as serious as I know how to be. I tell you most solemnly that if I and my gang find any gentlemen of the proscribed variety at Nortonstowe we shall quite literally throw them out of the place. If this be prevented by police action or if the proscribed variety are so dense on the ground that we cannot throw them out, then I warn you with equal solemnity that you will not get one single groat of co-operation from us. If you think I am overstressing this point, then I would say that I am only doing so because I know how extremely foolish politicians can be.'

'Thank you.'

'Not at all. Perhaps we can now come to the third stage. We need pencil and paper for this. I want you to note in detail, so that there can be no possibility of any mistake, every item of equipment that must be in place before I move in to Nortonstowe. Again I repeat that the equipment must reach Nortonstowe before I do. I shall *not* accept the excuse that there has been an unavoidable delay and that something or other will be coming along in a few days' time. Here, take this paper and start writing.'

Parkinson took long lists back to London with him. The following morning he had an important discussion with the Prime Minister.

'Well?' said the Prime Minister.

'Yes, and no,' was Parkinson's answer. 'I've had to promise to fit the place up as a regular scientific establishment.'

'That's no disadvantage. Kingsley was quite right in saying that we need more facts, and the sooner we get them the better.'

'I don't doubt that, sir. But I would have preferred it if Kingsley were not likely to be quite so important a figure in the new establishment.'

'Isn't he a good man? Could we have got someone better?'

'Oh, as a scientist he's good enough. It's not that which worries me.'

'I know it would have been far better if we had had to work with a more amenable type of person. But his interests seem to be pretty much the same as ours. So long as he doesn't sulk when he finds he can't get out of Nortonstowe.'

'Oh, he's quite realistic about that. He used the point as a strong bargaining counter.'

'What were the conditions?'

'For one thing that there are to be no civil servants, and no political liaison except through me.'

The Prime Minister laughed.

'Poor Francis. Now I see what the trouble is. Ah well, as for the civil servants that's not so serious, and as for the liaison, well we shall see what we shall see. Any tendency to make salaries – er – astronomical in magnitude?'

'None at all, except that Kingsley wants to use salaries as a bargaining counter to get people to Nortonstowe, until he can explain the real reason.'

'Then what *is* the trouble?'

'Nothing explicit that I can put my finger on, but I've got a sort of general sense of uneasiness. There are lots of small points, insignificant severally, but worrying when put together.'

'Come on, Francis, out with it!'

'Put in its most general terms, I've a feeling that it's we who are being manoeuvred, not we who are doing the manoeuvring.'

'I don't understand.'

'Neither do I really. On the face of it everything looks all right, but is it? Considering the level of Kingsley's intelligence, wasn't it just a bit too convenient that he took the trouble to register those letters?'

'It might have been a college porter who posted them for him.'

'It might have been, but if it was, Kingsley ought to have realized that the porter would register them. Then the letter to Leicester. It almost looked to me as if Kingsley expected us to intercept it, as if he wanted to force our hand. And didn't he rough-house poor old Harry [the Home Secretary] just a bit too much? Then look at these lists. They're incredibly detailed, as if everything had been thought out in advance. The food and fuel requirements I can understand, but why this enormous quantity of earth-moving equipment?'

'I haven't the least idea.'

'But Kingsley has, because he's already given a great deal of thought to it.'

'My dear Francis, what does it matter how much thought he has given to it? What we want to do is to get a highly competent team of scientists together, to isolate them, and to keep them happy. If Kingsley can be kept happy with these lists, then let him have the stuff. Why should we worry?'

'Well, there's a lot of electronic equipment down here, an awful lot of it. It could be used for radio transmission purposes.'

'Then you strike that out here and now. That he can't have!'

'Just a moment, sir, that isn't the whole story. I was suspicious about this stuff, so I got some advice on it, good advice, I think. The position is this. Every radio transmission takes place in some form of code, which has to be unscrambled at the receiving end. In this country the normal form of coding goes by the technical name of amplitude modulation, although the B.B.C. has recently also been using a somewhat different form of coding known as frequency modulation.'

'Ah, that's what frequency modulation is, is it? I've often heard people talking about it.'

'Yes, sir. Well, here's the point. The type of transmission that this equipment here of Kingsley's could give would be in a quite new form of code, a code that could not be unscrambled except by a specially designed receiving instrument. So although he might wish to send some message nobody could receive it.'

'Short of having this special receiver?'

'Exactly. Well now, do we allow Kingsley his electronic equipment or not?'

'What reason does he give for wanting it?'

'For radio astronomy. For observing this Cloud by radio.'

'Could it be used for that purpose?'

'Oh, yes.'

'Then what *is* the trouble, Francis?'

'It's just that there's an awful lot of it. Admittedly I'm not a scientist, but I can't swallow that this mass of stuff is really necessary. Well, do we let him have it or not?'

The Prime Minister thought for a few minutes.

'Check this advice of yours carefully. If what you've said about the coding turns out to be right, let him have it. In fact this transmission business may turn out to be an advantage. Francis, so far you've been thinking of all this from a national point of view – national as opposed to international, I mean?'

'Yes, sir?'

'I've been giving some attention to the wider aspects. The Americans must be finding themselves in much the same boat as ourselves. Almost certainly they will be thinking of forming a similar establishment to Nortonstowe. I think I shall try to persuade them of the advantage of a single co-operative effort.'

'But won't that mean that we shall go there, not them come here?' said Parkinson, somewhat ungrammatically. 'They will consider their men to be better than ours.'

'Perhaps not in this field of – er – radio astronomy, in which I gather that both we and the Australians rank very highly. Since radio astronomy seems to be of rather key importance in this business I shall use radio astronomy as a strong bargaining point.'

'Security,' groaned Parkinson. 'Americans think we have no security, and sometimes I think they are not far wrong.'

'Overweighed by the consideration that our population is more phlegmatic than theirs. I suspect that the American Administration may see an advantage in having all working scientists in this matter as far away from them as possible. Otherwise they will be sitting on a powder keg the whole time. Communication was my difficulty until a few moments ago. But if we could provide a radio link direct from Nortonstowe to Washington, using this new code of yours, that might solve the problem. I shall urge all this most strenuously.'

'You referred to international aspects a few moments ago. Did you really mean international or Anglo-American?'

'I meant international, the Australian radio astronomers for one thing. And I can't see things remaining between us and the Americans for very long. The heads of other Governments will have to be told, even the Soviets. Then I shall see that a few hints are dropped, to the effect that Dr this and Dr that have received letters from one Kingsley discussing details of the business and that we have since been obliged to confine Kingsley in a place called Nortonstowe. I shall also say that if Dr this and Dr that are sent to Nortonstowe we shall be glad to see that they cause no trouble to their respective Governments.'

'But the Soviets wouldn't fall for that!'

'Why not? We've seen ourselves how acutely embarrassing knowledge outside the Government can be. What wouldn't we have given yesterday to have been rid of Kingsley? Perhaps you'd still like to be rid of him. They'll rush their people over here as fast as aeroplanes can travel.'

'Possibly so. But why go to all this trouble, sir?'

'Well, has it struck you that Kingsley may all along have been picking the team? That those registered letters were his way of doing it? I think it's going to be important to us to have the strongest possible team. I have a hunch that in the days to come Nortonstowe may possibly become more important than the United Nations.'

Chapter Five

NORTONSTOWE

THE manor house of Nortonstowe is set in open parkland, high in the Cotswolds not far from the steep western scarp. The land around is fertile. When it was first proposed to turn the manor into 'one of those Government places' there was a considerable measure of opposition both locally and in newspapers throughout Gloucestershire. But the Government had its way, as it does in such matters. The 'locals' were somewhat mollified when they heard that the new 'place' was to be agricultural in orientation and that farmers could look to it for advice.

An extensive new estate was built in the grounds of Nortonstowe out of sight of the manor house about a mile and a half away. For the most part the new estate consisted of semi-detached dwellings to be used for the working staff, but there were also some separate houses for senior officials and supervisors.

Helen and Joe Stoddard lived in one of the semi-detached rows of whitewashed houses. Joe had got himself a job as one of the gardeners. Literally and metaphorically it suited him down to the ground. At the age of thirty-one it was work in which he had had almost thirty years' experience, for he had learned from his father, a gardener before him, almost as soon as he could walk. It suited Joe because it kept him out of doors the year round. It suited him because in an era of form-filling and letter-writing there was no paper work to be done, for, let it be said, Joe had difficulty both in reading and writing. His appreciation of seed catalogues was confined to a study of the pictures. But this was no disadvantage since all seeds were ordered by the head gardener.

In spite of a somewhat remarkable slowness of mind Joe was popular with his mates. No one ever found him out of countenance, he was never known to be 'down in the dumps'. When he was puzzled, as he often was, a smile would spread slowly across an amiable face.

Joe's control over the muscles of his powerful frame was as good as his control over his brain was poor. He played an excellent game of darts, although he left the business of scoring to others. At skittles he was the terror of the neighbourhood.

Helen Stoddard contrasted oddly with her husband: a slight pretty girl of twenty-eight, highly intelligent but uneducated. It was something of a mystery how Joe and Helen got on so well. Perhaps it was because Joe was so easy to manage. Or perhaps because their two small children seemed to have inherited the best of two worlds, the mother's intelligence and the father's toughness of physique.

But now Helen was angry with her Joe. Queer things were happening up at the big house. During the last fortnight hundreds of men had descended on the place. Old installations had been torn out to make way for new. A great tract of land had been cleared and strange wires were being erected all over it. It should have been easy for Joe to have discovered what it all meant, but Joe was so easily fobbed off with ridiculous explanations; that the wires were for training trees being the latest piece of nonsense.

Joe for his part couldn't understand what all the fuss was about. If it was very strange, as his wife said, well, most things were pretty odd anyway. 'They' must know all about it, and that was good enough for him.

Helen was angry because she had become dependent for information on her rival, Mrs Alsop. Peggy, Agnes Alsop's daughter, was employed as a secretary at the manor, and Peggy was endowed with a curiosity not even surpassed by Helen or by her mother. In consequence a steady stream of information flowed into the Alsop household. Thanks in part to this bounty and in part to the skilful way in which she dispensed it, Agnes Alsop's prestige ranked high among her neighbours.

To this must be added a gift for speculation. On the day that Peggy solved the mystery of the contents of the vast number of crates marked 'Fragile: with the Greatest Care' Mrs Alsop's stock attained a new high.

'Full of wireless valves, that's what they are,' she told her assembled court, 'millions of 'em.'

'But what would they want millions of valves for?' asked Helen.

'You might well ask,' answered Mrs Alsop. 'And what would

they want all those towers and wires in the five-hundred-acre field for? If you ask me, it's a death-ray that they're building.'

Subsequent events never shook her faith in this opinion.

Excitement in 'Highlands Estate' knew no bounds on the day 'they' arrived. Peggy became well nigh incoherent when she told her mother how a tall man with blue eyes had talked to important people from the Government 'as if they were office boys, Mum'. 'It's a death-ray all right,' breathed Mrs Alsop in ecstasy.

One of the tit-bits fell to Helen Stoddard after all, perhaps the most important tit-bit from a practical point of view. The day after 'they' moved in, she started off early in the morning to cycle to the neighbouring village of Far Striding only to discover that a barrier had been thrown across the road. The barrier was guarded by a sergeant of police. Yes, she would be allowed this once to go on to the village, but in future no one could come into or out of Nortonstowe unless a pass was shown. Passes were going to be issued later that day. Everyone was to be photographed and the photos would be added to the passes later in the week. What about the children going to school? Well, he believed that a teacher was being sent up from Stroud so that it wouldn't be necessary for the children to go into the village at all. He was sorry that he knew no more about it.

The death-ray theory gained further ground.

*

It was an odd commission. It came through Ann Halsey's agent. Would she accept an engagement on 25 February to play two sonatas, one by Mozart, the other by Beethoven, at some place in Gloucestershire? The fee named was high, very high even for an able young pianist. There would also be a quartet. No other details were given, except that a car would be waiting at Bristol for the 2 p.m. Paddington train.

It wasn't until Ann went along to the restaurant car for tea that she discovered the identity of the quartet, which turned out to be none other than Harry Hargreaves and his crowd.

'We're doing some Schönberg,' said Harry. 'Just to file their ear-drums down a bit. Who are they, by the way?'

'A country-house party, as far as I can gather.'

'Must be pretty wealthy, judging by the fees they're willing to pay.'

The drive from Bristol to Nortonstowe passed very pleasantly. There was already a hint of an early spring. The chauffeur took them into the manor house, along corridors, opened a door. 'The visitors from Bristol, sir!'

Kingsley had not been expecting anyone, but he recovered quickly.

'Hello, Ann! Hello, Harry! How nice!'

'Nice to see you, Chris. But what is all this? How did you come to turn yourself into a country squire? Lord, more like, considering the magnificence of this place – rolling acres and that sort of thing.'

'Well, we're on a special job for the Government. They apparently think we're in need of some cultural uplift. Hence your presence,' explained Kingsley.

The evening was a great success, both the dinner and the concert, and it was with great regret that the musicians prepared to leave the following morning.

'Well, good-bye, Chris, and thanks for the pleasant stay,' said Ann.

'Your car ought to be waiting. It's a pity that you should have to leave so soon.'

But there was neither chauffeur nor car waiting.

'No matter,' said Kingsley, 'I'm sure that Dave Weichart will be willing to run you to Bristol in his own car, although it'll be quite a squeeze with all those instruments.'

Yes, Dave Weichart would run them to Bristol, and it was quite a squeeze, but after about a quarter of an hour and much laughter they were under way.

Within half an hour the whole party was back again. The musicians were puzzled. Weichart was in a flaming rage. He marched the whole party into Kingsley's office.

'What's going on around here, Kingsley? When we got down to the guard's place, he wouldn't let us through the barrier. Said he had orders not to let anyone out.'

'We've all got engagements in London this evening,' said Ann, 'and if we don't get away soon we shall miss our train.'

'Well, if you can't get out of the front gate, there are lots of other ways out,' answered Kingsley. 'Let me make a few inquiries.'

He spent ten minutes at the phone while the others fretted and fumed. At length he put the receiver down.

'You're not the only ones in a bit of a temper. People from the estate have been trying to get out into the village, and they've all been stopped. It appears as if there's a guard around the whole perimeter. I think I'd better get on to London.'

Kingsley pressed a switch.

'Hello, is that the guard's office at the front gate? Yes, yes, I accept that you are only acting under the Chief Constable's orders. I understand that. What I want you to do is this. Listen carefully, I want you to ring Whitehall 9700. When you get that number you will give the code letters QUE and ask for Mr Francis Parkinson, Secretary to the Prime Minister. When Mr Parkinson comes on the line you will tell him that Professor Kingsley wishes to speak to him. Then you will put the call through to me. Please repeat these instructions.'

After a few minutes Parkinson came through. Kingsley began:

'Hello, Parkinson. I hear you sprang your trap this morning ... No, no, I'm not complaining. I expected it. You may put as many guards as you please on the perimeter of Nortonstowe, but I will have none of them inside. I am ringing now to tell you that communication with Nortonstowe will henceforth be on a different basis. There are to be no more telephone calls. We intend cutting all wires leading to the guard posts. If you wish to communicate with us you must use the radio link ... If you haven't finished the transmitter yet, that's your own affair. You shouldn't insist on the Home Secretary doing all the wiring ... You don't understand? Then you ought to. If you chaps are competent enough to run this country at a time of crisis you ought to be competent enough to build a transmitter, especially when we've given you the design. There's one other thing and I'd like you to take careful note of it. If you won't allow anyone to go out, we shall allow nobody to come into Nortonstowe. Or on second thoughts you yourself, Parkinson, may come in if you please, but you will not be allowed out. That's all.'

'But the whole thing's preposterous,' said Weichart. 'Why, it's practically like being imprisoned. I didn't know this could happen in England.'

'Anything can happen in England,' answered Kingsley, 'only the reasons that are given may be somewhat unusual. If you want to keep a body of men and women imprisoned in a country estate somewhere in England, you don't tell the guards that they are guarding a prison. You tell them that those inside need protection against desperate characters who are trying to break in from outside. Protection, not confinement, is the watchword here.'

And indeed the Chief Constable was under the impression that Nortonstowe held atomic secrets that would revolutionize the application of nuclear power to industry. He was also under the impression that foreign espionage would do its utmost to prise out these secrets. He knew that the most likely leak would be from someone actually working at Nortonstowe. It was therefore a simple deduction that the best form of security would be to prevent all access to, or egress from, the place. In this belief he had been confirmed by the Home Secretary himself. He was even willing to concede that it might be necessary to augment his police guard by calling in the military.

'But what has this, whatever it may mean, to do with us?' asked Ann Halsey.

'It'd be easy for me to pretend that you happened to be here by accident,' said Kingsley, 'but I don't think so. You're here as part of a plan. There are others here as well. You see George Fisher, the artist, was commissioned by the Government to do some drawings of Nortonstowe. Then there's John McNeil, a young physician, and Bill Price, the historian, working on the old library. I think we'd better try to rope 'em all in, and then I'll explain as best I can.'

When Fisher, McNeil, and Price had been added to their company, Kingsley gave the assembled non-scientists a general but fairly detailed account of the discovery of the Black Cloud, and of the events that had led up to the establishment of Nortonstowe.

'I can see why this explains the guards and so forth. But it doesn't explain why we're here. You said it wasn't an accident. Why us and not someone else?' asked Ann Halsey.

'My fault,' answered Kingsley. 'What I believe to have happened is this. An address book of mine was found by Government agents. In that book were the names of scientists that I consulted about the Black Cloud. What I presume to have happened is that when some of my contacts were discovered, the Government decided to take no chances. They simply roped in everybody in the address book. I'm sorry.'

'That was damned careless of you, Chris,' exclaimed Fisher.

'Well, frankly I've had quite a lot to worry about during the last six weeks. And after all your situation is really pretty good. You've said, without exception, what a nice place this is. And when the crisis comes you've a vastly better chance of surviving than you could possibly have had otherwise. We shall survive here if survival is at all possible. So at root you may think that you've been pretty fortunate.'

'This address book business, Kingsley,' said McNeil, 'doesn't seem to apply at all in my case. As far as I'm aware we never met until a few days ago.'

'Incidentally, McNeil, why are you here, if I may ask?'

'Cock and bull story evidently. I've been concerned with finding a site for a new sanatorium, and Nortonstowe was recommended to me. Ministry of Health suggested I might like to see the place for myself. But why me I can't imagine.'

'Perhaps so that we had a doctor on the spot.'

Kingsley got up and walked to the window. Cloud shadows were chasing each other across the meadows.

*

One afternoon in mid-April, Kingsley returned to the house after a brisk walk round the Nortonstowe estate, to find aniseed smoke pervading his room.

'What the ...!' he exclaimed. 'By all that's wonderful, Geoff Marlowe. I'd given up hopes of you getting here. How did you manage it?'

'By deception and treachery,' replied Marlowe between large mouthfuls of toast. 'Nice place you've got here. Have some tea?'

'Thanks, it's very kind of you.'

'Not at all. After you left we were moved down to Palomar,

where I was able to do a certain amount of work. Then we were all transported into the desert, with the exception of Emerson, who I believe was sent over here.'

'Yes, we've got Emerson, Barnett, and Weichart. I was rather afraid they'd given you the desert treatment. That's why I cleared out so quickly as soon as Herrick said he was going to Washington. Did he get a thick ear for allowing me to leave the country?'

'I gather so, but he didn't say much about it.'

'Incidentally, am I right in supposing that the A.R. was sent over to your side?'

'Yes, sir! The Astronomer Royal is Chief British Liaison Officer to the whole U.S. project.'

'Good for him. That'll be exactly up his alley, I expect. But you haven't told me how you managed to give the desert the slip, and why you decided to leave.'

'The why of it is easy. Because of the way we were organized to death.'

Marlowe took a handful of lumps out of the sugar bowl. He laid one on the table.

'This is the guy who does the work.'

'What do you call him?'

'I don't know that we call him anything in particular.'

'We call him a "bod" over here.'

'A "bod"?'

'That's right. Short for "body".'

'Well, even though we don't call him a "bod", he's a "bod" all right,' went on Marlowe. 'In fact he's a hell of a "bod", as you'll soon see.'

Next he laid down a row of sugar lumps.

'Above the "bod" comes his Section Leader. In view of my seniority I'm a Section Leader. Then comes the Deputy Director. Herrick became a Deputy Director in spite of his being in the doghouse. Then here's our old friend the Director himself. Above him comes the Assistant Controller, then who else but the Controller? They're the military, of course. Next comes the Project Coordinator. He's a politician. And so by degrees we come to the President's Deputy. After that I suppose comes the President, although I can't be sure because I never got as high as that.'

'You didn't like it, I suppose?'

'No, sir, I didn't,' continued Marlowe as he crunched another piece of toast. 'I was too near the bottom of the hierarchy to like it. Besides I could never find out what was going on outside my own section. The policy was to keep everything in watertight compartments. In the interests of security, they said, but more likely in the interests of inefficiency, I think. Well, I didn't like it as you can imagine. It isn't my way of going about a problem. So I started agitating for a transfer, a transfer to this show over here. I had an idea that things would be done a lot better here. And I see they are,' he added, as he took up another piece of toast.

'Besides I suddenly got a longing for a sight of green grass. When that comes on you it isn't to be denied.'

'This is all very well, Geoff, but it doesn't explain how you prised yourself loose from this formidable organization.'

'Pure luck,' answered Marlowe. 'The people over in Washington got the idea that maybe you people weren't telling everything you knew. And as I'd let it be known that I'd welcome a transfer, I was sent over here as a spy. That's where the treachery comes in.'

'You mean you're supposed to report on anything we may be concealing?'

'That's exactly the situation. And now that you know why I'm here, am I to be allowed to stay or are you going to throw me out?'

'It's the rule here that everyone who comes into Nortonstowe stays. We don't let anyone out.'

'Then it'll be all right if Mary comes along? She's been doing some shopping in London. But she'll be right along some time tomorrow.'

'That'll be fine. This is a big place. We've got plenty of room. We shall be glad to have Mrs Marlowe here. Frankly, there's an awful lot of work to be done, and far too few people to do it.'

'And maybe occasionally I might send a crumb of information to Washington, just to keep them happy?'

'You can tell 'em anything you like. I find the more I tell the politicians the more depressed they get. So it's our policy to tell

'em everything. There's no secrecy at all here. You can send anything you wish on the direct radio link to Washington. We got it
working about a week ago.'

'In that case maybe you'd give me an outline of what's been
happening at this end. Personally, I'm very little wiser than on the
day we talked out in the Mohave Desert. I have done a bit, but
it isn't optical work we need just now. By the fall we could get
something. But this is a business for the radio boys, as I think
we agreed.'

'We did. And I stirred up John Marlborough as soon as I got
back to Cambridge in January. It took some persuasion to start
him on the job, because I didn't tell him the real reason to begin
with – although he knows now of course. Well, we got out a temperature for the Cloud. It's a little above two hundred degrees,
two hundred degrees absolute of course.'

'That's pretty good. About what we'd hoped for. A bit cold,
but possible.'

'It's really better than it sounds. Because, as the Cloud approaches the Sun, internal motions must develop inside it. My
first calculations showed that the resulting rise of temperature
might be somewhere between fifty and a hundred per cent, making in total a temperature somewhere around freezing point. So it
looked as if we might be in for a frosty spell and nothing more.'

'Couldn't be better.'

'That's what I thought at the time. But I'm not really an expert
in gas dynamics, so I wrote off to Alexandrov.'

'My God, you were taking a chance in writing to Moscow.'

'I don't think so. The problem could be put in a purely aca-
demic form. And there's nobody better suited to tackle it than
Alexandrov. In any case it led to us getting him here. He regards
this as the best concentration camp in the world.'

'I see there's still a lot that I don't know. Go on.'

'At this time, still in January, I was feeling pretty clever. So I
decided to take the political authorities for a really rough trip. I
perceived that two things the politicians must have at all costs –
scientific information and secrecy. I determined to give both to
them, on my own conditions – the conditions you see around you
here at Nortonstowe.'

'I see, a pleasant place to live in, no military to badger you, no secrecy. And how was the team recruited?'

'Simply by indiscretions in the right quarters, like the letter to Alexandrov. What could be more natural than that everyone should be brought here who might have learned anything from me? I did play one dirty trick, and it still lies on my conscience. Sooner or later you will meet a charming girl who plays the piano extremely well. You will meet an artist, an historian, other musicians. It seemed to me that incarceration at Nortonstowe for over a year would be quite intolerable if there were only scientists here. So I arranged the appropriate indiscretions. Don't breathe a word of this, Geoff. In the circumstances I think perhaps I was justified. But it's better they shouldn't know that I was deliberately responsible for their being sent here. What the eye doesn't see, the heart doesn't grieve over.'

'And what about that cave you were talking about when we were in the Mohave? I suppose you've got that all lined up too.'

'Of course. You probably haven't seen it, but over there – just below that hillock – we've got a vast quantity of earth-moving machinery at work.'

'Who looks after it?'

'The chaps that live down on the new housing estate.'

'And who runs the house here, cooks the food, and so on?'

'The women from the new estate, and the girls do the secretarial work.'

'What happens to them when things get tough?'

'They come into the shelter, of course. It means that the shelter has to be far bigger than I originally intended. That's why we've started work on it so early.'

'Well, Chris, it seems to me as if you've arranged a pretty smooth trip for yourself. But I don't see where the politicians are getting their rough ride. After all they've got us boxed in here, and by what you told me a while ago they're getting all the information you can give 'em. So things look pretty smooth for them too.'

'Let me put it to you as I saw it in January and February. In February I planned to take over the control of world affairs.'

Marlowe laughed.

'Oh, I know it sounds ridiculously melodramatic. But I'm being serious. And I'm not suffering from megalomania either. At least I don't think I am. It was only to be for a month or two, after which I would retire gracefully back to scientific work. I'm not the stuff dictators are made of. I'm only really comfortable as an underdog. But this was a heaven-sent opportunity for the underdog to take a great big bite out of those who were hoofing him around.'

'Living in this mansion you certainly look pretty much the underdog,' said Marlowe, settling down to his pipe and still laughing.

'All this had to be fought for. Otherwise we'd have had the same sort of set-up that you objected to. Let me talk a bit of philosophy and sociology. Has it ever occurred to you, Geoff, that in spite of all the changes wrought by science – by our control over inanimate energy, that is to say – we will preserve the same old social order of precedence? Politicians at the top, then the military, and the real brains at the bottom. There's no difference between this set-up and that of Ancient Rome, or of the first civilizations in Mesopotamia for that matter. We're living in a society that contains a monstrous contradiction, modern in its technology but archaic in its social organization. For years the politicians have been squawking about the need for more trained scientists, more engineers, and so forth. What they don't seem to realize is that there are only a limited number of fools.'

'Fools?'

'Yes, people like you and me, Geoff. We're the fools. We do the thinking for an archaic crowd of nitwits and allow ourselves to be pushed around by 'em into the bargain.'

'Scientists of the world unite! Is that the idea?'

'Not exactly. It isn't just a case of scientists versus the rest. The matter goes deeper. It's a clash between two totally different modes of thinking. Society today is based in its technology on thinking in terms of numbers. In its social organization, on the other hand, it is based on thinking in terms of words. It's here that the real clash lies, between the literary mind and the mathematical mind. You ought to meet the Home Secretary. You'd see straight away what I mean.'

'And you had an idea for altering all this?'

'I had an idea for striking a blow for the mathematical mind. But I'm not sufficient of an ass to imagine that anything I could do would be of decisive importance. With luck I thought I might be able to provide a good example, a sort of *locus classicus*, to quote the literary boys, for how we ought to set about twisting the tails of the politicians.'

'My God, Chris, you talk about numbers and words, but I never knew a man who used so many words. Can you explain what you're up to in simple terms?'

'By that I suppose you mean in terms of numbers. Well, I'll try. Let's assume that survival is possible when the Cloud gets here. Although I say survival, it's pretty certain that the conditions won't be pleasant. We shall either be freezing or sweltering. It's obviously extremely unlikely that people will be able to move about in a normal way. The most we can hope for is that by staying put, by digging our caves or cellars and staying in them, we shall be able to hang on. In other words all normal travel of people from place to place will cease. So communication and the control of human affairs must come to depend on electrical information. The signalling will have to go by radio.'

'You mean that coherence in society – coherence so that we don't split up into a whole lot of disconnected individuals – will depend on radio communications?'

'That's right. There'll be no newspapers, because the newspaper staffs will be in shelter.'

'Is this where you come in, Chris? Is Nortonstowe going to become a pirate radio station? Oh boy, where are my false whiskers!'

'Now listen. When radio communication becomes of overriding importance, problems of quantity of information will become vital. Control will gradually pass to those people with the ability to handle the greatest volume of information, and I planned that Nortonstowe would be able to handle at least a hundred times as much as all other transmitters on the Earth put together.'

'This is fantasy, Chris! How about power supplies for one thing?'

'We've got our own diesel generators, and plenty of fuel.'

'But surely you can't generate the tremendous amount of power that would be needed?'

'We don't need a tremendous amount of power. I didn't say we would have a hundred times the power of all other transmitters put together. I said we would have a hundred times the information-carrying capacity, which is quite a different thing. We shan't be transmitting programmes to individual people. We shall be transmitting on quite low power to Governments all over the world. We shall become a sort of international information clearing-house. Governments will pass messages one to another through us. In short we shall become the nerve centre of world communication, and that is the sense in which we shall control world affairs. If that seems a bit of an anti-climax after my build-up, well, remember I'm not a melodramatic sort of person.'

'I'm coming to realize that. But how on earth do you propose to equip yourself with this information-carrying capacity?'

'Let me give you the theory of it first. It's quite well known really. The reason it hasn't been put into operation already is partly inertia, vested interest in existing equipment, and partly inconvenience – all messages have to be recorded before transmission.'

Kingsley settled himself comfortably in an armchair.

'Of course you know that, instead of transmitting radio waves continuously, as is usually done, it's possible to transmit in bursts, in pulses. Let's suppose that we can transmit three sorts of pulses: a short pulse, a medium pulse, and a long pulse. In practice the long pulse might last for perhaps twice the duration of the short pulse, and the medium pulse might be one and a half times as long. With a transmitter working in the range seven to ten metres – the usual range for long-distance work – and with the usual band width, it should be possible to transmit about ten thousand pulses per second. The three sorts of pulses could be arranged in any assigned order – ten thousand of 'em per second. Now suppose we use the medium pulses for indicating the ends of letters, words, and sentences. One medium pulse indicates the end of a letter, two medium pulses following each other indicate the end of a word, and three following each other indicate the end of a sentence. This leaves the long and the short pulses for transmitting letters. Suppose, for instance, we elect to use the Morse code. Then at an average, about three pulses are needed per letter. Reckoning on an average of five letters to a word, this means that about fifteen of the long and short pulses are required per word. Or, if we include the medium pulses for marking the letters, about twenty pulses are required per word. So at a rate of ten thousand pulses per second this gives a transmission rate of about five hundred words per second, compared with a normal transmitter which handles less than three words per second. So we should be at least a hundred times faster.'

'Five hundred words per second. My God, what a gabble!'

'Actually we will probably broaden our band width so that we can send upwards of a million pulses per second. We reckon that a hundred thousand words a second might be possible. The limitation lies in the compression and expansion of messages. Obviously no one can talk at a hundred thousand words per second, not even the politicians, thank goodness. So messages will have to be recorded on magnetic tape. The tape will then be scanned electronically at high speed. But there's a limit to the speed of the scanning, at any rate with our present equipment.'

'Isn't there one big snag in all this? What's to stop the various Governments throughout the world from building the same sort of equipment?'

'Stupidity and inertia. As usual, nothing will be done until the crisis is on us. My one fear is that the politicians will be so lethargic that they won't get single transmitters and receivers built, let alone whole batteries of stuff. We're pushing 'em as hard as we can. For one thing they want information from us, and we've refused to provide this except by radio link. Another thing is that the whole ionosphere may get altered so that shorter wavelengths have to be used. We're preparing here to go as short as one centimetre. This is a point that we're constantly warning 'em about, but they're devilishly slow, slow in action and slow in wit.'

'Who here, by the way, is doing all this?'

'The radio astronomers. You probably know that a whole crowd came in from Manchester, Cambridge, and Sydney. There were more than enough for doing the radio astronomy so that they were jumping on each others' heels. That was until they locked us in. Everybody got mad, the silly asses – as if it wasn't obvious we should be locked up. Then I pointed out, with my usual tact, that anger wouldn't help us, that the obvious thing to do was to lick the pants off the politicians by converting some of our radio astronomy stuff into communication equipment. It was, of course, discovered that we had far more electronic equipment than was necessary for radio astronomy purposes. So we soon had a veritable army of communication engineers at work. Already we could swamp the B.B.C. in the amount of information we could transmit, if we were so minded.'

'You know, Kingsley, I'm still bemused by this pulse business. It still seems to me incredible that our broadcasting system should go on pumping out two or three words a second, when they might be sending five hundred.'

'That's a very easy one, Geoff. The human mouth transmits information at some two words per second. The human ear can only receive information at rates less than about three words per second. The great brains that control our destinies therefore design their electronic equipment to comply with these limitations even though electronically no such limitation exists. Don't I keep telling everyone that our whole social system is archaic, with the real knowledge at the bottom and a whole crowd of hobbledehoys at the top?'

'Which makes a very fine exit line,' laughed Marlowe. 'Speaking for myself, I've got a feeling that you're in danger of oversimplifying things just a tiny bit!'

Chapter Six

THE CLOUD APPROACHES

THE Cloud was not visible during the following summer since it lay in the daytime sky, although it was keenly examined with the radio telescope at Nortonstowe.

The situation was better than the Prime Minister had expected. News from Nortonstowe suggested that the coming of the Cloud was not likely to lead to an impossible fuel crisis, for which he was heartily thankful. For the time being there was no fear of public alarm. With the exception of the Astronomer Royal, in whom he reposed great confidence, the threat from the scientists, particularly from Kingsley, had been safely canalized at Nortonstowe. True, ridiculous concessions had been made. Worst of all he had lost Parkinson. It had been necessary to send Parkinson to Nortonstowe to make sure that no hanky-panky was going on there. But apparently the reports he was receiving were quite above board, and for this reason the Prime Minister resolved to let sleeping dogs lie, in spite of urgent suggestions to the contrary by some of his Ministers. Occasionally the Prime Minister wavered in this decision, for he found it intensely difficult to swallow the frequent messages from Kingsley advising him to secrecy.

In point of fact Kingsley's innuendos were shrewdly conceived, for Government security was not good. At each level of the political hierarchy, individuals regarded it as safe to impart information to their immediate subordinates. The outcome was that a knowledge of the approach of the Cloud filtered slowly downwards, until by the early autumn it reached almost to the parliamentary level. In short it had almost become available to the Press. But the moment was not quite ripe yet for the Cloud to become headline news.

The autumn was stormy and the skies in England were overcast. So although by October the Cloud had obscured a portion of the constellation of Lepus no alarm was given until November. It came from the clear skies of Arabia. Engineers of a large oil company were drilling in the desert. They noticed the concern with which their men were examining the sky. The Arabs pointed to the Cloud, or rather to a blackness in the sky, which by now was about seven degrees across, looking like a yawning circular pit. They said the pit should not be there, and that it was a sign in the sky. What the sign meant was not clear, but the men were frightened. Certainly none of the engineers remembered any such blackness, but none of them knew the disposition of the stars well enough to be certain. One of them had a star map back at base, however. When the drilling expedition was over he consulted the map. Sure enough, something was wrong. Letters to newspapers in England followed.

The newspapers took no immediate action. But within a week a whole series of similar stories came to hand. As often happens, one report was the signal for a host of others, rather as a single raindrop heralds the outbreak of a storm. The London papers sent special correspondents equipped with cameras and star maps to North Africa. The reporters set out in high spirits, thinking it a wonderful relief to a drab November. They returned in a chastened mood. The black hole in the sky did not encourage frivolity. No photographs were brought back. Newspaper editors had not realized that it is extremely difficult to photograph the stars with an ordinary camera.

The British Government was in some difficulty to know whether or not to prevent reports appearing in the Press. It was eventually decided that no action be taken, since any suggestion of suppression could only emphasize the gravity of the situation.

Editors were surprised at the tone of the reports submitted to them. They gave orders for a lighter and more frivolous touch, and it was in banal headlines such as

APPARITION APPEARS IN SKY
CELESTIAL BLACK-OUT DISCOVERED IN N. AFRICA
NO STARS FOR CHRISTMAS, SAY ASTRONOMERS

that the first news reached the public towards the end of November. A campaign was run. Photographs came in from several observatories, both in Great Britain and elsewhere. These appeared on front pages of the dailies (on the last page of course in the case of *The Times*), in some cases after a generous degree of touching up. Articles by well-known scientists were featured.

The people were informed of the existence of the highly tenuous interstellar gas, the gas that occupies the vast regions of space between the stars. Mixed up with this gas, it was pointed out, were myriads of fine grains, probably grains of ice, no more than about one hundred-thousandth part of an inch in their dimensions. It was these grains that produced the dozens of dark patches to be seen along the Milky Way. Photographs of such dark patches were displayed. The new apparition was simply one of these patches seen from near by. The fact that the solar system occasionally passed close to, or even through, such accumulations had been known to astronomers for some time. Indeed encounters of this sort formed the basis of one well-known theory of the origin of comets. Photographs of comets were also displayed.

Scientific circles were not wholly soothed by this information. The Cloud became a frequent topic of conversation and speculation in laboratories everywhere. The argument given by Weichart a year earlier was rediscovered. It was soon realized that the density of the material of the Cloud was a critical factor. The general tendency was to set this much too low, but some scientists remembered Kingsley's remarks at the meeting of the British Astronomical Association. Significance was also attached to the disappearance from the universities of the group at Nortonstowe. It was generally felt that the circumstances justified a measure of alarm. No doubt this apprehension would have grown rapidly stronger had it not been for the increasing call of the Governments, both in Britain and elsewhere, on scientists in general. They were asked to take a part in organizing the emergency preparations that were then gaining real momentum, preparations particularly concerned with food, fuel, and shelter.

The alarm did communicate itself to the public in some degree, however. During the first fortnight of December there were signs of a growing uneasiness. Well-known columnists, demanding an informed statement from the Government, used much the same trenchant terms that they had employed several years earlier concerning the Burgess–Maclean episode. But this first wave of apprehension spent itself in a curious way. The third week of December was frosty and clear. In spite of the cold, people streamed by car and bus out of the towns to get a view of the night sky. But no apparition, no hole in the sky, was visible. Few stars could be seen at all because of bright moonlight. In vain did the Press point out that the Cloud was invisible except when projected against a background of stars. As an item of news the Cloud, for the time being at least, was dead. In any case Christmas was only a few days off.

The Government had good reason to be heartily thankful for this early demise of the Cloud, for they received in December an alarming report from Nortonstowe. The circumstances underlying this report are worth mentioning.

During the summer the organization at Nortonstowe settled down into a smooth pattern. The scientists divided into two groups, those concerned with 'Cloud investigations' and those concerned with the communication problems that Kingsley had explained to Marlowe. The non-scientists dealt with the business of the estate and with the building of the shelter. It was the practice for each of the three sections to hold a weekly meeting which everyone might attend. In this way it was possible to know how all affairs were developing without the necessity of going into details concerning the problems of other groups.

Marlowe worked on the 'Cloud investigations', using the Schmidt telescope taken from Cambridge. By October he and Roger Emerson had solved the problem of the direction of motion of the Cloud. Marlowe explained the matter in rather more detail than was perhaps necessary to the meeting that had been called to hear the latest results. He concluded:

'So it seems as if the Cloud must have practically zero angular momentum about the Sun.'

'And what in practical terms does that mean?' asked McNeil.

'It means that both the Sun and the Earth are certain to be engulfed. If there had been any appreciable angular momentum, the Cloud would have swung aside at the last moment. But now it's quite clear that this won't happen. The Cloud is moving straight in at the Sun.'

'Isn't that a bit odd, that it should just happen to be lined up so accurately on the Sun?' persisted McNeil.

'Well, it's got to be moving somehow,' answered Bill Barnett. 'And it's quite as likely to be moving one way as another.'

'But I can't help feeling that it's queer that the Cloud should just happen to be going straight for the Sun,' continued the tenacious Irishman.

Alexandrov stopped trying to persuade one of the secretaries to sit on his knee.

'Damn queer,' he announced. 'But lots of things damn queer. Damn queer that Moon looks just same size as Sun. Damn queer that I'm here, isn't it so?'

'Damned unfortunate,' muttered the secretary.

After a few minutes of further somewhat inconsequential discussion, Yvette Hedelfort stood up and addressed the meeting.

'I'm in trouble,' she announced.

There were grins and a voice was heard to remark: 'Damn queer, isn't it so?'

'I don't mean that sort of trouble,' the girl continued. 'I mean a proper kind of trouble. Dr Marlowe says the Cloud is made of hydrogen. Measurements give a density inside the Cloud a little greater than 10^{-10} gm. per cm^3. I estimate that if the Earth moves through such a cloud for about one month the amount of hydrogen that will be added to our atmosphere will exceed a hundred grams for each square centimetre of the earth's surface. Is this right, please?'

There was a silence as the implication of these remarks dawned on the meeting, or at any rate on some of the scientists.

'We'd better check that right away,' muttered Weichart. He figured on a pad of paper for perhaps five minutes.

'It's right, I guess,' he announced.

Almost without comment the meeting broke up. Parkinson came up to Marlowe.

'But, Dr Marlowe, what does all this mean?'

'My God, isn't it obvious? It means that enough hydrogen is going to come into the Earth's atmosphere to combine with all the oxygen. Hydrogen and oxygen are a violently unstable chemical mixture. The whole atmosphere will blow sky-high. Trust a woman to spot that.'

Kingsley, Alexandrov, and Weichart spent the afternoon arguing. In the evening they collected Marlowe and Yvette Hedelfort and went to Parkinson's room.

'Look, Parkinson,' began Kingsley, after drinks had been poured, 'I think it's up to you to decide what London, Washington, and all the other cities of sin are to be told. Things aren't quite as simple as they seemed this morning. I'm afraid the hydrogen isn't really as important as you thought, Yvette.'

'I didn't say it was important, Chris. I simply asked a question.'

'And you were quite right to do so, Miss Hedelfort,' broke in Weichart. 'We've been giving far too much attention to the temperature problem and overlooking the effect of the Cloud on the Earth's atmosphere.'

'Not clear until Dr Marlowe finished work that Earth would be in Cloud,' grunted Alexandrov.

'That's true enough,' agreed Weichart. 'But now the decks are cleared we can get into action. The first point is one of energy. Each gram of hydrogen that enters the atmosphere can liberate energy in two ways, first by its impact with the atmosphere and second by combination with oxygen. Of these the first yields more energy and is therefore more important.'

'My God, this only makes its worse,' exclaimed Marlowe.

'Not necessarily. Think what'll happen when the gas of the Cloud hits the atmosphere. The very outside of the atmosphere'll become extremely hot, because it's on the outside where the impact will take place. We've calculated that the temperature of the outer parts of the atmosphere'll go racing up to hundreds of thousands of degrees, perhaps even to millions of degrees. The next point is that the Earth and the atmosphere are spinning round and that the Cloud will be hitting the atmosphere from one side only.'

'From what side?' asked Parkinson.

'The Earth's position in its orbit will be such that the Cloud will come at us from the approximate direction of the Sun,' explained Yvette Hedelfort.

'Although the Sun itself won't be visible,' added Marlowe.

'So the Cloud will be hitting the atmosphere during what would normally be the daytime?'

'That's right. And it will not be hitting the atmosphere during the night.'

'And that's the crux of the matter,' continued Weichart.

'Because of the very high temperature I was talking about, the outer parts of the atmosphere will tend to blow outwards. This won't happen during the "daytime" because the impact of the Cloud will hold it in, but at "night" the upper atmosphere will stream outwards into space.'

'Oh, I see what you're meaning,' said Yvette Hedelfort. 'Hydrogen will come into the atmosphere during the "daytime" but it will blow out again during the "night". So there will not be any cumulative addition of hydrogen from day to day.'

'That's exactly right.'

'But can we be sure that all the hydrogen will be evaporated off in this way, Dave?' asked Marlowe. 'If even a small proportion of it were retained, say one per cent or a tenth per cent, the effect would be disastrous. We've got to keep in mind how very small a disturbance – small from the astronomical point of view – could still wipe us out of existence.'

'I'd feel confident in predicting that effectively all the hydrogen will be evaporated away. The danger is rather the other way, that too much of the other gases of the atmosphere will also get evaporated into space.'

'How can that be? You said only the outer parts of the atmosphere would be heated.'

Kingsley took up the argument.

'The situation is this. To begin with, the top of the atmosphere will be hot, extremely hot. The bottom of the atmosphere, the part where we live, will be cool to start with. But there'll be a gradual downward transfer of energy, tending to heat up the lower parts.'

Kingsley put down his glass of whisky.

'The whole point is to decide how fast the downward transference of energy will be. As you say, Geoff, only a very slight effect would be utterly disastrous. The lower atmosphere might be heated sufficiently to cook us, quite literally to cook us, all done to a turn quite slowly, politicians included, Parkinson!'

'You're forgetting that we shall survive longest, because our skins are thickest.'

'Excellent, a point to you! Of course the downward transfer of energy might be fast enough to cause the whole of the atmosphere to be blown off into space.'

'Can this be decided?'

'Well, there are three ways of transferring energy, they're just our old friends, conduction, convection, and radiation. We can be pretty sure already that conduction isn't going to be important.'

'Nor convection either,' broke in Weichart. 'There'll be a stable atmosphere with a rising temperature as you go outwards. So there can be no convection.'

'So that leaves radiation,' concluded Marlowe.

'And what will the effect of radiation be?'

'We don't know,' said Weichart. 'It'll have to be calculated.'

'You can do that?' queried the persistent Parkinson.

Kingsley nodded.

'Can calculate,' affirmed Alexandrov. 'Will be bloody great calculation.'

*

Three weeks later Kingsley asked Parkinson to see him.

'We've got the results from the electronic computer,' he said. 'Good thing I insisted on having that computer. It looks as though we're all right so far as radiation is concerned. We've got a factor of about ten in hand and that should be safe enough. There's going to be an awful lot of lethal stuff coming downward from the top of the atmosphere though – X-rays and ultra-violet light. But it seems as if it won't get through to the bottom of the atmosphere. We shall be pretty well shielded down at sea-level. But the situation won't be so good in the high mountains. I think people will have to be brought down. Places like Tibet will be impossible.'

'But, by and large, you think we'll be all right?'

'I just don't know. Frankly, Parkinson, I'm worried. It's not this radiation business. I think we're all right there. But I don't agree with Dave Weichart about convection, and I don't think he's as confident as he was. You remember his point about there being no convection because of the temperature increasing outwards. That's all very well under ordinary conditions. Temperature inversions, as they're called, are well known, particularly in Southern California, where Weichart comes from. And it's quite true that there's no vertical movement of the air in a temperature inversion.'

'Well then, what are you worried about?'

'The top of the atmosphere, the part that the Cloud is hitting. There must be convection at the top, because of the impact from outside. This convection certainly won't penetrate through to the bottom of the atmosphere. Weichart's right there. But it must penetrate downwards a little way. And in the region in which it does there'll be a big transference of heat.'

'But so long as the heat doesn't get to the bottom will that matter?'

'It may do. Consider things as they'll occur day by day. The first day there'll be a little penetration of the currents. Then at night we shall lose not only the hydrogen that has come in during the day but also the part of the atmosphere down to which the currents have penetrated. So in the first day and night we shall lose an outer skin of our atmosphere, quite in addition to the hydrogen. Then the next day and night we shall lose another skin. And so on. Day by day the atmosphere will be stripped off in a series of skins.'

'Will it last for a month?'

'That's exactly the problem. And I can't tell you the answer. Maybe it won't last ten days. Maybe it'll last a whole month quite easily. I just don't know.'

'Can't you find out?'

'I can try, but it's horribly difficult to make sure that every important factor is included in the calculations. It's much worse than the radiation problem. Undoubtedly we can get some sort of answer but I don't know that I'd give it much weight. I can tell you right now that it's going to be a touch-and-go business. Frankly again, I don't believe we shall be much wiser six months from now.

This is probably one of those things that are too complicated for
direct calculation. We shall have to wait and see, I'm afraid.'

'What am I to tell London?'

'That's up to you. You certainly ought to tell 'em about
evacuating high mountain districts even though there aren't any
high enough to matter in Britain. But I leave it to your judgement
how much of the rest you tell 'em.'

'Not very nice, is it?'

'No. If you find it getting you down I'd recommend a talk with
one of the gardeners, Stoddard by name. He's so slow that nothing would worry him, not even the atmosphere being sprayed off.'

*

By the third week in January the fate of Man was to be read in the
skies. The star Rigel of Orion was obscured. The sword and belt
of Orion and the bright star Sirius followed in subsequent weeks.
The Cloud might have blotted out almost any other constellation,
except perhaps the Plough, without its effect being so widely noted.

The Press revived its interest in the Cloud. 'Progress reports'
were published daily. Bus companies were finding their Night-
time Mystery Tours increasingly popular. 'Listener research'
showed a threefold increase in the audience for a series of B.B.C.
talks on astronomy.

At the end of January perhaps one person in four had actually
observed the Cloud. This was not a sufficient proportion to control public opinion, but it was sufficient to persuade the majority
that it was high time that they took a look for themselves. Since
it was scarcely possible for a majority of town dwellers to move
at night into the country, suggestions were made for the shutting
off of town lighting systems. These were at first resisted by muni-
cipal authorities, but resistance only served to change polite suggestions into strident demands. Wolverhampton was the first
town in Britain to impose a nightly black-out. Others quickly followed, and by the end of the second week in February the London
authorities capitulated. Now at last the population at large was
starkly aware of the Black Cloud, as it clutched like a grasping
hand at Orion, the Hunter of the Heavens.

A closely similar pattern of events was repeated in the U.S., and indeed in every industrialized country. The U.S. had the additional problem of evacuating much of the western states, since a considerable area of populated territory there lies above 5,000 feet, the safe limit set in the Nortonstowe report. The U.S. Government had of course referred the matter to its own experts, but their conclusions turned out not to differ significantly from those of Nortonstowe. The U.S. also undertook to organize the evacuation of the Andean republics of South America.

The agrarian countries of Asia were strangely unmoved by the information supplied to them through the United Nations. Theirs was a 'wait and see' policy, which might really be said to have been the wisest course of all. For thousands of years the Asian peasant had been accustomed to natural disasters – 'acts of God' as the lawyers of the West called them. To the oriental mind drought and flood, marauding tribes, plagues of locusts, disease, were to be suffered passively, and so was the new thing in the sky. In any case life offered them little and consequently was not set at an unduly high price.

The evacuation of Tibet, Sinkiang, and Outer Mongolia was left to the Chinese. With cynical indifference nothing at all was done by them. The Russians, on the other hand, were punctilious and prompt in their evacuation of the Pamirs and of their other highland areas. Indeed genuine efforts were made to shift the Afghans, but Russian emissaries were driven out of Aghanistan at pistol point. India and Pakistan also spared no effort to ensure the evacuation of the part of the Himalaya south of the main watershed.

With the coming of spring in the northern hemisphere the Cloud passed more and more from the night sky to the day sky. So, although it was spreading rapidly outside the constellation of Orion, which was now completely obscured, its presence was far less obvious to the casual observer. The British still played cricket, and dug their gardens, as indeed did the Americans.

The widespread interest in gardening was favoured by an exceptionally early summer which started in mid-May. Apprehension was widespread certainly, but it was lulled to a vague outline by week after week of wonderfully clear sunny weather. Vegetable crops were ready for eating in late May.

The Government was not nearly so pleased by the excellent weather. The reason underlying it was ominous. Since its first detection, the Cloud had by now completed about ninety per cent of the journey to the Sun. It had of course been realized that more and more radiation would be reflected by the Cloud as the Sun was approached, and that a consequent rise of temperature would take place on the Earth. Marlowe's observations suggested that there would be little or no increase in the amount of visible light, a prediction that turned out to be correct. Throughout the whole of the brilliant spring and early summer there was no noticeable increase in the brightness of the sky. What was happening was that light from the Sun was impinging on the Cloud and being re-radiated as invisible heat. Fortunately, not all the light impinging on the Cloud was re-radiated in this fashion, otherwise the Earth would have become entirely uninhabitable. And fortunately quite a large fraction of the heat never penetrated inwards through our atmosphere. It was reflected and bounced back into space.

By June it became clear that the temperature of the Earth was likely to be raised everywhere by some thirty degrees Fahrenheit. It is not commonly realized how near the death temperature a large fraction of the human species lives. Under very dry atmospheric conditions a man can survive up to air temperatures of about 140° Fahrenheit. Such temperatures are in fact attained in a normal summer in low-lying regions of the Western American desert and in North Africa. But under highly humid conditions, the death temperature is only about 115° Fahrenheit. Temperatures at high humidity up to 105° Fahrenheit are attained in a normal summer down the eastern seaboard of the U.S. and sometimes in the Middle West. Curiously, temperatures at the equator do not usually run above 95° Fahrenheit, although conditions are highly humid. This oddity arises from a denser cloud cover at the equator, reflecting more of the Sun's rays back into space.

It will accordingly be appreciated that the margin of safety over much of the Earth amounts to no more than 20°, and in some places to very much less than this. An additional rise of 30° could be viewed therefore only with the greatest apprehension.

It may be added that death results from the inability of the body to get rid of the heat that it is constantly generating. This is necessary in order to maintain the body at its normal working temperature of about 98° Fahrenheit. An increase of body temperature to 102° produces illness, 104° produces delirium, and 106° or thereabouts produces death. It may be wondered how the body can manage to rid itself of heat when it happens to be immersed in a hotter atmosphere, say in an atmosphere at 110°. The answer is by evaporation of sweat from the skin. This happens best when the humidity is low, which explains why a man can survive at higher temperatures in low humidity, and indeed why hot weather is always pleasanter when the humidity is low.

Evidently much would depend in the days to come on the behaviour of the humidity. Here there were grounds for hope. The heat rays from the Cloud would raise the temperature of the surface of the land more rapidly than the sea, and the air temperature would rise with the land while the moisture content of the air would rise more slowly with the sea. Hence the humidity would fall as the temperature rose, at any rate to begin with. It was just this initial fall of humidity that produced the unprecedented clarity of the spring and early summer in Britain.

First estimates of the heat rays from the Cloud underrated their importance. Otherwise the American Government would never have placed their scientific advisory establishment in the western desert. They were now obliged to evacuate men and equipment. This made them more dependent for information on Nortonstowe, which therefore increased in importance. But Nortonstowe had its own difficulties.

Alexandrov summed up the general opinion at a meeting of the Cloud investigation group.

'Result impossible,' he said. 'Experiment wrong.'

But John Marlborough averred that he was not wrong. To avoid an impasse it was agreed that the work should be repeated by Harry Leicester, who otherwise was concerning himself with communication problems. The work was repeated and ten days later Leicester reported back to a crowded meeting.

'To go back to the early phases. When the Cloud was first discovered it was found to be moving in towards the Sun at a speed of slightly less than seventy kilometres per second. It was estimated that the speed would gradually increase as the Sun was approached, and that the average speed eventually attained would be around eighty kilometres per second. The upshot of observations reported a fortnight ago by Marlborough is that the Cloud is not behaving as we expected. Instead of speeding up as it approaches the Sun it is actually slowing down. As you know, it was decided to repeat Marlborough's observation. The best thing will be to show a few slides.'

Only one person was pleased with the slides – Marlborough. His work was confirmed.

'But damn it all,' said Weichart, 'the Cloud must speed up as it falls through the Sun's gravitational field.'

'Unless it gets rid of momentum in some way,' countered Leicester. 'Let's look at that last slide again. You see these tiny pips right away over here. They're so small that they might be a mistake, I'll grant you. But if they're real they represent motions of about five hundred kilometres per second.'

'That's very interesting,' grunted Kingsley. 'You mean the Cloud is firing off small blobs of material at very high speed, and that's what is making it slow down?'

'You could interpret the results in that way,' answered Leicester.

'At least it's an interpretation that conforms with the laws of mechanics, and which preserves sanity in some degree.'

'But why should the Cloud behave in such a darned fashion?' asked Weichart.

'Because bastard inside, maybe,' suggested Alexandrov.

Parkinson joined Marlowe and Kingsley that afternoon as they were walking in the grounds.

'I've been wondering whether things are going to be altered in any important way by these new discoveries,' he said.

'Difficult to say,' answered Marlowe, puffing smoke. 'Too early to say. From now on we must keep our eyes wide open.'

'Our time schedule may get changed,' remarked Kingsley. 'We reckoned that the Cloud would reach the Sun in early July, but if this slowing down goes on it'll take longer for the Cloud to move in. It may be late July or even August before things begin to happen. And I don't give much for our estimates on heating inside the Cloud either. Changes of speed are going to alter all that.'

'Do I understand that the Cloud is slowing down in rather the same way that a rocket might slow down, by firing off bits of material at high speed?' asked Parkinson.

'That's what it looks like. We were just discussing possible reasons for it.'

'What sort of thing have you in mind?'

'Well,' continued Marlowe, 'it's quite likely that there's a pretty strong magnetic field inside this Cloud. We're already getting quite big perturbations of the Earth's magnetic field. Might of course be corpuscles from the Sun, the usual sort of magnetic storm. But I've a hunch that it's the magnetic field of the Cloud that we're beginning to detect.'

'And you think this business might be bound up with magnetism?'

'It may be so. Some process caused by an interaction of the magnetic field of the Sun with that of the Cloud. It's not at all clear just what *is* happening, but out of all the explanations we've been able to think of this seems the least unlikely.'

As the three men turned a corner, a stocky man touched his cap.

'Afternoon, gentlemen.'

'Wonderful weather, Stoddard. How's the garden?'

'Yes, sir, wonderful weather. Tomatoes are ripening already. Never known it before, sir.'

When they passed Kingsley said:

'To be frank, if it were given to me to changes places with that chap for the next three months, you know I wouldn't hesitate. What a relief to have no horizon but the ripening of tomatoes!'

*

Throughout the rest of June and July temperatures rose steadily all over the Earth. In the British Isles the temperature climbed through the eighties, into the nineties, and moved towards the hundred mark. People grumbled, but there was no serious distress.

The death-roll in the U.S. remained quite small, thanks largely to the air-conditioning units that had been fitted during previous years and months. Temperatures rose to the lethal limit throughout the whole country and people were obliged to remain indoors for weeks on end. Occasionally air-conditioning units failed and it was then that fatalities occurred.

Conditions were utterly desperate throughout the tropics as may be judged from the fact that 7,943 species of plants and animals became totally extinct. The survival of Man himself was only possible because of the caves and cellars he was able to dig. Nothing could be done to mitigate the stifling air temperature. The number who perished during this phase is unknown. It can only be said that in all phases together more than seven hundred million persons are known to have lost their lives. And but for various fortunate circumstances still to be recounted the number would have been far greater still.

Eventually the temperature of the surface waters of the sea rose, not so fast as the air temperature it is true, but fast enough to produce a dangerous increase of humidity. It was indeed this increase that produced the distressing conditions just remarked. Millions of people between the latitudes of Cairo and the Cape of Good Hope were subjected to a choking atmosphere that grew damper and hotter inexorably from day to day. All human movement ceased. There was nothing to be done but to lie panting, as a dog pants in hot weather.

By the fourth week of July conditions in the tropics lay balanced between life and total death. Then quite suddenly rain clouds condensed over the whole globe. Within three days not a break was anywhere to be found. The Earth was as completely cloud-shrouded as normally is the planet Venus. The temperature declined a little, owing no doubt to the clouds' reflecting more of the Sun's radiation back into space. But conditions could not be said to have improved. Warm rain fell everywhere, even as far north as Iceland. The insect population increased enormously, since the torrid hot atmosphere was as favourable to them as it was unfavourable to Man and the other mammals.

Plant life flourished to a fantastic degree. The deserts flowered as they had never done at any time while Man had walked the Earth. Ironically no advantage could be taken of the sudden fertility of hitherto barren soils. No crops were planted. Except in north-west Europe and the far northlands it was all Man could do to exist. No initiative could be taken. The lord of creation was beaten to his knees by his environment, the environment that for the previous fifty years he had prided himself on being able to control.

But although there was no improvement, conditions got no worse. With little or no food, but now with plenty of water, many of those exposed to the extreme heat managed to survive. The death rate had climbed to a wholly grotesque level, but it rose no further.

*

A discovery of some astronomical interest was made at Norton-stowe about a week before the great cloudbank spread itself over the Earth. The existence of vast drifts of dust on the Moon was confirmed in a dramatic fashion.

The rising temperature in July changed Britain's usual cool summer to a tropical heat but no worse. The grass was soon burned and the flowers died. By the standards that prevailed over most of the Earth, Britain might be considered to have been little affected, even though the daytime temperature rose to 100° and fell during the night only to about 90°. Seaside resorts were crowded and caravans were to be found everywhere along the coast.

Nortonstowe was now fortunate in possessing a large air-conditioned shelter in which more and more of the party were finding it preferable to sleep at night. Otherwise life proceeded normally, except that walks in the grounds were taken at night instead of in the heat of the Sun.

One moonlit night Marlowe, Emerson, and Knut Jensen were strolling abroad when gradually the light seemed to change. Looking up, Emerson said:

'You know, Geoff, that's darned queer. I don't see any cloud.'

'Probably very high-level ice particles.'

'Not in this heat!'

'No, I suppose it can't be.'

'And there's a queer yellow look that wouldn't be ice crystals,' added Jensen.

'Well, there's only one thing to do. When in doubt take a look. Let's go along to the telescope.'

They made their way to the dome that housed the Schmidt. Marlowe directed the six-inch finder telescope on the Moon.

'My God,' he exclaimed, 'it's boiling!'

Emerson and Jensen took a look. Then Marlowe said:

'Better go up to the house and call 'em all down. This is the sight of a lifetime. I'm going to take photographs on the Schmidt itself.'

Ann Halsey accompanied the group that hurried to the telescope in response to the urgent call from Emerson and Jensen. When it came to her turn to look through the finder Ann did not know at all what to expect. True she had a general idea of the grey, scarred, sterile surface of the Moon, but she had no knowledge of its detailed topography. Nor did she understand the meaning of the excited remarks that were passing between the astronomers. It was rather in the sense of a duty to be done that she went to the telescope. As she adjusted the focusing knob, a wholly fantastic world jumped into view. The Moon was a lemon-yellow colour. The usual sharp details were dulled by a giant cloud that appeared to extend over and beyond the circular outline. The cloud was fed by jets that sprang out of the darker areas. Every now and then new jets would emerge from these areas, which all the time were rippling and shimmering in an astonishing fashion.

'Come on, Ann, don't hog it. We'd like a look before the night's over,' said someone. Reluctantly she yielded her place.

'What does it mean, Chris?' Ann asked Kingsley as they walked towards the shelter.

'Do you remember what we were saying the other day about the Cloud slowing down? That it's slowing down as it gets nearer the Sun instead of speeding up?'

'I remember that everybody was worried about it.'

'Well, the Cloud is slowing down by firing out blobs of gas at very high speed. We don't know why it's doing this or how, but the work that Marlborough and Leicester are doing shows pretty certainly that it is so.'

'You're not going to tell me that one of these blobs has hit the Moon?'

'That's exactly what I think it is. Those dark areas are gigantic drifts of dust, drifts perhaps two or three miles deep. What is happening is that the impact of the high-speed gas is causing the dust to be squirted hundreds of miles upwards from the surface of the Moon.'

'Is there any chance that one of these blobs might hit us?'

'I wouldn't have thought the chance was very great. The Earth must be a very small target. But then the Moon is an even smaller target and one of 'em has just hit the Moon!'

'What would happen if ...?'

'If one hit us? I hardly like to think. We're worried enough about what's likely to happen if the Cloud hits us at a speed of perhaps fifty kilometres a second. It would be appalling if we were hit at the speed of one of those blobs, which must be the best part of a thousand kilometres a second. I suppose the whole of the Earth's atmosphere would simply be sprayed outwards into space, just like the Moon's dust.'

'What I can't understand about you, Chris, is how you can know all these things and yet get so worked up about politics and politicians. It seems so unimportant and trivial.'

'Ann, my dear, if I spent my time thinking about the situation as it really is, I should be off my head in a couple of days. Some men would go off their heads. Others'd take to drink. My form of escapism is to roar at politicians. Old Parkinson knows perfectly well that it's only a sort of game we're playing. But quite seriously, from now on survival is to be measured in hours.'

She moved in closer to him.

'Or perhaps I should put it more poetically,' he murmured.

> 'Come kiss me, sweet and twenty,
>   Life's a stuff will not endure.'

Chapter Seven

ARRIVAL

FROM the end of July a night watch was kept at the Norton-stowe shelter. Joe Stoddard was on the rota, as was natural since his work as a gardener had ceased by that time. Gardening was not an activity suited to the tropical heat.

It came about that Joe's watch fell on the night of 27 August. No dramatic action took place. Yet at 7.30 the following morning Joe knocked hesitantly on Kingsley's bedroom door. The previous evening Kingsley together with quite a number of other worthies had caroused somewhat heartily. So at first he was scarcely aware that Joe was trying to give him some message. Gradually he realized that the cheerful gardener was unusually solemn.

'It's not there, sir, it's not there.'

'What's not there? For heaven's sake go and fetch me a cup of tea. I've got a mouth like the bottom of a parrot's cage.'

'Cup of tea, sir!' Joe hesitated but stood his ground stolidly. 'Yes, sir. It's just that you said I was to report anything unusual, and it really isn't there.'

'Look here, Joe, much as I have regard for you, I say most solemnly that I'll disembowel you, here and now, unless you tell me what it is that isn't there.' Kingsley spoke slowly and loudly. '*What isn't there?*'

'The day, sir! There's no Sun!'

Kingsley grabbed his watch. It was about 7.42 a.m., long after dawn in August. He rushed out of the shelter into the open. It was pitch black, unrelieved even by starlight, which was unable to penetrate the thick cloud cover. An unreasoning primitive fear seemed to be abroad. The light of the world had gone.

In England and the western lands generally the shock was cushioned by night, for to them it was during the night hours that the light of the Sun became extinguished. One evening the light faded slowly away as is normally the case. But eight hours later there was no dawn. The advancing wall of the Cloud had reached the Sun during the intervening hours.

The people of the eastern hemisphere experienced in full measure the horror of the fading light. To them the total unrelieved blackness fell in what should have been full day. In Australia for instance, the sky began darkening about noon, and by three o'clock not a glimmer was to be seen, except where artificial illuminations had been switched on. There was fierce wild rioting in many of the world's major cities.

For three days the Earth lived as a black world, except for those pockets of humanity that possessed the technological sufficiency to provide their own lighting. Los Angeles and the other American cities lived in the artificial blaze of millions of electric bulbs. But this did not entirely protect the American people from the terror that gripped the rest of mankind. Indeed one might say that Americans had more leisure and opportunity to appreciate the situation as they sat huddled over television sets, waiting for the latest pronouncements of authorities who were powerless to understand or control the march of events.

After three days two things happened. Light appeared again in the day sky, and the rains began to fall. The light was at first very faint, but day by day it increased in strength until eventually the intensity reached a level about midway between full moonlight and full sunlight. It is doubtful whether on balance the light brought any easement to the acute psychological stress that afflicted Man everywhere, for its deep red tone showed beyond all doubt that it was not a natural light.

At first the rains were warm, but the temperature fell slowly and steadily. The precipitation was enormous. The air had been so hot and humid that a vast quantity of moisture had been stored in it. With the lowering of temperature following the extinction of the Sun's radiation, more and more of this moisture fell out as rain. Rivers rose swiftly and flooded their banks, destroying communications and rendering whole multitudes homeless. After weeks of heat exhaustion, the fate of those millions throughout the world who were thus overtaken by raging waters can scarcely be imagined. And always with them, reflected a dark red in the flood, was the unearthly half-light.

Yet this flooding was of minor consequence compared with the storms that swept over the Earth. The release of energy in the atmosphere, caused by the condensation of vapour into rain-drops, was beyond all precedent. It was sufficient to cause enormous fluctuations of atmospheric pressure, leading to hurricanes on a scale beyond human memory, and indeed beyond all credence.

*

The manor house at Nortonstowe was largely destroyed in one such hurricane. Two workmen were killed in the tumbling ruins. The fatalities at Nortonstowe were not limited to this tragedy. Knut Jensen and his Greta, the same Greta Johannsen that Kingsley had written to, were caught in a fierce storm and killed by a falling tree. They were buried together, hard by the old manor.

The temperature fell more and more. Rain changed to sleet and then to snow. The flooded fields were covered by ice and, as September wore on, the brawling rivers were gradually silenced as they were changed to immutable cascades of ice. The snow-covered land spread slowly down into the tropics. And as the whole Earth fell into the iron grip of frost, snow, and ice, the clouds cleared from the skies. Once more men could see out into space.

It was now manifest that the weird red light of day did not come from the Sun. The light was spread almost uniformly from horizon to horizon, without any special point of focus. Every bit of the day sky was glowing a faint dull red. People were told by radio and television that the light was coming from the Cloud, not from the Sun. The light was caused, so scientists said, by the heating of the Cloud as it swept around the Sun.

By the end of September the first gossamer-thin outposts of the Cloud reached the Earth. The impact heated the upper regions of the Earth's atmosphere, as reports from Nortonstowe had predicted. But so far the incident gas was too diffuse to cause heating to hundreds of thousands or to millions of degrees. Even so, temperatures rose to some tens of thousands of degrees. This was sufficient to cause the upper atmosphere to radiate a shimmering blue light, easily visible by night. Indeed the nights became indescribably beautiful, although it is to be doubted whether many people were able to appreciate the beauty, for in truth beauty needs ease and leisure for its proper enjoyment. Yet perhaps here and there some hardy northern shepherd guarding his flocks may have regarded the violet-streaked night with wonder and awe.

So as time went on, a pattern of dark red days and scintillating blue nights became established, a pattern in which neither Sun nor Moon played any part. And always the temperature fell lower and lower.

Except in the heavily industrialized countries, vast legions of people lost their lives during this period. For weeks they had been exposed to well-nigh unbearable heat. Then many had died by flood and storm. With the coming of intense cold, pneumonia became fiercely lethal. Between the beginning of August and the first week of October roughly a quarter of the world's population died. The volume of personal tragedy was indescribably enormous. Death intervened to part husband from wife, parent from child, sweetheart from sweetheart with irreversible finality.

The Prime Minister was angry with the scientists at Nortonstowe. His irritation caused him to make a journey there, a journey that was bitterly cold and miserable and which did not improve his temper.

'It appears that the Government has been very seriously misled,' he told Kingsley. 'First you said that the emergency might be expected to last for a month and no more. Well, the emergency has now lasted for more than a month and there is still no sign of an end. When may we expect this business to be over?'

'I haven't the slightest idea,' answered Kingsley.

The Prime Minister glowered at Parkinson, Marlowe, Leicester, then most ferociously at Kingsley.

'What, may I ask, is the explanation of this appalling misinformation? Might I point out that Nortonstowe has been afforded every facility? Not to put too fine a point on it, you have been cosseted – feather-bedded as some of my colleagues would say. In return we have every right to expect a reasonable standard of competence. I may say that living conditions here are a great deal superior to the conditions in which the Government itself is obliged to work.'

'Of course conditions are superior here. They are superior because we had the foresight to see what was coming.'

'And that seems to have been the only foresight you have shown, a foresight for your own comfort and safety.'

'In which we have followed a course remarkably similar to that of the Government.'

'I fail to understand, sir.'

'Then let me put the position more plainly. When this matter of the Cloud was first broached, the immediate concern of your Government, and indeed of all other Governments so far as I am aware, was to prevent the relevant facts becoming known to the people. The real object of this supposed secrecy was, of course, to prevent the people from choosing a more effective set of representatives.'

The Prime Minister was thoroughly angry now.

'Kingsley, let me tell you without reserve that I shall feel obliged to take steps that you will scarcely welcome when I return to London.'

Parkinson noticed a sudden hardening in Kingsley's easy-going, insulting manner.

'I fear you will not be returning to London, you will be staying here.'

'I can scarcely believe that even you, Professor Kingsley, can have the effrontery to suggest that I am to be kept a prisoner!'

'Not a prisoner, my dear Prime Minister, no such thing,' said Kingsley with a smile. 'Let us rather put it this way. In the coming crisis you will be far safer at Nortonstowe than in London. Let us therefore say that we feel it preferable, in the public interest of course, that you should remain at Nortonstowe. And now as no doubt you and Parkinson have a great deal to talk over together, you will, I imagine, wish Leicester, Marlowe, and myself to withdraw.'

Marlowe and Leicester were in something of a daze as they followed Kingsley out of the room.

'But you simply can't do it, Chris,' said Marlowe.

'I can and I will do it. If he's allowed to go back to London things will be done that'll endanger the lives of everybody here from yourself, Geoff, down to Joe Stoddard. And that I simply will not allow. Heaven knows we've little enough chance as it is without making matters worse.'

'But if he doesn't go back to London they'll send for him.'

'They won't. We'll send a radio message to say that the roads here are temporarily impassable and that there may be a couple of days' delay in his return. The temperature is dropping so quickly now – you remember what I told you when we were out in the Mohave Desert about the temperature going cracking down, well, it's happening right now – in a few days the roads will be genuinely impassable.'

'I don't see that. There's not likely to be more snow.'

'Of course not. But soon the temperature will be too low for internal combustion engines to work. There'll be no motorized transport either by road or air. I know that special engines can be made, but by the time they get round to that, things will have become so bad that nobody'll give much thought to whether the Prime Minister is in London or not.'

'I reckon that's right,' said Leicester. 'We've only got to bluff for a week or so and then everything will be fine. I must say I wouldn't welcome being winkled out of our cosy little shelter, especially after all the trouble we had building it.'

Parkinson had seldom before seen the Prime Minister really angry. He had previously dealt with these situations by such yes-yessing and no-noing as seemed most appropriate. But this time he felt that he must take the full broadside of the Prime Minister's wrath.

'I'm sorry, sir,' he said, after listening for some minutes, 'but I fear you brought it on yourself. You shouldn't have called Kingsley incompetent. The charge wasn't justified.'

The Prime Minister spluttered.

'Not justified! Do you realize, Francis, that on the basis of that one month of Kingsley's we've taken no special fuel precautions? Do you realize what sort of a position that puts us in?'

'The one-month crisis wasn't due to Kingsley alone. We got exactly the same advice from America.'

'One piece of incompetence doesn't excuse another.'

'I don't agree, sir. When I was in London we always sought to minimize the situation. Kingsley's reports always had a gravity that we were unwilling to accept. We were always trying to persuade ourselves that things were better than they seemed. We never considered the possibility that they might be worse than they seemed. Kingsley may have been wrong, but he was nearer being right than we were.'

'But why was he wrong? Why were all the scientists wrong? That's what I've been trying to find out, and nobody will tell me.'

'They would have told you, if you'd taken the trouble to ask, instead of roaring their heads off.'

'I'm beginning to think you've lived here for a little too long, Francis.'

'I've lived here long enough to realize that scientists don't claim to be infallible, that it's really we laymen who attach infallibility to their statements.'

'For heaven's sake, stop this philosophy, Francis. Please be good enough to tell me in plain terms what it is that has gone wrong.'

'Well, as I understand it, the Cloud is behaving in a way that nobody expected and that nobody understands. Every scientist thought that it would gain speed as it approached the Sun, that it would sweep past the Sun and recede again into the distance. Instead it slowed down and by the time it reached the Sun it had slowed to practically no speed at all. So instead of sweeping outwards again it's simply sitting there around the Sun.'

'But how long is it going to stop there? That's what I want to know.'

'Nobody can tell you. It might stop a week, a month, a year, a millennium, or millions of years. Nobody knows.'

'But good God, man, do you realize what you're saying? Unless that Cloud moves out we can't carry on.'

'Do you think Kingsley doesn't know that? If the Cloud stays a month, a lot more people will die, but quite a few will survive. If it stays two months, very few people will survive. If it stays three months, we at Nortonstowe will die in spite of all our preparations, and we shall be among the last to die. If it stays a year, not a living thing on the Earth will survive. As I say, Kingsley knows all this and that's why he doesn't take the political aspects of the matter very seriously.'

Chapter Eight

CHANGE FOR THE BETTER

ALTHOUGH nobody realized it at the time, the occasion of the Prime Minister's visit was very nearly the worst moment in the whole episode of the Black Cloud. The first evidence of improving conditions was discovered by the radio astronomers, appropriately so since at no time did they discontinue their observations of the Cloud, even though this meant working out of doors in most distressing conditions. On 6 October John Marlborough called a meeting. Word went round that something important was in the offing, so the meeting was well attended.

Marlborough showed how his observations indicated that the amount of gas lying between the Earth and the Sun had been decreasing steadily throughout the previous ten days or so. It seemed as if the amount of gas had halved about every three days. If this behaviour continued for another fortnight the Sun would come clear altogether – but of course there was no certainty that it would continue.

Marlborough was asked if the Cloud seemed to be moving away from the Sun altogether. To this he answered that there was no such evidence. What appeared to be happening was that the material of the Cloud was distributing itself in such a fashion that the Sun would be able to shine through in our direction, but not of course in all other directions.

'Isn't it a bit too much to hope that the Cloud will just happen to come clear in our direction?' asked Weichart.

'It's odd certainly,' answered Marlborough. 'But I'm only giving you the evidence for what it's worth. I'm not giving any interpretation.'

What eventually turned out to be the correct explanation was suggested by Alexandrov, although nobody took much notice at the time, probably because of the way Alexandrov chose to express himself.

'Disk stable configuration,' said he. 'Probably Cloud settling into ... disk.'

There were grins and someone exclaimed:

'Need we have these military adjectives, Alexis?'

Alexandrov looked surprised.

'Not military. Am scientist,' he insisted.

After this diversion the Prime Minister said:

'If I may return to more parliamentary language, do I understand from what has been said that the present crisis will be at an end in a fortnight from now?'

'If the present trend continues,' answered Marlborough.

'Then we must keep a close watch and have ourselves apprised of the situation.'

'Masterly conclusion!' groaned Kingsley.

It is safe to say that never in the history of science had measurements been made more anxiously than those conducted during the following days by the radio astronomers. The curve on which they plotted their results became quite literally a curve of life or death. If it continued to decline it meant life; if the decline ceased and the curve started to climb it meant death.

A new point was added to the graph every few hours. All persons capable of appreciating the issues were to be found hanging around waiting for the next point, throughout the night as well as during the dusky, faint daytime. For four days and nights the curve continued to decline but on the fifth day the decline eased off, while on the sixth day there were signs of the decline changing to a rise. Scarcely anyone spoke, except for an occasional terse sentence. The tension was indescribably fierce. Then on the seventh day the decline was resumed and on the eighth day the curve was descending more steeply than ever. The intense stress was followed by violent reaction. By ordinary human standards, behaviour at Nortonstowe might have seemed somewhat promiscuous at all times and perhaps decidedly so at that time, although to those concerned, to those who experienced the anguish of the sixth day, nothing seemed at all untoward.

Thereafter the curve continued its descent and as it did so the amount of gas between the Earth and Sun dwindled more and more. On 19 October a focus of yellow light could be seen in the day sky. It was still faint, but it moved across the sky as the hours passed. Without question it was the Sun, seen for the first time since the beginning of August, still seen through a veil of gas and dust. But the veil was getting thinner and thinner. By 24 October the Sun shone again in full strength on a frozen Earth.

Those who have experienced the coming of sunrise after a cold night in the desert will have a faint idea of the joy brought by the dawn of 24 October 1965. A word about religion may be in order. During the approach of the Cloud all manner of religious beliefs had flourished mightily. During the spring, the Jehovah's Witnesses had robbed all other speakers in Hyde Park of their audiences. Incumbents of the Church of England had been astonished to find themselves preaching to overflowing congregations. All this was swept aside on 24 October. Everyone, men and women of all creeds – Christian, Atheist, Mohammedan, Buddhist, Hindu, Jew – all became pervaded to their innermost beings with the emotional complex of the old Sun-worshippers. True, Sunworship never became an established religion, for it had no central organization, but the undertones of the ancient religion were set vibrating and were never again damped out.

Tropical areas were the first to thaw. Ice disappeared from the rivers. Snow melted with more flooding, but the effects were marginal compared with what had gone before. The thaw in North America and in Europe was only partial, for in the ordinary way of things winter was coming on.

Vast as was the human suffering in the heavily industrialized countries, industrial populations fared far better than the less fortunate peoples, emphasizing the importance of inanimate energy and of the control of machines. It should be added that the situation in this respect might have been very different if the cold had continued to deepen, for relief came at a time when industrialization was on the verge of widespread collapse.

Somewhat paradoxically, among non-industrialized peoples, those of the tropics were hardest hit, while the genuinely nomadic Esquimaux came off best of all. In many parts of the tropics and semi-tropics as many as one person in two lost his life. Among the Esquimaux there was comparatively little loss of life, comparatively little more than in the normal way of things, that is to say. The heat had not been so great in the far north. The Esquimaux had found it highly unpleasant but no worse. Melting ice and

snow interfered with their freedom of movement, thereby seriously reducing the area over which they could hunt. But the heat
was not so great as to be lethal to them. Nor was the intense cold.
They simply dug themselves into the snow and waited, and in this
they were better off in many respects than the people of England.

Governments everywhere were in a shaky condition. Now, if
ever, was the time for Communism to sweep the world. Now was
the time for the United States to stamp out Communism. Now
was the time for dissident groups to capture their Governments.
But nothing of the sort happened. In the days immediately following 24 October everyone was too overcome with relief and too
beaten down to contemplate such seemingly trivial matters. And
by the middle of November the opportunity had passed. Humanity had begun to organize itself again into its respective communities.

The Prime Minister returned to London, feeling less unfavour-
ably disposed towards Nortonstowe than might perhaps be expected. For one thing he had passed the time of the crisis far more
comfortably than he would have done at Downing Street. For
another he had shared the agony of suspense with the scientists
at Nortonstowe and there is always a bond between those who
have shared a common stress.

Before the Prime Minister left he was warned that there was no
reason to suppose that the emergency was at an end. At a discussion, held in one of the laboratories attached to the shelter, it had
been generally agreed that Alexandrov's prognostication was
correct. Marlborough said:

'It seems fairly certain that the Cloud is settling into a disk at a
pretty high inclination to the ecliptic.'

'Disk stable configuration. Obvious,' grunted Alexandrov.

'It may be obvious to you, Alexis,' broke in Kingsley, 'but
there's an awful lot about this business that's not obvious to me.
By the way, what would you put the outer radius of the disk at?'

'About three-quarters of the radius of the Earth's orbit, about
the same as the radius of the orbit of Venus,' answered Marlborough.

'This settling down into a disk must be a relative way of speaking,' Marlowe began. 'I suppose you mean that the bulk of the

material of the Cloud is settling into a disk. But there must be quite a lot of material spread through the whole of the Earth's orbit. This is obvious from the stuff that's hitting our atmosphere all the time.'

'God-awful cold in shadow of disk,' announced Alexandrov.

'Yes, thank goodness we're clear of the disk, otherwise there'd still be no Sun,' Parkinson said.

'But remember that we shall not stay clear of the disk' – this from Kingsley.

'What d'you mean by that?' asked the Prime Minister.

'Simply that the Earth's motion around the Sun will carry us into the shadow of the disk. Of course we shall come out of the shadow again.'

'Damn cold in shadow,' grunted Alexandrov.

The Prime Minister was worried, and with some justice.

'And how often, may I ask, is this appalling state of affairs likely to arise?'

'Twice a year! According to the present position of the disk, in February and August. The lengths of time for which the Sun will be eclipsed depends on how thin the disk gets. Probably the eclipses will last for somewhere between a fortnight and a month.'

'The implications of this are certain to be extremely far-reaching,' sighed the Prime Minister.

'For once we agree,' remarked Kingsley. 'Life on the Earth is not going to be impossible but it'll have to be carried on in far less favourable circumstances. For one thing people will have to get used to living together in quite large numbers. We shall no longer be able to afford to live in individual houses.'

'I don't follow.'

'Well, heat is lost from a building at its surface. Is that clear?'

'Yes, of course.'

'On the other hand, the number of people that can be housed and sheltered in a building depends essentially on its volume. Since the ratio of surface to volume is much less for a large building than for a small one it follows that large buildings will house people at a far lower fuel consumption per head. If there is to be an endless repetition of periods of intense cold, our fuel resources will admit of no other arrangement.'

'Why do you say "if ", Kingsley?' asked Parkinson.

'Because so many queer things have happened. I won't be satisfied with our predictions of what is going to happen next, until I can really understand what has happened already.'

'It might be worth while mentioning the possibility of long-term climatic changes,' remarked Marlowe. 'Although this may not be of very great importance in the next year or two, I can't see how it can fail to be vitally important in the long run – assuming we're going to have these bi-annual eclipses of the Sun.'

'What have you in mind, Geoff?'

'Well, surely we can't avoid moving into a new Ice Age. Past Ice Ages show how delicately the Earth's climate is balanced. Two periods of intense cold, one in winter and the other in summer, must tip the balance on the Ice Age side – the Ice Age plus side, I would say.'

'You mean that ice sheets will sweep down over Europe and North America?'

'I can't see how it can be otherwise, although it won't happen in the next year or two. It'll be a slow cumulative process. As Chris Kingsley says, Man'll have to come to terms with his environment. And I guess the terms won't be altogether to his liking.'

'Ocean currents,' said Alexandrov.

'I don't understand,' said the Prime Minister.

'What I imagine Alexis means,' Kingsley remarked, 'is that there is no certainty that the present pattern of ocean currents will be maintained. If it isn't, the effects might be completely disastrous. And this might happen quite quickly, quicker than an Ice Age.'

'You said it,' nodded Alexandrov. 'Gulf Stream go, gets bloody cold.'

The Prime Minister felt he had heard enough.

*

During November the pulse of mankind quickened. And as Governments got matters more and more in hand the desire for communication between the various pockets of humanity strengthened. Telephone lines and cables were repaired. But it was to radio that men turned in the main. Long wave radio transmitters were soon working normally, but of course they were useless for long distance communication. For this, short wave transmitters were put into operation. But the short wave transmitters failed to work, and for a reason that was soon discovered. The ionization of the atmospheric gases at a height of about fifty miles turned out to be abnormally high. This was giving rise to an excessive amount of collisional damping, as the radio engineers called it. The excessive ionization was caused by the radiation from the very hot upper reaches that were still producing the blue shimmering nights. In short, radio fade-out conditions were operative.

There was only one thing to be done: to shorten the transmitting wave-length. This was tried down to a wave-length of about one metre, but still the fade-out continued; and no suitable transmitters on still lower wave-lengths were available, since lower wave-lengths were never widely used before the coming of the Cloud. Then it was remembered that Nortonstowe possessed transmitters that would work from one metre down as far as one centimetre. Moreover the Nortonstowe transmitters were capable of handling an enormous quantity of information, as Kingsley was not slow to point out. It was accordingly decided to make Nortonstowe a world information clearing-house. Kingsley's plan had borne fruit at last.

Intricate calculations had to be performed and, as they had to be done quickly, the electronic computer was put into operation. The problem was to find the best wave-length. If the wave-length was too long the fade-out trouble would continue. If the wave-length was too short the radio waves would stream out of the atmosphere away into space instead of being bent round the Earth, as they must be to travel from London to Australia, let us say. The problem was to compromise between these extremes. Eventually a wave-length of twenty-five centimetres was decided on. This was thought to be short enough to overcome the worst of the fade-out difficulty, and yet not to be so short that too much power would get squirted out into space, although it was recognized that some loss must occur.

The Nortonstowe transmitters were switched on during the

first week of December. Their information-carrying capacity turned out to be prodigious, as Kingsley had predicted. Less than half an hour on the first day was sufficient to clear the whole back-log of information. To begin with, only a few Governments possessed a transmitter and receiver, but the system worked so well that soon many other Governments were lashing up equipment at all speed. Partly for this reason the volume of traffic through Nortonstowe was quite small at first. Also it was difficult to appreciate initially that an hour's talk occupied a transmission time of a small fraction of a second. But as time went on, conversation and messages became longer, and more Governments joined in. So transmission at Nortonstowe rose gradually from a few minutes a day to an hour or more.

One afternoon, Leicester, who had organized the building of the transmission system, rang Kingsley and asked him to come along to the transmitting lab.

'What's the panic, Harry?' asked Kingsley.

'We've done a fade!'

'What!'

'Yes, right out. You can see it over here. A message was coming through from Brazil. Look how the signal has gone completely.'

'It's fantastic. Must be an extremely rapid burst of ionization.'

'What d'you think we ought to do?'

'Wait, I suppose. It may be a transient effect. In fact it looks rather like it.'

'If it goes on we might shorten the wave-length.'

'Yes, we might. But scarcely anybody else could. The Americans could work up a new wave-length pretty quickly, and probably the Russians as well. But it's doubtful if many of the others could. We've had enough trouble getting 'em to build their present transmitters.'

'Then there's nothing to do but hang on?'

'Well, I don't think I should try transmitting, because you'll never know if the messages get through. I should just leave the receiver on recorder. Then we shall have any stuff that happens to come through – if conditions improve, that is to say.'

There was a brilliant aurora-type display that night, which the Nortonstowe scientists took to be associated with the sudden burst of ionization high in the atmosphere. They had no idea of the cause of the ionization, however. Very large disturbances of the Earth's magnetic field were also noted.

Marlowe and Bill Barnett discussed the matter as they strolled around, admiring the display.

'My God, look at those orange-coloured sheets,' said Marlowe.

'What baffles me, Geoff, is that this is obviously a low-level display. You can tell that from the colours. I suppose we ought to have a shot at getting a spectrum, although I'd swear to it from what we can see right now. I'd say that all this is going on not more than fifty miles up, probably less. It's in just the place where we've been getting all the excessive ionization.'

'I know what you're thinking, Bill. That it's easy to imagine a sudden puff of gas hitting the extreme outside of the atmosphere. But that would produce a disturbance much higher up. It's difficult to believe this is due to impact.'

'No, I don't think it possibly can be. It looks to me much more like an electrical discharge.'

'The magnetic disturbances would check with that.'

'But you see what this means, Geoff? This isn't from the Sun. Nothing like it from the Sun has ever happened before. If it's an electrical disturbance, it must come from the Cloud.'

*

Leicester and Kingsley hurried along to the communication lab after breakfast the following morning. A short message from Ireland had come in at 6.20. A long message from the U.S. had started at 7.51, but after three minutes there had been a fade and the rest of the message was lost. A short message from Sweden was received about midday, but a longer message from China was interrupted by fade-out soon after two o'clock.

Parkinson joined Leicester and Kingsley at tea.

'This is a most disturbing business,' he said.

'I can imagine so,' answered Kingsley. 'And it's another queer business.'

'Well, it's certainly annoying. I thought we'd got this communication problem in hand. In what way is it queer?'

'In that we seem to be on the verge of transmission the whole time. Sometimes messages come through and sometimes they don't, as if the ionization is oscillating up and down.'

'Barnett thinks that electrical discharges are going on. So wouldn't you expect oscillations?'

'You're becoming quite a scientist, aren't you, Parkinson?' laughed Kingsley. 'But it isn't as easy as that,' he went on. 'Oscillation yes, but hardly oscillations like the ones we've been getting. Don't you see how odd it is?'

'No, I can't say I do.'

'The messages from China and the U.S., man! We got a fadeout on each of 'em. That seems to show that when transmission is possible it's only barely possible. The oscillations seem to be making transmission just possible but only by the slightest margin. That might happen once by chance but it's very remarkable that it should happen twice.'

'Isn't there a flaw there, Chris? Leicester chewed his pipe, and then pointed with it. 'If discharges are going on, the oscillations might be quite rapid. Both the messages from the U.S. and China were long, over three minutes. Perhaps the oscillations last about three minutes. Then you can understand why we get short messages complete, like those from Brazil and Iceland, while we never get a complete long message.'

'Ingenious, Harry, but I don't believe it. I was looking at your signal record of the U.S. message. It's quite steady, until the fadeout starts. That doesn't look like a deep oscillation, otherwise the signal would vary even before the fade-out. Then if oscillations are going on every three minutes, why aren't we getting a lot more messages, or at any rate fragments of them? I think that's a fatal objection.'

Leicester chewed his pipe again.

'It certainly looks like it. The whole thing's damn strange.'

'What do you propose to do about it?' asked Parkinson.

'It might be a good idea, Parkinson, if you were to ask London to cable Washington asking for transmissions to be sent for five minutes every hour, starting on the hour. Then we shall know what messages are not being received, as well as those that do come through. You might also like to apprise other Governments of the situation.'

*

No further transmissions were received during the next three days. Whether this was due to fade-out or because no messages were sent was not known. In this unsatisfactory state of affairs a change of plan was decided on. As Marlowe told Parkinson:

'We've decided to look into this business properly, instead of depending on chance transmissions.'

'How do you intend to do that?'

'We're arranging to point all our aerials upwards, instead of more or less towards the horizon. Then we can use our own transmissions to investigate this unusual ionization. We'll pick up reflections of our own transmissions, that is to say.'

For the next two days the radio astronomers were hard at work on the aerials. It was late in the afternoon of 9 December by the time every arrangement had been made. Quite a crowd assembled in the lab to watch results.

'O.K. Let her rip,' said someone.

'What wave-length shall we start on?'

'Better try one metre first,' suggested Barnett. 'If Kingsley is right in supposing that twenty-five centimetres is on the verge of transmission, and if our ideas on collision damping are correct, this ought to be about critical for vertical propagation.'

The one-metre transmitter was switched on.

'It's going through,' Barnett remarked.

'How do you know that?' Parkinson asked Marlowe.

'There's nothing but very weak return signals,' answered Marlowe. 'You can see that on the tube. Most of the power is being absorbed or is going right through the atmosphere into space.'

The next half hour was spent in gazing at electrical equipment and in technical talk. Then there was a rustle of excitement.

'Signal's going up.'

'Look at it!' exclaimed Marlowe. 'It's going up with a rush!'

The return signal continued to grow for about ten minutes.

'It's saturated. We're getting total reflection now, I'd say,' said Leicester.

'Looks as though you were right, Chris. We must be quite near the critical frequency. Reflection is coming from a height of just under fifty miles, more or less where we expected it. Ionization there must be a hundred to a thousand times normal.'

A further half-hour was spent in measurements.

'Better see what ten centimetres does,' remarked Marlowe.

There was a pressing of switches.

'We're on ten centimetres now. It's going right through, as of course it ought to,' announced Barnett.

'This is unbearably scientific,' said Ann Halsey. 'I'm going off to make tea. Come and help, Chris, if you can leave your meters and dials for a few minutes.'

Some time later while they were drinking tea and conversing generally, Leicester gave a startled cry.

'Heavens above! Look at this!'

'It's impossible!'

'But it's happening.'

'The ten-centimetre reflection is rising. It must mean that the ionization is going up at a colossal rate,' Marlowe explained to Parkinson.

'The damn thing's saturating again.'

'It means the ionization has increased a hundredfold in less than an hour. It's incredible.'

'Better put the one-centimetre transmitter on, Harry,' Kingsley said to Leicester.

So the ten-centimetre transmission was changed to a one-centimetre transmission.

'Well, that's going through all right,' someone remarked.

'But not for long. In another half hour the one-centimetre will be trapped, mark my words,' said Barnett.

'Incidentally what message is being sent?' asked Parkinson.

'None,' answered Leicester, 'we're only sending C.W. – continuous wave.'

'As if that explained everything,' thought Parkinson.

But although the scientists sat around for a couple of hours or more nothing further of note happened.

'Well, it's still going through. We'll see what it looks like after dinner,' said Barnett.

After dinner the one-centimetre transmission was still going through.

'It might be worth switching back to ten centimetres,' suggested Marlowe.

'O.K. Let's try again.' Leicester flicked the switches. 'That's interesting,' he said. 'We're going through on ten centimetres now. The ionization seems to be dropping, and pretty rapidly too.'

'Negative ion formation probably' – from Weichart.

Ten minutes later Leicester whooped with excitement.

'Look, the signal's coming in again!'

He was right. During the next few minutes the reflected signal grew rapidly to a maximum value.

'Complete reflection now. What shall we do? Go back to one centimetre?'

'No, Harry,' said Kingsley. 'My revolutionary suggestion is that we go upstairs to the sitting-room, where we drink coffee and where we listen to music played by Ann's fair hand. I'd like to switch off for an hour or two and come back later.'

'What on earth is the idea, Chris?'

'Oh, just a hunch, a crazy idea, I suppose. But perhaps you'll indulge me for once in a way.'

'For once in a way!' chuckled Marlowe. 'You've been indulged, Chris, from the day you were born.'

'That may be so, but it's scarcely polite to remark on it, Geoff. Come on, Ann. You've been waiting to try out the Beethoven Opus 106 on us. Now's your chance.'

It was an hour and a half or so later, with the opening chords of the great sonata still ringing in their heads, that the company made its way back to the transmitting lab.

'Try the one-metre first, just for luck,' said Kingsley.

'Bet you that one-metre is completely trapped,' Barnett said as he clicked on various switches.

'No, it's not, by John Brown's body,' he exclaimed a few minutes later, when the equipment had warmed up. 'It's going through. It just isn't believable, and yet it's as plain as a pikestaff on the tube.'

'What's your betting, Harry, on what's going to happen next?'

'I'm not betting, Chris. This is worse than "spot the lady".'

'I'm betting it's going to saturate.'

'Any reasons?'

'If it saturates I'll have reasons, of course. If it doesn't there won't be any reasons.'

'Playing safe, eh?'

'Signal going up,' sang out Barnett. 'Looks as though Chris is going to be right. Up it goes!'

Five minutes later the one-metre signal saturated. It was completely trapped by the ionosphere, no power getting away from the Earth.

'Now try ten centimetres,' Kingsley commanded.

For the next twenty or thirty minutes the equipment was watched keenly, all comment silenced. The earlier pattern repeated. Very little reflection was obtained at first. The reflected signal then increased rapidly in intensity.

'Well, there it is. At first the signal penetrates the ionosphere. Then after a few minutes the ionization rises and we get complete trapping. What's it mean, Chris?' asked Leicester.

'Let's go back upstairs and think about it. If Ann and Yvette will be kind-hearted and make another brew of coffee, perhaps we can do something towards licking this business into shape.'

McNeil came in while coffee was being prepared. He had been attending a sick child while the experiments had been going on.

'Why the air of great solemnity? What's been happening?'

'You're just in time, John. We're going to run over the facts. But we've promised not to start until the coffee arrives.'

The coffee came, and Kingsley began his summing up.

'For John's benefit I'll have to start a long way back. What happens to radio waves when they're transmitted depends on two things, the wave-length and the ionization in the atmosphere. Suppose we choose a particular wave-length for transmission and consider what happens as the degree of ionization increases. To begin with, for low ionization the radio energy streams out of the atmosphere, with very little of it getting reflected. Then as the ionization increases there is more and more reflection until quite suddenly the reflection goes up very steeply until eventually all the radio energy is reflected, none of it getting away from the Earth. We say that the signal saturates. Is that all clear, John?'

'Up to a point. What I don't see is how the wave-length comes into it.'

'Well, the lower the wave-length, the more ionization is needed to produce saturation.'

'So while one wave-length might be completely reflected by the atmosphere, some shorter wave-length might penetrate almost completely into outer space.'

'That's exactly the situation. But let me go back to my particular wave-length for a moment, and to the effect of rising ionization. For convenience in talking, I'd like to call it "pattern of events A".'

'You'd like to call it what?' asked Parkinson.

'This is what I mean:

1. A low ionization allowing almost complete penetration.
2. A rising ionization giving a reflected signal of increased strength.
3. An ionization so high that reflection becomes complete.

This is what I call "pattern A".'

'And what is pattern B?' asked Ann Halsey.

'There won't be any pattern B.'

'Then why bother with the A?'

'Preserve me from the obtuseness of women! I can call it pattern A because I want to, can't I?'

'Of course, dear. But why do you want to?'

'Go on, Chris. She's only pulling your leg.'

'Well, here's a list of what happened this afternoon and evening. Let me read it out to you as a table.'

Transmission wave-length	Approximate time of switching on	Event
1 metre	2.45 p.m.	Pattern A taking approximately half an hour.
10 centimetres	3.15 p.m.	Pattern A taking approximately half an hour.
1 centimetre	3.45 p.m.	Complete penetration of ionosphere over a period of three hours roughly.
10 centimetres	7.0 p.m.	Pattern A taking approximately half an hour.
No transmissions from 7.30 p.m. to 9.0 p.m.		
1 metre	9.0 p.m.	Pattern A taking half an hour.
10 centimetres	9.30 p.m.	Pattern A taking half an hour.

'It certainly looks horribly systematic when it's all put together like that,' said Leicester.

'It does, doesn't it?'

'I'm afraid I'm not getting this' – Parkinson.

'Nor am I,' admitted McNeil.

Kingsley spoke slowly.

'As far as I'm aware, these events can be explained very simply on one hypothesis, but I warn you it's an entirely preposterous hypothesis.'

'Chris, will you please stop trying to be dramatic, and tell us in simple words what this preposterous hypothesis is?'

'Very well. In one breath – that on any wave-length from a few centimetres upwards our own transmissions automatically produce a rise of ionization which continues to the saturation point.'

'It simply isn't possible.' Leicester shook his head.

'I didn't say it was possible,' answered Kingsley. 'I said it explained the facts. And it does. It explains the whole of my table.'

'I can half see what you're driving at,' remarked McNeil.

'Am I to suppose that the ionization falls as soon as you cease transmission?'

'Yes. When we stop transmission the ionizing agent is cut off, whatever it may be – perhaps Bill's electrical discharges. Then the ionization falls very rapidly. You see the ionization we're dealing with is abnormally low in the atmosphere, where the gas density is large enough to give an extremely rapid rate of formation of negative oxygen ions. So the ionization dries up very quickly as soon as it isn't being renewed.'

'Let's go into this in a bit more detail,' Marlowe began, speaking out of a haze of aniseed smoke. 'It seems to me that this hypothetical ionizing agency must have pretty good judgement. Suppose we switch on a ten-centimetre transmission. Then according to your idea, Chris, the agency, whatever it is, drives the ionization up until the ten-centimetre waves remain trapped inside the Earth's atmosphere. And – here's my point – the ionization goes no higher than that. It's all got to be very nicely adjusted. The agency has to know just how far to go and no further.'

'Which doesn't make it seem very plausible,' said Weichart.

'And there are other difficulties. Why were we able to go on so

long with the twenty-five centimetre communication? That lasted
for quite a number of days, not for only half an hour. And why
doesn't the same thing happen – your pattern A as you call it –
when we use a one-centimetre wave-length?'

'Bloody bad philosophy,' grunted Alexandrov. 'Waste of
breath. Hypothesis judged by prediction. Only sound method.'

Leicester glanced at his watch.

'It's well over an hour since our last transmission. If Chris is
right we ought to get his pattern A, if we switch on again at ten
centimetres, that is to say, and possibly at one metre also. Let's
try.'

Leicester and about half a dozen others went off to the lab.
Half an hour later they were back.

'Still complete reflection at one metre. Pattern A on ten centimetres,' Leicester announced.

'Which looks as if it supports Chris.'

'I'm not sure that it does,' remarked Weichart. 'Why didn't the
one metre give pattern A?'

'I might make some suggestions, but in a way they're even more
fantastic, so I won't bother with 'em just for the moment. The
fact is, and I insist it is a fact, that whenever we have switched on
our ten-centimetre transmitter there has always been a sharp rise
of atmospheric ionization, and whenever we switched off there
has been a decline of ionization. Does anyone deny that?'

'I don't deny that what has happened so far agrees with what
you say,' Weichart argued. 'I agree that no denial is possible
there. It's when it comes to inferring a causal connexion between
our transmissions and the fluctuations of ionization that I dig my
toes in.'

'You mean, Dave, that what we found this afternoon and this
evening was coincidence?' asked Marlowe.

'That's what I mean. I grant you that the odds against such a
series of coincidences are pretty big, but Kingsley's causal connexion seems to me an out-and-out impossibility. What I feel is
that the improbable can happen but the impossible cannot.'

'Impossible is too strong,' insisted Kingsley. 'And I'm sure
that Weichart couldn't really defend his use of the word. What
we're faced with is a choice between two improbabilities – I said

that my hypothesis seemed improbable when I first trotted it out. Moreover I agree with what Alexis said earlier on, that the only way to test a hypothesis is by its predictions. It's about three-quarters of an hour since Harry Leicester did his last transmission. I'm going to suggest that he goes right now and does another ten-centimetre transmission.'

Leicester groaned. 'Not again!'

'I predict,' went on Kingsley, 'that my pattern A will be repeated. What I'd like to know is what Weichart predicts.'

Weichart didn't quite like the turn of the argument, and he attempted to hedge. Marlowe laughed.

'He's pinching you, Dave! You've got to stand up and take it. If you're right about it being coincidence before, you've got to agree that Kingsley's present prediction is very unlikely to be right.'

'Of course it's unlikely, but it might happen that way all the same.'

'Come off it, Dave! What do you predict? Where d'you put your money?'

And Weichart was forced to admit that he put his money on Kingsley's prediction being wrong.

'All right. Let's go and see,' said Leicester.

While the company were filing out, Ann Halsey said to Parkinson:

'Will you help me to make more coffee, Mr Parkinson? They'll be wanting some when they get back.'

As they busied themselves, she went on:

'Did you ever hear such a lot of talk? I used to think that scientists were of the strong silent type, but never did I hear such a gibble-gabble. What is it that Omar Khayyám says about the doctors and saints?'

'I believe it goes something like this,' answered Parkinson:

> 'Myself when young did eagerly frequent
> Doctor and Saint, and heard great argument
> About it and about, but evermore
> Came out by the same door as in I went.'

'It isn't so much the volume of talk that surprises me,' he laughed. 'We get plenty of that in politics. It's the number of mistakes they've made, how often things have turned out differently to what they've expected.'

When the party reassembled it was obvious at a glance how things had gone. Marlowe took a cup of coffee from Parkinson.

'Thanks. Well, that's that. Chris was right and Dave was wrong. Now I suppose we must get down to trying to decide what it means.'

'Your move, Chris,' said Leicester.

'Let's suppose then that my hypothesis is right, that our own transmissions are producing a marked effect on the atmospheric ionization.'

Ann Halsey handed Kingsley a mug of coffee.

'I'd be a lot happier if I knew what ionization meant. Here, drink this.'

'Oh, it means that the outer parts of the atoms are stripped away from the inner parts.'

'And how does this happen?'

'It can happen in many ways, by an electrical discharge, as in a flash of lightning, or in a neon tube – the sort of strip lighting we've got here. The gas in these tubes is being partially ionized.'

'I suppose energy is the real difficulty? That your transmissions have far too little power to produce this rise of ionization?' said McNeil.

'That's right,' answered Marlowe. 'It's completely impossible that our transmissions should be the primary cause of the fluctuations in the atmosphere. My God, they'd need a fantastic amount of power.'

'Then how can Kingsley's hypothesis be right?'

'Our transmissions are not the primary cause, as Geoff says. That's wholly impossible. I agree with Weichart there. My hypothesis is that our transmissions are acting as a trigger, whereby some very large source of power is released.'

'And where, Chris, do you suppose this source of power is to be located?' asked Marlowe.

'In the Cloud, of course.'

'But surely it's quite fantastic to imagine that we can cause the Cloud to react in such a fashion, and to do it with such reproducibility? You'd have to suppose that the Cloud was equipped with a sort of feedback mechanism,' argued Leicester.

'On the basis of my hypothesis that's certainly a correct inference.'

'But don't you see, Kingsley, that it's utterly mad?' Weichart exclaimed.

Kingsley looked at his watch.

'It's almost time to go and try again, if anyone wants to. Does anyone want to?'

'In heaven's name, no!' said Leicester.

'Either we go or we stay. And if we stay it means that we accept Kingsley's hypothesis. Well, boys, do we go or do we stay?' remarked Marlowe.

'We stay,' said Barnett. 'And we see how the argument goes. We've got as far as some sort of a feedback mechanism in the Cloud, a mechanism set to churn out an enormous amount of power as soon as it receives a trickle of radio emission from outside itself. The next step, I suppose, is to speculate on how the feedback mechanism works, and why it works as it does. Anybody got any ideas?'

Alexandrov cleared his throat. Everybody waited to catch one of his rare remarks.

'Bastard in Cloud. Said so before.'

There were wide grins and a giggle from Yvette Hedelfort. Kingsley, however, remarked quite seriously:

'I remember you did. Were you serious about it, Alexis?'

'Always serious, damn it,' said the Russian.

'Without frills, what exactly do you mean, Chris?' someone asked.

'I mean that the Cloud contains an intelligence. Before anybody starts criticizing, let me say that I know it's a preposterous idea and I wouldn't suggest it for a moment if the alternative weren't even more outrageously preposterous. Doesn't it strike you how often we've been wrong about the behaviour of the Cloud?'

Parkinson and Ann Halsey exchanged an amused glance.

'All our mistakes have a certain hallmark about them. They're just the sort of mistake that it'd be natural to make if, instead of the Cloud being inanimate, it were alive.'

Chapter Nine

CLOSE REASONING

I T is curious in how great a degree human progress depends on the individual. Humans, numbered in thousands of millions, seem organized into an ant-like society. Yet this is not so. New ideas, the impetus of all development, come from individual people, not from corporations or states. New ideas, fragile as spring flowers, easily bruised by the tread of the multitude, may yet be cherished by the solitary wanderer.

Among the vast host that experienced the coming of the Cloud, none except Kingsley arrived at a coherent understanding of its real nature, none except Kingsley gave the reason for the visit of the Cloud to the solar system. His first bald statement was greeted with outright disbelief even by his fellow scientists – Alexandrov excepted.

Weichart was frank in his opinion.

'The whole idea is quite ridiculous,' he said.

Marlowe shook his head.

'This comes of reading science fiction.'

'No bloody fiction about Cloud coming straight for dam' Sun. No bloody fiction about Cloud stopping. No bloody fiction about ionization,' growled Alexandrov.

McNeil, the physician, was intrigued. The new development was more in his line than transmitters and aerials.

'I'd like to know, Chris, what you mean in this context by the word "alive".'

'Well, John, you know better than I do that the distinction between animate and inanimate is more a matter of verbal convenience than anything else. By and large, inanimate matter has a simple structure and comparatively simple properties. Animate or living matter on the other hand has a highly complicated structure and is capable of very involved behaviour. When I said the Cloud may be alive I meant that the material inside it may be organized in an intricate fashion, so that its behaviour and consequently the behaviour of the whole Cloud is far more complex than we previously supposed.'

'Isn't there an element of tautology there?' – from Weichart.

'I said that words such as "animate" and "inanimate" are only verbal conveniences. If they're pushed too far they do appear tautological. In more scientific terms I expect the chemistry of the interior of the Cloud to be extremely complicated – complicated molecules, complicated structures built out of molecules, complicated nervous activity. In short I think the Cloud has a brain.'

'A dam' straightforward conclusion,' nodded Alexandrov.

When the laugh had subsided, Marlowe turned to Kingsley.

'Well, Chris, we know what you mean, at any rate we know near enough. Now let's have your argument. Take your time. Let's have it point by point, and it'd better be good.'

'Very well then, here goes. Point number one, the temperature inside the Cloud is suited to the formation of highly complicated molecules.'

'Right! First point to you. In fact, the temperature is perhaps a little more favourable than it is here on the Earth.'

'Second point, conditions are favourable to the formation of extensive structures built out of complicated molecules.'

'Why should that be so?' asked Yvette Hedelfort.

'Adhesion on the surface of solid particles. The density inside the Cloud is so high that quite large lumps of solid material – probably mostly ordinary ice – are almost certainly to be found inside it. I suggest that the complicated molecules get together when they happen to stick to the surfaces of these lumps.'

'A very good point, Chris,' agreed Marlowe.

'Sorry, I don't pass this round.' McNeil was shaking his head. 'You talk of complicated molecules being built up by sticking together on the surface of solid bodies. Well, it won't do. The molecules out of which living material is made contain large stores of internal energy. Indeed the processes of life depend on this internal energy. The trouble with your sticking together is that you don't get energy into the molecules that way.'

Kingsley seemed unperturbed.

'And from what source do the molecules of living creatures

here on the Earth get their internal supplies of energy?' he asked McNeil.

'Plants get it from sunlight, and animals get it from plants, or from other animals of course. So in the last analysis the energy always comes from the Sun.'

'And where is the Cloud getting energy from now?'

The tables were turned. And as neither McNeil nor anyone else seemed disposed to argue, Kingsley went on:

'Let's accept John's argument. Let's suppose that my beast in the Cloud is built out of the same sort of molecules that we are. Then the light from some star is required in order that the molecules be formed. Well, of course starlight is available far out in the space between the stars, but it's very feeble. So to get a really strong supply of light the beast would need to approach close to some star. And that's just what the beast has done!'

Marlowe became excited.

'My God, that ties three things together, straight away. The need for sunlight, number one. The Cloud making a bee-line for the Sun, number two. The Cloud stopping when it reached the Sun, number three. Very good, Chris.'

'It is a very good beginning, yes, but it leaves some things obscure,' Yvette Hedelfort remarked. 'I do not see,' she went on, 'how it was that the Cloud came to be out in space. If it has need of sunlight or starlight, surely it would stay always around one star. Do you suppose that this beast of yours has just been born somewhere out in space and has now come to attach itself to our Sun?'

'And while you're about it, Chris, will you explain how your friend the beast controls its supplies of energy? How did it manage to fire off those blobs of gas with such fantastic speed when it was slowing down?' asked Leicester.

'One question at a time! I'll take Harry's first, because it's probably easier. We tried to explain the expulsion of those blobs of gas in terms of magnetic fields, and the explanation simply didn't work. The trouble was that the required fields would be so intense that they'd simply burst the whole Cloud apart. Stated somewhat differently, we couldn't find any way in which large quantities of energy could be localized through a magnetic agency in comparatively small regions. But let's now look at the problem from this new point of view. Let's begin by asking what method we ourselves would use to produce intense local concentrations of energy.'

'Explosions!' gasped Barnett.

'That's right, explosions, either by nuclear fission, or more probably by nuclear fusion. There's no shortage of hydrogen in this Cloud.'

'Are you being serious, Chris?'

'Of course I'm being serious. If I'm right in supposing that some beast inhabits the Cloud, then why shouldn't he be at least as intelligent as we are?'

'There's the slight difficulty of radioactive products. Wouldn't these be extremely deleterious to living material?' asked McNeil.

'If they could get at the living material, certainly they would. But although it isn't possible to produce explosions with magnetic fields, it is possible to prevent two samples of material mixing with each other. I imagine that the beast orders the material of the Cloud magnetically, that by means of magnetic fields he can move samples of material wherever he wants inside the Cloud. I imagine that he takes very good care to keep the radioactive gas well separated from the living material – remember I'm using the term "living" for verbal convenience. I'm not going to be drawn into a philosophical argument about it.'

'You know, Kingsley,' said Weichart, 'this is going far better than I thought it would. What I suppose you would say is that whereas basically we assemble materials with our hands, or with the aid of machines that we have made with our hands, the beast assembles materials with the aid of magnetic energy.'

'That's the general idea. And I must add that the beast seems to me to have far the better of it. For one thing he's got vastly more energy to play with than we have.'

'My God, I should think so, billions of times more, at the very least,' said Marlowe. 'It's beginning to look, Chris, as if you're winning this argument. But we objectors over here in this corner are pinning our faith to Yvette's question. It seems to me a very good one. What can you offer in answer to it?'

'It is a very good question, Geoff, and I don't know that I can give a really convincing answer. The sort of idea I've got is that perhaps the beast can't stay for very long in the close proximity of a star. Perhaps he comes in periodically to some star or other, builds his molecules, which form his food supply as it were, and then pushes off again. Perhaps he does this time and time again.'

'But why shouldn't the beast be able to stay permanently near a star?'

'Well, an ordinary common or garden cloud, a beastless cloud, if it were permanently near a star, would gradually condense into a compact body, or into a number of compact bodies. Indeed, as we all know, our Earth probably condensed at one time from just such a cloud. Obviously our friend the beast would find it extremely embarrassing to have his protective Cloud condense into a planet. So equally obviously he'll decide to push off before there's any danger of that happening. And when he pushes off he'll take his Cloud with him.'

'Have you any idea how long that will be?' asked Parkinson.

'None at all. I suggest that the beast will push off when he's finished recharging his food supply. That might be a matter of weeks, months, years, millennia for all I know.'

'Don't I detect a slight smell of rat in all this?' Barnett remarked.

'Possibly. I don't know how keen your sense of smell is, Bill. What's your trouble?'

'I've got lots of troubles. I should have thought that your remarks about condensing into a planet apply only to an inanimate cloud. If we grant that the Cloud is able to control the distribution of material within itself, then it could easily prevent condensation from taking place. After all, condensation must be a sort of instability process and I would have thought that quite a moderate degree of control on the part of your beast could prevent any condensation at all.'

'There are two replies to that. One is that I believe the beast will lose his control if he stays too long near the Sun. If he stays too long, the magnetic field of the Sun will penetrate into the Cloud. Then the rotation of the Cloud round the Sun will twist up the magnetic field to blazes. All control would then be lost.'

'My God, that's an excellent point.'

'It is, isn't it? And here's another one. However different our beast is to life here on Earth, one point he must have in common with us. We must both obey the simple biological rules of selection and development. By that I mean that we can't suppose that the Cloud started off by containing a fully-fledged beast. It must have started with small beginnings, just as life here on Earth started with small beginnings. So, to start with, there would be no intricate control over the distribution of material in the Cloud. Hence if the Cloud had originally been situated close to a star, it could not have prevented condensation into a planet or into a number of planets.'

'Then how do you visualize the early beginnings?'

'As something that happened far out in interstellar space. To begin with, life in the Cloud must have depended on the general radiation field of the stars. Even that would give it more radiation for molecule-building purposes than life on the Earth gets. Then I imagine that as intelligence developed it would be discovered that food supplies – i.e. molecule-building – could be enormously increased by moving in close to a star for a comparatively brief period. As I see it, the beast must be essentially a denizen of interstellar space. Now, Bill, have you any more troubles?'

'Well, yes, I've got another problem. Why can't the Cloud manufacture its own radiation? Why bother to come in close to a star? If it understands nuclear fusion to the point of producing gigantic explosions, why not use nuclear fusion for producing its supply of radiation?'

'To produce radiation in a controlled fashion requires a slow reactor, and of course that's just what a star is. The Sun is just a gigantic slow nuclear fusion reactor. To produce radiation on any real scale comparable with the Sun, the Cloud would have to make itself into a star. Then the beast would get roasted. It'd be much too hot inside.'

'Even then I doubt whether a cloud of this mass could produce very much radiation,' remarked Marlowe. 'Its mass is much too small. According to the mass-luminosity relation it'd be down as compared with the Sun by a fantastic amount. No, you're barking up a wrong tree there, Bill.'

'I've a question that I'd like to ask,' said Parkinson. 'Why do you always refer to your beast in the singular? Why shouldn't there be lots of little beasts in the Cloud?'

'I have a reason for that, but it'll take quite a while to explain.'

'Well, it looks as if we're not going to get much sleep tonight, so you'd better carry on.'

'Then let's start by supposing that the Cloud contains lots of little beasts instead of one big beast. I think you'll grant me that communication must have developed between the different individuals.'

'Certainly.'

'Then what form will the communication take?'

'You're supposed to be telling us, Chris.'

'My question was purely rhetorical. I suggest that communication would be impossible by our methods. We communicate acoustically.'

'You mean by talking. That's certainly your method all right, Chris,' said Ann Halsey.

But the point was lost on Kingsley. He went on:

'Any attempt to use sound would be drowned by the enormous amount of background noise that must exist inside the Cloud. It would be far worse than trying to talk in a roaring gale. I think we can be pretty sure that communication would have to take place electrically.'

'That seems fair enough.'

'Good. Well, the next point is that by our standards the distances between the individuals would be very large, since the Cloud by our standards is enormously large. It would obviously be intolerable to rely on essentially D.C. methods over such distances.'

'D.C. methods? Chris, will you please try to avoid jargon?'

'Direct current.'

'That explains it, I suppose!'

'Oh, the sort of thing we get on the telephone. Roughly speaking, the difference between D.C. communication and A.C. communication is the difference between the telephone and radio.'

Marlowe grinned at Ann Halsey.

'What Chris is trying to say in his inimitable manner is that communication must occur by radiative propagation.'

'If you think that makes it clearer ...'

'Of course it's clear. Stop being obstructive, Ann. Radiative propagation occurs when we emit a light signal or a radio signal. It travels across space through a vacuum at a speed of 186,000 miles per second. Even at this speed it would still take about ten minutes for a signal to travel across the Cloud.

'My next point is that the volume of information that can be transmitted radiatively is enormously greater than the amount that we can communicate by ordinary sound. We've seen that with our pulsed radio transmitters. So if this Cloud contains separate individuals, the individuals must be able to communicate on a vastly more detailed scale than we can. What we can get across in an hour of talk they might get across in a hundredth of a second.'

'Ah, I begin to see light,' broke in McNeil. 'If communication occurs on such a scale then it becomes somewhat doubtful whether we should talk any more of separate individuals!'

'You're home, John!'

'But *I'm* not home,' said Parkinson.

'In vulgar parlance,' said McNeil amiably, 'what Chris is saying is that individuals in the Cloud, if there are any, must be highly telepathic, so telepathic that it becomes rather meaningless to regard them as being really separate from each other.'

'Then why didn't he say so in the first place?' – from Ann Halsey.

'Because like most vulgar parlance, the word "telepathy" doesn't really mean very much.'

'Well, it certainly means a great deal more to me.'

'And what does it mean to you, Ann?'

'It means conveying one's thoughts without talking, or of course without writing or winking or anything like that.'

'In other words it means – if it means anything at all – communication by a non-acoustic medium.'

'And that means using radiative propagation,' chipped in Leicester.

'And radiative propagation means the use of alternating currents, not the direct currents and voltages we use in our brains.'

'But I thought we were capable of some degree of telepathy,' suggested Parkinson.

'Rubbish. Our brains simply don't work the right way for tele-pathy. Everything is based on D.C. voltages, and radiative trans-mission is impossible that way.'

'I know this is rather a red herring, but I thought these extra-sensory people had established some rather remarkable correla-tions,' Parkinson persisted.

'Bloody bad science,' growled Alexandrov. 'Correlations ob-tained after experiments done is bloody bad. Only prediction in science.'

'I don't follow.'

'What Alexis means is that only predictions really count in science,' explained Weichart. 'That's the way Kingsley downed me an hour or two ago. It's no good doing a lot of experi-ments first and then discovering a lot of correlations after-wards, not unless the correlations can be used for making new predictions. Otherwise it's like betting on a race after it's been run.'

'Kingsley's ideas have many very interesting neurological im-plications,' McNeil remarked. 'Communication for us is a matter of extreme difficulty. We ourselves have to make a translation of the electrical activity – essentially D.C. activity – in our brains. To do this, quite a bit of the brain is given over to the control of the lip muscles and of the vocal chords. Even so our translation is very incomplete. We don't do too badly perhaps in conveying simple ideas, but the conveying of emotions is very difficult. Kingsley's little beasts could, I suppose, convey emotions too, and that's another reason why it's rather meaningless to talk of separate individuals. It's rather terrifying to realize that every-thing we've been talking about tonight and conveying so inade-quately from one to another could be communicated with vastly greater precision and understanding among Kingsley's little beasts in about a hundredth of a second.'

'I'd like to follow the idea of separate individuals a little further,' said Barnett, turning to Kingsley. 'Would you think of each individual in the Cloud as building a radiative transmitter of some sort?'

'Not as *building* a transmitter. Let me describe how I see bio-logical evolution taking place within the Cloud. At an early stage

I think there would be a whole lot of more or less separate disconnected individuals. Then communication would develop, not by a deliberate inorganic building of a means of radiative transmission, but through a slow biological development. The individuals would develop a means of radiative transmission as a biological organ, rather as we have developed a mouth, tongue, lips, and vocal chords. Communication would improve to a degree that we can scarcely contemplate. A thought would no sooner be thought than it would be communicated. An emotion would no sooner be experienced than it would be shared. With this would come a submergence of the individual and an evolution into a coherent whole. The beast, as I visualize it, need not be located in a particular place in the Cloud. Its different parts may be spread through the Cloud, but I regard it as a neurological unity, interlocked by a communication system in which signals are transmitted back and forth at a speed of 186,000 miles a second.'

'We ought to get down to considering those signals more closely. I suppose they'd have to have a longish wave-length. Ordinary light presumably would be useless since the Cloud is opaque to it,' said Leicester.

'My guess is that the signals are radio waves,' went on Kingsley. 'There's a good reason why it should be so. To be really efficient one must have complete phase control in a communication system. This can be done with radio waves, but not, so far as we know, with shorter wave-lengths.'

McNeil was excited.

'Our radio transmissions!' he exclaimed. 'They'd have interfered with the beast's neurological control.'

'They would if they'd been allowed to.'

'What d'you mean, Chris?'

'Well, the beast hasn't only to contend with our transmissions, but with the whole welter of cosmic radio waves. From all quarters of the Universe there'd be radio waves interfering with its neurological activity unless it had developed some form of protection.'

'What sort of protection have you in mind?'

'Electrical discharges in the outer part of the Cloud causing sufficient ionization to prevent the entry of external radio waves. Such a protection would be as essential as the skull is to the human brain.'

Aniseed smoke was rapidly filling the room. Marlowe suddenly found his pipe too hot to hold and put it down gingerly.

'My God, you think this explains the rise of ionization in the atmosphere, when we switch on our transmitters?'

'That's the general idea. We were talking earlier on about a feedback mechanism. That, I imagine, is just what the beast has got. If any external waves get in too deeply, then up go the voltages and away go the discharges until the waves can get in no farther.'

'But the ionization takes place in our own atmosphere.'

'For this purpose I think we can regard our atmosphere as a part of the Cloud. We know from the shimmering of the night sky that gas extends all the way from the Earth to the denser parts of the Cloud, the disk-like parts. In short we're inside the Cloud, electronically speaking. That, I think, explains our communication troubles. At an earlier stage, when we were outside the Cloud, the beast didn't protect itself by ionizing our atmosphere, but through its outer electronic shield. But once we got inside the shield the discharges began to occur in our own atmosphere. The beast has been boxing-in our transmissions.'

'Very fine reasoning, Chris,' said Marlowe.

'Hellish fine,' nodded Alexandrov.

'How about the one-centimetre transmissions? They went through all right,' Weichart objected.

'Although the chain of reasoning is getting rather long there's a suggestion that one can make on that. I think it's worth making because it suggests the next action we might take. It seems to me most unlikely that this Cloud is unique. Nature doesn't work in unique examples. So let's suppose there are lots of these beasts inhabiting the Galaxy. Then I would expect communication to occur between one cloud and another. This would imply that some wave-lengths would be required for external communication purposes, wave-lengths that could penetrate into the Cloud and would do no neurological harm.'

'And you think one centimetre may be such a wave-length?'

'That's the general idea.'

'But then why was there no reply to our one-centimetre transmission?' asked Parkinson.

'Perhaps because we sent no message. There'd be no point in replying to a perfectly blank transmission.'

'Then we ought to start sending pulsed messages on the one centimetre,' exclaimed Leicester. 'But how can we expect the Cloud to decipher them?'

'That's not an urgent problem to begin with. It will be obvious that our transmissions contain information – that will be clear from the frequent repetition of various patterns. As soon as the Cloud realizes that our transmissions have intelligent control behind them I think we can expect some sort of reply. How long will it take to get started, Harry? You're not in a position to modulate the one centimetre yet, are you?'

'No, but we can be in a couple of days, if we work night shifts. I had a sort of presentiment that I wasn't going to see my bed tonight. Come on, chaps, let's get started.'

Leicester stood up, stretched himself, and ambled out. The meeting broke up. Kingsley took Parkinson on one side.

'Look, Parkinson,' he said, 'there's no need to go gabbling about this until we know more about it.'

'Of course not. The Prime Minister suspects I'm off my head as it is.'

'There is one thing that you might pass on, though. If London, Washington, and the rest of the political circus could get ten-centimetre transmitters working, it's just possible that they might avoid the fade-out trouble.'

When Kingsley and Ann Halsey were alone later that night, Ann remarked:

'How on earth did you come on such an idea, Chris?'

'Well, it's pretty obvious really. The trouble is that we're all inhibited against such thinking. The idea that the Earth is the only possible abode of life runs pretty deep in spite of all the science fiction and kids' comics. If we had been able to look at the business with an impartial eye we should have spotted it long ago. Right from the first, things have gone wrong and they've gone wrong according to a systematic sort of pattern. Once I overcame the psychological block, I saw all the difficulties could be removed by one simple and entirely plausible step. One by one the bits of the puzzle fitted into place. I think Alexandrov probably had the same idea, only his English is a bit on the terse side.'

'On the bloody terse side, you mean. But seriously, do you think this communication business will work?'

'I very much hope so. It's quite crucial that it should.'

'Why do you say that?'

'Think of the disasters the Earth has suffered so far, without the Cloud taking any purposive steps against us. A bit of reflection from its surface nearly roasted us. A short obscuration of the Sun nearly froze us. If the merest tiny fraction of the energy controlled by the Cloud should be directed against us we should be wiped out, every plant and animal.'

'But why should that happen?'

'How can one tell? Do you think of the tiny beetle or the ant that you crush under your foot on an afternoon's walk? One of those gas bullets that hit the Moon three months ago would finish us. Sooner or later the Cloud will probably let fly with some more of 'em. Or we might be electrocuted in some monstrous discharge.'

'Could the Cloud really do that?'

'Easily. The energy that it controls is simply enormous. If we can get some sort of a message across, then perhaps the Cloud will take the trouble to avoid crushing us under its foot.'

'But why should it bother?'

'Well, if a beetle were to say to you, "Please, Miss Halsey, will you avoid treading here, otherwise I shall be crushed," wouldn't you be willing to move your foot a trifle?'

Chapter Ten

COMMUNICATION ESTABLISHED

FOUR days later after thirty-three hours of transmission from Nortonstowe the first communication from the Cloud came through. It would be idle to attempt to describe the prevailing excitement. Suffice it to say that frenzied attempts were made to decode the incoming message, for message it obviously was, judging from regular patterns that could be discovered among the rapid pulses of radio signal. The attempts were not successful. Nor was this surprising, for, as Kingsley remarked, it can be difficult enough to discover a code when the message has initially been thought out in a known language. Here the language of the Cloud was entirely unknown.

'That seems good sense to me,' remarked Leicester. 'Our problem isn't likely to be any easier than the Cloud's problem, and the Cloud won't understand our messages until it's discovered the English language.'

'The problem's probably a great deal worse than that,' said Kingsley. 'We've every reason to believe that the Cloud is more intelligent than we are, so its language – whatever it may be – is likely to be a lot more complicated than ours. My proposal is that we stop bothering trying to decipher the messages we've been receiving. Instead I propose we rely on the Cloud being able to decipher our messages. Then when it's learned our language it can reply in our own code.'

'Dam' good idea. Always force foreigner to learn English,' said Alexandrov to Yvette Hedelfort.

'To begin with, I think we should stick as much as possible to science and mathematics because these are likely to be the best common denominator. Later on we can try sociological stuff. The big job will be to record all the material we want to transmit.'

'You mean that we ought to transmit a sort of basic course in science and mathematics, and in basic English?' said Weichart.

'That's the idea. And I think we ought to get down to it right away.'

The policy was successful, too successful. Within two days the first intelligible reply was received. It read:

'Message received. Information slight. Send more.'

For the next week almost everyone was kept busy reading from suitably chosen books. The readings were recorded and then transmitted. But always there came short replies demanding more information, and still more information.

Marlowe said to Kingsley:

'It's no good, Chris, we shall have to think up a new idea. This brute'll soon exhaust the lot of us. My voice is getting as hoarse as an old crow with this constant reading.'

'Harry Leicester's working on a new idea.'

'I'm glad of that. What is it?'

'Well, it may kill two birds with one stone. The slowness of our present methods isn't the only trouble. Another difficulty is that a great deal of what we're sending must seem shockingly unintelligible. A whole multitude of words in our language refer to objects that we see and touch and hear. Unless the Cloud knows what those objects are I don't see how it can make sense of a great deal of the stuff we're churning out. If you haven't ever seen an orange or come in contact with an orange in some way, I don't see how you could possibly know what the word "orange" means, however intelligent you were.'

'I can see that. What d'you propose to do?'

'It was Harry's idea. He thinks he can use a television camera. Luckily I got Parkinson to lay some in. Harry thinks he can hook one up to our transmitter, and what's more he's pretty confident that he can modify it to do something like 20,000 lines instead of the miserable 450 or so lines of ordinary television.'

'That's because of the much lower wave-length?'

'Yes, of course. We ought to be able to transmit an excellent picture.'

'But the Cloud doesn't have a television tube!'

'Of course not. How the Cloud decides to analyse our signals is entirely its own business. What we must make sure of is that we're transmitting all relevant information. So far, we've been doing a pretty poor job and the Cloud's been quite right to complain.'

'How do you propose to use the television camera?'

'We'll start by going through a whole list of words, demonstrating various nouns and verbs. This will be preliminary. It's got to be carefully done but it shouldn't take too long to go through about five thousand words – perhaps a week. Then we can transmit the contents of whole books by scanning the pages with the camera. It should be possible to deal with the whole *Encyclopaedia Britannica* in a few days by this method.'

'That certainly ought to satisfy the brute's thirst for knowledge. Well, I suppose I'd better get back to my reading! Tell me when the camera's going to be ready. I can't estimate how glad I'll be to get rid of this chore.'

Later Kingsley could be seen in contact with Leicester. 'I'm sorry, Harry,' he said, 'but I've got some other problems.'

'Then I hope you'll keep them to yourself. We're right under the surface here in this department.'

'I'm sorry but they concern you, and I'm afraid they'll mean more work.'

'Look here, Chris, why don't you take your coat off and start doing some real work instead of interrupting the good intentions of the proletariat? Well, what's the trouble? Let's hear it.'

'The trouble is we're not giving enough attention to the receiving end, to us here as the receiving end, I mean. Once we start to transmit with the television camera we shall presumably get replies in the same form as we transmit. That's to say a received message would appear as words on a television tube.'

'Well, what's the matter with that? It'll be nice and easy to read.'

'Yes, that's all right so far as it goes. But remember that we can only read about a hundred and twenty words a minute, whereas we're hoping to transmit at least a hundred times faster than that.'

'We shall have to tell Johnny Boy up there to slow down the speed of his replies, that's all. We'll tell him that we're such dimwits that we can only deal with a hundred and twenty words a minute, instead of the tens of thousands that he seems capable of gobbling up.'

'All very good, Harry, I'm not quarrelling with anything you say.'

'Only you're wanting me to do more work, eh?'

'That's right. How did you guess? My idea is that it'd be nice to hear the Cloud's messages acoustically, as well as to read 'em off a tube. We'll get much more tired reading than listening.'

'To quote Alexis, I think it's a bloody awful idea. You realize what it involves?'

'It means you'll have to keep sight and sound equivalents. We could use the electronic computer for that. We've only got to store about five thousand words.'

'Only!'

'I don't see it's going to mean very much work at all. We shall have to go over individual words quite slowly to the Cloud. I'm reckoning about a week for it. As we show off each word we put some key part of our T.V. signal on to punched tape. That shouldn't be difficult. You can also put the sound of the words on to punched tape, using a microphone, of course, to get the sound into an electrical form. Once we've got it all on tape we can put it into the computer any time we like. There'll be quite a lot of storage needed so we'll use the magnetics. It'll be easily fast enough. And we'll put a conversion programme in the high-speed store. Then we can either read the Cloud's messages on a television tube or hear 'em over a loud-speaker.'

'I'll say this for you, Chris. I never knew anyone who was better at finding work for other people. I take it that you'll write the conversion programme.'

'Of course.'

'A nice armchair job, eh? Meanwhile us poor devils can slave away with our soldering irons, burning holes in our trousers and heaven knows what. What voice shall I use for the sound?'

'Your own, Harry. That's your reward for having all those holes burned in your trousers. We shall all be listening to you for hours on end!'

As time went on, the idea of a conversion of the Cloud's messages into sound seemed to commend itself more and more to Harry Leicester. After a few days he began to go around with a more or less permanent grin on his face, but nobody could discover the joke.

The television system turned out highly successful. After four days of transmission a message was received that read:

'Congratulations on improvement of technique.'

This message appeared on the television tube since the sound-conversion system was not yet working.

The transmission of individual words proved rather more difficult than had been expected, but eventually it was accomplished. The transmission of scientific and mathematical works turned out a simple matter. Indeed it soon became clear that these transmissions were only serving to acquaint the Cloud with the state of human development, rather as a child shows off its attainments to an adult. Books dealing with social issues were then run through. Their choice was a matter of some difficulty and in the end a large and rather random sample was televised. It became clear that the Cloud was having more difficulty in absorbing this material. At length the message came, still read on the television tube:

'Later transmissions appear most confused and strange. I have many questions to ask, but would prefer to deal with them at some future time. Incidentally your transmissions are interfering very seriously, on account of the proximity of your transmitter, with various external messages that I wish to receive. For this reason I am providing you with the following code. In future always use this code. I intend setting up an electronic shield against your transmitter. The code will serve as a signal that you wish to penetrate the shield. If it is convenient you will be allowed to do so. You may expect to receive a further transmission from me in approximately forty-eight hours from now.'

An intricate pattern of lights flashed across the television tube. They were followed by a further message:

'Please confirm that you have received this code and can use it.'

Leicester dictated the following reply:

'We have made a recording of your code. We believe that we can use it but are not certain. We will confirm at your next transmission.'

There was a delay of about ten minutes. Then the reply came:

'Very well. Good-bye.'

Kingsley explained to Ann Halsey:

'The delay is due to the time required for the transmission to reach the Cloud and for the reply to get back here. These delays are going to make short speeches rather unprofitable.'

But Ann Halsey was less interested in the delays than in the tone of the Cloud's messages.

'It sounded just like a human,' she said, wide-eyed with amazement.

'Of course it did. How could it have done otherwise? It's using our language and our phrases, so it's bound to sound human.'

'But the "good-bye" sounded so nice.'

'Nonsense! To the Cloud "good-bye" is probably just a code word for ending a transmission. Remember that it's learned our language from scratch in about a fortnight. That doesn't look very human to me.'

'Oh, Chris, you're exactly what the Americans call a "sad sack". Isn't he, Geoff?'

'What, Chris a sad sack? I should just say he is, ma'am, the biggest god-almighty sad sack in Christendom. Yes, sir! Seriously, Chris, what did you think of it?'

'I thought the sending of a code was a very good sign.'

'So did I. Very good for our morale. Heaven knows we need it. This last year hasn't been easy. I think I feel better than I've felt since the day I picked you up at Los Angeles airport, and that seems at least a lifetime ago.'

Ann Halsey wrinkled her nose.

'I can't understand why you go all goofy over a code, and why you poured cold water on my "good-bye".'

'Because, my dear,' answered Kingsley, 'the sending of the code was a reasonable rational thing to do. It was a point of contact, of understanding, quite unconnected with language, whereas the "good-bye" was only a superficial linguistic gloss.'

Leicester walked across to join them.

'This two-day delay is rather fortunate. I think we can get the sound system working by then.'

'How about the code?'

'I'm pretty sure it's all right, but I thought it'd be best to be on the safe side.'

*

Two days later in the evening the whole company assembled in
the transmitting lab. Leicester and his friends busied themselves
with last-minute adjustments. It was nearly eight o'clock when
preliminary flashes appeared on the tube. Words soon began to
appear.

'Let's have some sound,' said Leicester.

There were broad grins and laughter as a voice came over the
loud-speaker, for it was the voice of Joe Stoddard that spoke. For
a minute or so most people thought of a hoax, but then it was
noticed that the voice and the words on the tube were the same.
And decidedly the sentiments were not those of Joe Stoddard.

Leicester's joke had some advantage. Of necessity he had not
been given sufficient time to include voice inflexions: each word
was always pronounced the same way, and the words were always
spoken at the same rate, except at the end of sentences where
there was always a slight pause. These disadvantages of the sound
reproduction were to some extent compensated by the fact that in
natural speech Joe Stoddard did not show much inflexion anyway. And Leicester had cleverly timed the rate of delivery of the
words to agree pretty closely with Joe's natural speech. So although the Cloud's speech was obviously an artificial imitation
of Joe, the imitation was quite a good one. Nobody ever really
got used to the Cloud speaking with the easy slow burr of the
West Country, and nobody ever quite got over the indescribably
comic effect of some of Joe's mispronunciations. Ever afterwards
the Cloud was known as Joe.

Joe's first message ran roughly as follows:

'Your first transmission came as a surprise, for it is most unusual to find animals with technical skills inhabiting planets,
which are in the nature of extreme outposts of life.'

Joe was asked why this should be so.

'For two quite simple reasons. Living on the surface of a solid
body, you are exposed to a strong gravitational force. This greatly
limits the size to which your animals can grow and hence limits
the scope of your neurological activity. It forces you to possess
muscular structures to promote movement, and it also forces you
to carry protective armour against sharp blows – as for instance
your skulls are a necessary protection for your brains. The extra

weight of muscle and armour still further reduces the scope of your neurological activities. Indeed your very largest animals have been mostly bone and muscle with very little brain. As I have already said, the strong gravitational field in which you live is the cause of this difficulty. By and large, one only expects intelligent life to exist in a diffuse gaseous medium, not on planets at all.

'The second unfavourable factor is your extreme lack of basic chemical foods. For the building of chemical foods on a large scale starlight is necessary. Your planet, however, absorbs only a very minute fraction of the light from the Sun. At the moment I myself am building basic chemicals at about 10,000,000,000 times the rate at which building is occurring on the whole entire surface of your planet.

'This shortage of food chemicals leads to a tooth-and-claw existence in which it is difficult for the first glimmerings of intellect to gain a foothold in competition with bone and muscle. Of course once intelligence becomes firmly established, competition with sheer bone and muscle becomes easy, but the first steps along the road are excessively difficult – so much so that your own case is a rarity among planetary life forms.'

'And so much for the space travel enthusiasts,' said Marlowe. 'Ask him, Harry, to what we owe the emergence of intelligence here on the Earth.'

The question was put, and after a time the answer came:

'Probably to the combination of several circumstances, among which I would rate as most important the development about fifty million years ago of an entirely new type of plant: the plant that you call grass. The emergence of this plant caused a drastic reorganization of the whole animal world, owing to the peculiarity that grass can be cropped to ground level, in distinction from all other plants. As the grasslands spread over the Earth those animals that could take advantage of this peculiarity survived and developed. Other animals declined or became extinct. It seems to have been in this major reshuffle that intelligence was able to gain its first footing on your planet.

'There are several very unusual factors that made the decoding of your method of communication a matter of some difficulty,' went on the Cloud. 'Particularly I find it most strange that your communication symbols do not bear any really close connexion with the neurological activity in your brains.'

'We'd better say something about that,' remarked Kingsley.

'I bet we had. I didn't think you'd be able to keep quiet for long, Chris,' Ann Halsey remarked.

Kingsley explained his idea about A.C. and D.C. communication, and asked whether Joe himself operated on an A.C. basis. Joe confirmed that this was so and continued:

'This is not the only quaint feature. Your outstanding oddity is the great similarity of one individual to another. This allows you to use a very crude method of communication. You attach labels to your neurological states – anger, headache, embarrassed, happy, melancholy – these are all labels. If Mr A wishes to tell Mr B that he is suffering from a headache he makes no attempt to describe the neurological disruption in his head. Instead he displays his label. He says:

"I have a headache."

'When Mr B hears this he takes the label "headache" and interprets it in accordance with his own experience. Thus Mr A is able to acquaint Mr B of his indisposition even though neither party may have the slightest idea what a "headache" really consists of. Such a highly singular method of communication is of course only possible between nearly identical individuals.'

'Could I put it this way?' said Kingsley. 'Between two absolutely identical individuals, if that were possible, no communication at all would be necessary because each individual would automatically know the experience of the other. Between nearly identical individuals a quite crude method of communication suffices. Between two widely different individuals a vastly more complicated communication system is required.'

'That is exactly what I was trying to explain. The difficulty I had in decoding your language will now be clear. It is a language suited to nearly similar individuals, whereas you and I are widely separated, much more widely than you probably imagine. Fortunately your neurological states seem rather simple. Once I had managed to understand them in some degree, the decoding became possible.'

'Do we have anything neurological in common? Do you, for

instance, have anything that corresponds to our "headache"?'
asked McNeil.

The reply came:

'In a broad sense we share the emotions of pleasure and pain.
But this is only to be expected of any creature that possesses a
neurological complex. Painful emotions correspond to a sharp
disruption of neurological patterns, and this can happen with me
as well as with you. Happiness is a dynamic state in which neurological patterns are being extended, not disrupted, and this too
can happen with me as well as with you. Although there are these
similarities, I imagine that my subjective experiences are very
different from yours, except in one particular – like you I regard
painful emotions as emotions that I wish to avoid, and *vice versa*
for happy emotions.

'More specifically, your headaches arise from a faulty blood
supply that destroys the precision of the electrical firing sequences
in your brain. I experience something very akin to a headache if
radio-active material gets into my nervous system. It causes electrical discharges in much the way that happens in your Geiger
counters. These discharges interfere with my timing sequences
and produce an extremely unpleasant subjective experience.

'Now I wish to inquire into quite a different matter. I am interested in what you call "the arts". Literature I can understand
as the art of arranging ideas and emotions in words. The visual
arts are clearly related to your perception of the world. But I do
not understand at all the nature of music. My ignorance in this
respect is scarcely surprising, since as far as I am aware you have
transmitted no music. Will you please repair this deficiency?'

'Here's your chance, Ann,' said Kingsley. 'And what a chance!
No musician ever played to an audience like this!'

'What shall I play?'

'How about the Beethoven you played the other night?'

'The Opus 106? It's a bit fierce for a beginner.'

'Come on, Ann. Give old Joe the works,' encouraged Barnett.

'There's no need to play if you don't want to, Ann. I took a
recording,' said Leicester.

'What's the quality like?'

'As good as we'll get it from a technical point of view. If you were satisfied with the performance we can start transmitting more or less straight away if you wish.'

'I think I'd prefer you to use the recording. It sounds ridiculous, but I've an idea that I might be nervous if I started to play to that thing, whatever it is.'

'Don't be silly. Old Joe won't bite.'

'Perhaps he won't but I'd still prefer to use the recording.'

And so the recording was transmitted. At the end came the message:

'Very interesting. Please repeat the first part at a speed increased by thirty per cent.'

When this had been done, the next message was:

'Better. Very good. I intend to think this over. Good-bye.'

'My God, you've finished him, Ann!' exclaimed Marlowe.

'It defeats me how music can have any appeal for Joe. After all, music is sound and we've agreed that sound oughtn't to mean anything to him,' remarked Parkinson.

'I don't agree there,' said McNeil. 'Our appreciation of music has really nothing to do with sound, although I know that at first sight it seems otherwise. What we appreciate in the brain are electrical signals that we receive from the ears. Our use of sound is simply a convenient device for generating certain patterns of electrical activity. There is indeed a good deal of evidence that musical rhythms reflect the main electrical rhythms that occur in the brain.'

'That's very interesting, John,' Kingsley exclaimed. 'So you might say that music gives the most direct expression of the activities of our brains.'

'No, I wouldn't put it as strongly as that. I would say that music gives the best index of the large-scale patterns in the brain. But words give a better index of the fine-scale patterns.'

And so the discussion continued until far into the night. All aspects of the Cloud's statements were argued over. Perhaps the most striking remark came from Ann Halsey.

'The first movement of the B flat major Sonata bears a metronome marking requiring a quite fantastic pace, far faster than any normal pianist can achieve, certainly far faster than I can manage. Did you notice that request for an increase of speed? It makes me feel a little shivery, although probably it was only some queer coincidence, I suppose.'

*

At this stage it became generally agreed that information concerning the Cloud's real nature should be passed to the political authorities. Various Governments were again getting radio communication to work. It was found that, provided a three-centimetre transmission was propagated vertically, the ionization in the atmosphere could be maintained at a value favourable for communication at a wave-length of about ten centimetres. Once more Nortonstowe became an information clearing-house.

Nobody was really happy at disseminating information about the Cloud. Everybody felt that communication with the Cloud would be taken out of Nortonstowe's control. And there was so much that the scientists wished to learn. Kingsley was strongly opposed to passing information to the political authorities, but on this point he was overruled by general opinion, which felt that, regrettable as it might be, secrecy should no longer be maintained.

Leicester had made recordings of the conversations with the Cloud and these were broadcast over the ten-centimetre channels. Governments everywhere had no scruples themselves about maintaining secrecy however. The man-in-the-street never learned of the existence of life in the Cloud, for as time went on events took such a turn as to make secrecy quite imperative.

No Government at this time possessed a one-centimetre transmitter and receiver of appropriate design. For the time being at least, therefore, communication with the Cloud had to be made from Nortonstowe. Technicians in the U.S. pointed out, however, that ten-centimetre transmission to Nortonstowe and thence by one centimetre would allow the U.S. Government and others to establish contact with the Cloud. It was decided that Nortonstowe should become a clearing-house, not only for conveying information over the Earth but also for communication with the Cloud.

The personnel at Nortonstowe divided into two roughly equal camps. Those who supported Kingsley and Leicester wished to veto the politicians' plan openly and violently by telling the various Governments to go to hell. The others, led by Marlowe and Parkinson, argued that nothing was to be gained by such defiance, since the politicians could if necessary secure their own way by main force. A few hours before a communication from the Cloud was expected the argument between the two groups became acute. It was resolved by compromise. It was decided that a technical hitch would prevent any ten-centimetre transmissions being received at Nortonstowe. Thus the Governments would be able to hear the Cloud, but they wouldn't be able to talk to it.

And so it came to pass. That day the highest and most honoured of the human species listened to the Cloud and were unable to reply. It turned out that the Cloud made a bad impression on its august audience, for Joe began talking frankly about sex.

'Will you please resolve this paradox?' he said. 'I notice that a very large portion of your literature is concerned with what you call "love", "profane love" mostly. Indeed, from the specimens available to me I estimate that nearly forty per cent of literature is concerned with this subject. Yet nowhere in literature could I find out what "love" consists of, always the issue is very carefully avoided. This led me to believe that "love" must be some rare remarkable process. Can you imagine my surprise when at last I learnt from medical textbooks that "love" is only a very simple ordinary process shared by a great variety of other animals?'

There were some protests at these remarks from the highest and most honoured of the human species. They were silenced by Leicester who cut their transmissions from the loud-speakers.

'Aw, dry out,' he said. Then he handed a microphone to McNeil. 'I reckon this is your turn, John. You'd better try to give Joe an answer.'

McNeil did his best:

'Viewed from a wholly logical point of view the bearing and rearing of children is a thoroughly unattractive proposition. To a woman it means pain and endless worry. To a man it means extra work extending over many years to support his family. So, if we were wholly logical about sex, we should probably not bother to reproduce at all. Nature takes care of this by making us utterly and wholly irrational. If we were not irrational we simply wouldn't be able to survive, contradictory as this may sound. It's probably the same with all the other animals too.'

Joe was speaking again:

'This irrationality, which I suspected and which I am glad to hear you recognize, has a serious, more grim, aspect. I have already warned you that the supply of chemical foods is pitifully limited on your planet. It is only too likely that an irrational attitude towards reproduction will lead to more individuals being born than can possibly be supported by such slender resources. Such a situation would carry great dangers with it. Indeed it is more than likely that the rarity of intelligent life on planets as a whole arises from the general existence of such irrationalities in their relation to food shortage. I consider it not unlikely that your species may shortly become extinct. This view is confirmed, I find, by the far too rapid rate at which human populations are now increasing.'

Leicester pointed at a group of winking lights.

'The politicians are trying to get through – Moscow, Washington, London, Paris, Timbuctoo, Uncle Tom Cobbly, and all. Shall we let 'em through, Chris?'

Alexandrov made the first political speech of his life.

'Do b—s in Kremlin good to listen,' he said.

'Alexis, you've got the word wrong,' remarked Kingsley. 'In polite society we say "beggars".'

'I think we ought to recommend Alexis to study the writings of the celebrated Dr Bowdler. But it's time we got back to Joe,' said Marlowe.

'Certainly don't let the politicians in, Harry. Keep their throats cut. John, ask Joe how he reproduces himself' – from Kingsley.

'That's what I've been wanting to ask,' said McNeil.

'Then carry on. Let's see how delicate he gets when it comes to his turn.'

'Chris!'

McNeil put his question to the Cloud:

'It would be of interest to us to know how our reproductive system compares with your own case.'

'Reproduction in the sense of giving rise to a new individual proceeds in our case along entirely different lines. Barring accidents, or an overwhelming desire for self-destruction – which happens sometimes with us as with you – I can live indefinitely, you see. Therefore I am not under the necessity, as you are, of generating some new individual to take over at my death.'

'How old in fact are you?'

'Rather more than five hundred million years.'

'And was your birth, your origin, that is to say, a consequence of spontaneous chemical action, as we believe life here on the Earth to have been?'

'No, it was not. As we travel around the Galaxy we keep a look-out for suitable aggregations of material, suitable clouds in which we can plant life. We do this in rather the way that you might grow saplings from a tree. If I, for instance, were to find a suitable cloud not already endowed with life I would plant a comparatively simple neurological structure within it. This would be a structure that I myself had built, a part of myself.

'The multitude of hazards with which the spontaneous origin of intelligent life is faced is overcome by this practice. Let me take an example. Radio-active materials must be rigorously excluded from my nervous system for a reason that I explained in an earlier conversation. To ensure that this is so I possess an elaborate electromagnetic screen that serves to prevent the ingress of any radio-active gas into my neurological regions – into my brain in other words. Should this screen fail to operate, I would experience great pain and would soon die. A screen-failure is one of the possible accidents I mentioned a little while ago. The point of this example is that we can provide our "infants" both with screens and with the intelligence to operate them, whereas it would be most improbable that such screens would develop in the course of a spontaneous origin of life.'

'But it must have happened when the first member of your species arose,' suggested McNeil.

'I would not agree that there ever was a "first" member,' said the Cloud. McNeil did not understand this remark, but Kingsley and Marlowe exchanged a glance as if to say: 'Oh-ho, there we go. That's one in the eye for the exploding-universe boys.'

'Apart from providing such protective devices,' the Cloud went on, 'we leave our "infants" free to develop as they think best. Here I must explain an important difference between us and you. The number of cells in your brain is more or less fixed at birth. Your development then consists of learning to use a brain of fixed capacity in the best possible way. With us the case is quite different. We are free to increase the capacity of our brains as we find best. And of course worn or defective parts can be removed or replaced. Thus development with us consists in extending the brain in the best way, as well as in learning to use it in the best way – by the best way I mean of course in the way best suited to the solution of problems as they arise. You will realize therefore that as "infants" we start with comparatively simple brains and as we grow older our brains become very much larger and more complicated.'

'Could you describe, in a way we could understand, how you would go about building a new part to your brain?' asked McNeil.

'That I think I can do. First, I build chemical foods into complicated molecules of the required types. A supply of these is always kept on hand. Then the molecules are carefully laid down in an appropriate neurological structure on the surface of a solid body. The material of the body is adjusted so that its melting point is not too low – ice, for instance, would have a dangerously low melting point – and so that it is electrically a very good insulator. The outer part of the solid has also to be carefully prepared so that it will anchor the neurological material – the brain stuff as you might say – firmly in position.

'The design of the neurological structure is of course the really difficult part of the business. This is arranged so that the new brain acts as a unit for attaining some specified purpose. It is also arranged that the new unit does not come spontaneously into operation, but only when signals are received from the previously existing part of my brain. These signals have a variety of points of entry into the new structure. Likewise the output of the new unit has a host of connexions to the older part of my brain. In this way its activity can be controlled and integrated into the whole of my neurological activity.'

'There are two other points,' said McNeil. 'How do you

recharge your neurological material with energy? This is done in the human case by the blood supply. Do you have an equivalent to our blood supply? Secondly, what would be the rough size of the units that you build?'

The answer came:

'The size is variable according to what particular end the unit is designed for. The underlying solid may measure anything from a yard or two up to several hundred yards.

'Yes, I do have an equivalent to a blood supply. A supply of appropriate substances is maintained by a flow of gas that streams constantly past the units of which I am composed. The flow is maintained by an electromagnetic pump instead of by a "heart", however. That is to say, the pump is of an inorganic nature. This is another facility that we always provide when we plant new life. The gas flows from the pump to a supply of chemical foods, then past my neurological structure, which absorbs the sundry materials that are required for my brain operation. These materials also deposit their waste products in the gas. The gas then makes its way back to the pump, but before it does so it passes through a filter that removes the waste products – a filter that is rather akin to your kidneys.

'There is an important advantage in my having heart, kidneys, and blood that are essentially inorganic in their mode of operation. Failure of operation can readily be allowed for. If my "heart" goes wrong I simply switch over to a spare "heart" which I always keep in readiness. If my "kidneys" go wrong I do not die as your musician Mozart did. I again switch over to spare "kidneys". And I can make new "blood" in vast quantities.'

Shortly afterwards Joe went off the air.

'The thing which staggers me is the astonishing similarity in the principles on which life is maintained,' remarked McNeil. 'The details are of course wildly different: gas instead of blood, electromagnetic heart and kidneys, and so on. But the logic of the lay-out is the same.'

'And the logic of brain-building seems to have some relation to our programming of a computer,' said Leicester.

'Did you notice that, Chris? It sounded almost like designing some new sub-routine.'

'I think the similarities are genuine. I've heard it said that the knee-joint of a fly is very similar in its construction to our own knee-joints. Why? Because there is just one good way to construct a knee-joint. Similarly there is just one logic, and just one way of designing the general lay-out of intelligent life.'

'But why do you think there should be this unique logic?' McNeil asked Kingsley.

'It's a little difficult for me to explain, because this is as near as I go to the expression of religious sentiment. We know that the Universe possesses some inner basic structure, this is what we are finding out in our science or trying to find out. We tend to give ourselves a sort of moral pat on the back when we contemplate our successes in this respect, as if to say that the Universe is following *our* logic. But this is surely to put the cart before the horse. It isn't the Universe that's following our logic, it's *we* that are constructed in accordance with the logic of the Universe. And that gives what I might call a definition of intelligent life: something that reflects the basic structure of the Universe. We do, and so does Joe, and that's why we appear to have so much in common, why we can talk together on something like a common basis, even though we're so wildly different in our detailed construction. We're both constructed in a way that reflects the inner pattern of the Universe.'

'Those political bastards are still trying to get through. Damn it, I'll switch those lights off,' remarked Leicester.

He walked over to the bank of lights monitoring the various transmissions that were being received. A minute later he returned to his seat, shaking with laughter.

'Here's a fine thing,' he gurgled. 'I forgot to stop our conversation going out on ten centimetres. They've been hearing everything we've been saying – Alexis's reference to the Kremlin, Chris's remark about cutting their throats. No wonder they're in a rage! I reckon the fat's in the fire now, all right.'

No one seemed quite to know what to do. At length Kingsley walked over to the control board. He flicked a number of switches, and said into a microphone:

'This is Nortonstowe, Christopher Kingsley speaking. If you have any message, get on with it.'

An angry voice came over the loud-speaker:

'So you're there, are you, Nortonstowe! We've been trying to get through to you for the last three hours.'

'Who is that speaking?'

'Grohmer, U.S. Secretary for Defence. I might tell you that you are talking to a very angry man, Mr Kingsley. I am waiting for an explanation of tonight's outrageous conduct.'

'Then you will go on waiting, I fear. I will give you another thirty seconds, and if your statements have not assumed some reasonably cogent form by then, I shall switch off again.'

The voice became quieter, and more threatening:

'Mr Kingsley, I have heard before of your insufferable obstructiveness, but this is the first time I have encountered it myself. For your information, I intend that it shall be the last time. This is not a warning. I am simply telling you here and now that very shortly you will be removed from Nortonstowe. Where you will be removed to, I shall leave to your own imagination.'

'I am anxious that in your plans for me, Mr Grohmer, you have given full consideration to one very important point.'

'And what is that, may I ask?'

'That it is within my power to obliterate the whole continent of America. If you doubt this statement ask your astronomers what happened to the Moon on the evening of 7 August. You might also like to take into account that it would take me substantially less than five minutes to implement this threat.'

Kingsley clicked off a group of switches and the lights at the control panel went off. Marlowe was white-faced and there were little beads of sweat on his forehead and on his upper lip. 'Chris, that was not well done, it was not well done,' he said. Kingsley was genuinely disturbed.

'I'm sorry, Geoff. It never occurred to me while I was speaking that America is your country. I say again that I'm sorry, but by way of excuse you must know that I'd have said the same thing to London, or to Moscow, or to anybody.'

Marlowe shook his head.

'You've got me wrong, Chris. I'm not objecting because America is my country. In any case I know you were only putting up a bluff. What worries me is that the bluff may turn out to be damn dangerous.'

'Nonsense. You're giving an exaggerated importance to a storm in a tea-cup. You still haven't got over the idea that politicians are important because the newspapers tell you so. They'll probably realize that I might be bluffing but while there's just the possibility that I could make good my threat they'll lay off the strong arm stuff. You'll see.'

But in this matter Marlowe was right and Kingsley wrong, as events soon showed.

Chapter Eleven

THE HYDROGEN ROCKETS

KINGSLEY was roused from sleep about three hours later.

'Sorry to waken you, Chris, but something important has happened,' said Harry Leicester. When he was satisfied that Kingsley was sufficiently alert he went on:

'There's a call from London for Parkinson.'

'They're certainly not wasting much time.'

'We can't let him take it, can we? It'd be taking too big a risk.'

Kingsley was quiet for a few moments. Then, evidently making up his mind:

'I think we must take the risk, Harry, but we'll stand over him while he takes the call. In fact we'll make sure that he doesn't give anything away. The point is this. Although I've no doubt that the long arm of Washington could extend as far as Nortonstowe, I can't believe that our Government can relish being told what to do on their own territory. Therefore we start with the advantage of some sympathy from our own people. If we stop Parkinson answering the call we cancel that advantage straight away. Let's go along and see him.'

When they had wakened Parkinson and told him of the call, Kingsley said:

'Look here, Parkinson, I'm going to do some plain speaking. By our own lights we've played this game pretty clean so far. It's true that we made a lot of conditions when we came here, and we've insisted on those conditions being honoured. But in return we've quite genuinely supplied your people with the best information we had. Again it's true that we haven't always been right, but the reason for our mistakes is now only too clear. The Americans set up a corresponding establishment and this was run on the politicians' terms not on the scientists' terms, and the amount of information that came from that establishment was less than it has been from Nortonstowe. In fact, you know very well that but for our information the death roll in recent months would have been even vaster than it is.'

'Where is all this leading, Kingsley?'

'I'm simply showing you that however much it might at times have seemed otherwise we've played very straight. We've played straight even to the extent of revealing the real nature of the Cloud, and of passing on the information we've received from it. But where I do dig my toes in is at the thought of losing valuable communication time. We can't expect that the Cloud is going to give endless time to talking to us, it's got bigger fish to fry. And I'm emphatically not going to let what time we can get go by in political chit-chat if I can help it. We've got too much still to learn. Besides, if the politicians started up with their Geneva stuff and arguing about agendas, it's more than likely that the Cloud would sign off altogether. It's not going to waste its time talking to gibbering idiots.'

'I never cease being flattered at your opinion of us. But I still don't see where this is leading.'

'It's leading to this. London is calling you, and we're going to be there when you answer. If you breathe a word of doubt over my suggestion of an alliance between us and the Cloud I'll hit you over the head with a spanner. Come on, let's get it over.'

It turned out that Kingsley had misjudged the situation somewhat. All the Prime Minister really wanted to know from Parkinson was whether in his opinion there was any doubt that the Cloud could obliterate a continent if it really wished. Parkinson was in no difficulty over his answer. He answered quite genuinely and without hesitation that he had every reason to believe that it could. This satisfied the Prime Minister, and after a few unrelated remarks he went off the air.

'Very odd,' said Leicester to Kingsley after Parkinson had returned to bed.

'Too much Clausewitz,' he went on. 'They're only interested in fire power.'

'Yes, it's apparently never occurred to them that anybody might possess an overwhelming weapon and still decline to use it.'

'Particularly in a case like this.'

'What d'you mean, Harry?'

'Well, isn't it axiomatic that any non-human intelligence must be evil?'

'I suppose it is. Now I come to think of it, ninety-nine per cent of stories about non-human intelligences treat 'em as being entirely villainous. I'd always supposed that was because it's so difficult to invent a really convincing villain, but perhaps it may run deeper.'

'Well, people are always frightened of what they don't understand, and I don't suppose the political boys have understood much of what's been going on. Still you'd think that they'd have realized that we're on pretty matey terms with Old Joe, wouldn't you?'

'Unless they've interpreted it as evidence of a devil's compact.'

*

The first move of the U.S. Government after Kingsley's threat, and after London had confirmed the Cloud's potential destructive power, was to give overriding priority to the building of a one-centimetre transmitter and receiver of the Nortonstowe design (which thanks to the information supplied by Nortonstowe at an earlier date was available to them). So excellent was American technical ability that the work was finished in an extremely short time. But the outcome was wholly disappointing. The Cloud did not reply to the American transmissions, nor were any messages that the Cloud addressed to Nortonstowe intercepted. There were two distinct reasons for these failures. Failure to intercept was due to a serious technical difficulty. Once communication between the Cloud and Nortonstowe became conversational there was no need for a very rapid transmission of information, as for instance there had been during the period when the Cloud was learning of our human scientific knowledge and cultural patterns. This enabled transmission band widths to be greatly reduced, which was desirable from the Cloud's point of view, since interference with messages from other galactic denizens was thereby vastly lessened. Indeed so narrow was the band width and so low was the power used in the transmissions that the Americans were quite unable to discover the correct exact wave-length on which interception might have been achieved. The reason why the Cloud did not reply to the American transmissions was simpler. The Cloud would not reply unless a correctly coded signal was transmitted at the beginning of a message, and the U.S. Government did not possess the code.

Failure of communication led to other plans being followed. The nature of these plans came as a shock to Nortonstowe. News of them came through Parkinson, who rushed one afternoon into Kingsley's office.

'Why are there so many fools in the world?' he exclaimed in a rather wild tone.

'Good, you've seen the light at last, have you?' was Kingsley's comment.

'And you're among them, Kingsley. Now we're in an incredible mess, thanks to your imbecility combined with the cretin wits of Washington and Moscow.'

'Here, Parkinson, have a cup of coffee and calm down!'

'To hell with a cup of coffee. Listen to this. Let's go back to the situation of 1958 before anybody had ever heard of the Cloud. You remember the arms race, with the U.S. and the Soviets competing furiously to see who could produce an intercontinental rocket first, all fitted up with hydrogen war heads of course? And as a scientist you'll realize that to fire a rocket six or seven thousand miles from one point of the Earth's surface to another is much the same problem as to fire a rocket right off the Earth altogether out into space.'

'Parkinson, you're not trying to tell me ...'

'I'm telling you that work in the U.S. and in Russia on this problem has advanced much farther than the British Government realized. We've only learned about it in the last day or two. We only learned of it when both the U.S. Government and the Soviets announced that they've fired off rockets, fired them at the Cloud.'

'The incredible fools. When did this happen?'

'Within the last week. Apparently there's been an undercover competition that we knew nothing about. The U.S. has been trying to outdo the Soviets and *vice versa* of course. They're reckoning to show each other what they can do, quite apart from killing the Cloud.'

'We'd better get Marlowe, Leicester, and Alexandrov along and see what we can manage to salvage from the wreck.'

McNeil happened to be talking to Marlowe, so he joined the group when they assembled. After Parkinson had gone over his story again Marlowe said:

'It's happened. This is what I feared when I blew up at you the other day, Chris.'

'You mean you foresaw this?'

'Oh, not this exactly, so far as the details go. I'd no idea of how far they'd got with their miserable rockets. But I felt in my bones that something of this sort would happen. You see you're too logical, Chris. You don't understand people.'

'How many of these rockets have been sent?' asked Leicester.

'As far as our information goes, upwards of a hundred from the U.S. and perhaps fifty or so from the Russians.'

'Well, I don't see that it's so important,' Leicester remarked. 'The energy in a hundred hydrogen bombs may seem a lot to us, but it's surely only microscopic compared to the energy in the Cloud. I should have thought that this business is sillier than trying to kill a rhino with a tooth-pick.'

Parkinson shook his head.

'As I understand it, they're not trying to blow the Cloud to pieces, they're trying to poison it!'

'Poison it! How?'

'With radio-active materials. You heard the Cloud describe what could happen if radio-active materials penetrated its screen. They got all that from the Cloud's own statements.'

'Yes, I suppose a few hundred tons of highly radio-active stuff might be a different story.'

'Radio-active particles start ionization in wrong place. Discharges, more ionization, and whole bloody works goes sky high,' said Alexandrov.

Kingsley nodded.

'The point goes back to the old business of us working on D.C. and the Cloud on A.C. To work an A.C. system high voltages are necessary. We don't have high voltages in the body, and that's of course why we're obliged to work on D.C. But the Cloud must have high voltages in order to operate its A.C. communication over big distances. And if there are high voltages, a few electrified particles in the wrong places among insulating material can cause a devil of a mess, as Alexis says. Incidentally, Alexis, what's your feeling about it all?'

The Russian was even briefer than was his usual wont.

'Don't like,' he said.

'What about the Cloud screen? Won't that prevent the stuff going through?' Marlowe asked.

'I think that's where the nasty part of the plan comes in,' Kingsley answered. 'The screen probably works on gas, not on solids, so it won't stop the rockets. And there won't be any radiative material until they explode, and I expect the idea is that they won't explode until they get through the screen.'

Parkinson confirmed this.

'That's right,' he said. 'They're set to home on any substantial solid body. So they'll go straight for the Cloud's neurological centres. At least that's the idea.'

Kingsley got up and paced the room, talking as he walked.

'Even so, it's a mad-dog scheme. Consider the objections. First, it may not work, or suppose it works just enough to annoy the Cloud seriously but not to kill it. Then come the reprisals. The whole of life on the Earth might be wiped out with as little compunction as we would have in swatting a fly. The Cloud never sounded to me to have any real enthusiasm for life on planets.'

'But it always sounded pretty reasonable in discussions,' cut in Leicester.

'Yes, but its outlook might be changed by a fierce headache. In any case I can't believe that discussions with us have occupied more than a tiny fraction of the Cloud's whole brain. It's probably doing a thousand and one other things at the same time. No, I don't think we've the slightest reason to believe that it's going to be nice about it. And that's only the first risk. There'll be an equally grave risk even if they're successful in killing the Cloud. The break-up of its neurological activity is bound to lead to the most terrifying outbursts – what we might call death throes. From a terrestrial point of view the amount of energy held at the Cloud's disposal is simply colossal. In the event of sudden death all this energy will be released, and once again our chance of survival will be remote in the extreme. It'll be like being shut in a stable with a thrashing elephant, only incomparably worse – to use an Irishism. Finally and overwhelmingly, if the Cloud is killed and we are lucky enough to survive against all the probabilities, we'll have to live permanently with a disk of gas around the Sun. And as everyone knows, that's not going to be pleasant. So whichever way you look, it seems impossible to understand this business. Do you understand the psychology of it, Parkinson?'

'Curiously enough I believe I do. As Geoff Marlowe was saying a few moments ago, you always argue logically, Kingsley, and it's not logic you need now, it's an understanding of people. Let's take your last point first. From what we've learned from the Cloud we've every reason to believe that it's going to stay around the Sun for somewhere between fifty and a hundred years. To most people that is as good as saying that it is staying permanently.'

'It's not the same thing at all. In fifty years there'll be a considerable change of the Earth's climate, but it won't be the same overwhelming change that'll take place if the Cloud were to stay here permanently.'

'I'm not doubting it. What I'm saying is that to the great majority of people what happens after fifty years, or a hundred years if you like, isn't of the slightest consequence. And I'll deal with your other two points by admitting the grave risks that you've mentioned.'

'Then you admit my argument.'

'I admit nothing of the sort. Under what circumstances would you follow a policy that involved great risks? No, don't try to answer. I'll tell you. The answer is that you would follow a dangerous policy if all alternatives seemed worse.'

'But the alternatives are not worse. There was the alternative of doing nothing, and that would have involved no risk.'

'There would have been the risk of you becoming dictator of the world!'

'Catfish, man! I'm not the stuff dictators are made of. My only aggressive trait is that I can't suffer fools. Do I look like a dictator?'

'You do, Chris,' said Marlowe. 'Not to us, you don't,' he continued hastily lest Kingsley should burst apart, 'but to Washington you probably do. When a man starts talking to them as if they were backward schoolboys, and when it seems as if that same man possesses untold physical power, why then you can't blame them for jumping to conclusions.'

'And there's another reason why they would never reach any other conclusion,' added Parkinson. 'Let me tell you the story of my life. I went to the right sort of schools, prep school and public school. In these schools the brightest boys are usually encouraged to study the Classics and, although it shouldn't be I that say so, that's what happened to me. I won a scholarship to Oxford, did reasonably well there, and found myself at the age of twenty-one with a head stuffed full of unmarketable knowledge, or at any rate unmarketable unless you're very clever indeed, and I wasn't that clever. So I entered the Administrative Civil Service, which course led me by stages to my present position. The moral of my life story is that I got into politics quite by accident, not by design. This happens with others too – I'm not unique and don't aspire to be. But we accidental fishes are very much in the minority and we don't usually occupy the most influential offices. The great majority of politicians are where they are because they want to be, because they like the limelight, because they like the idea of administering the masses.'

'This is indeed a confession, Parkinson!'

'Now do you see my point?'

'I'm beginning to see through a glass darkly. You mean that the mental make-up of a leading politician is likely to be such that he couldn't dream it possible that anyone could find the prospect of becoming a dictator wholly unpalatable.'

'Yes, I can see it all, Chris,' Leicester grinned. 'Graft everywhere, executions just for the laughs, no wife or daughter safe. I must say I'm glad I'm in on this.'

'In on it?' said the Russian in some surprise. 'Likely to get throat cut.'

'Yes, Alexis, we'll not go into that just now!'

'Some things are getting a little clearer, Parkinson.' Kingsley went on pacing. 'I still don't understand, however, why the prospect of us dictating to the world, ridiculous as we know it to be, should seem a worse alternative than this dreadful course they've actually taken.'

'To Kremlin losing power worst thing,' said Alexis.

'Alexis puts it in a nutshell as usual,' answered Parkinson. 'Losing power, utterly and completely, is the most dreadful prospect that a politician can think of. It overshadows everything else.'

'Parkinson, you shock me. I mean it. Heaven knows I think little enough of politicians but I cannot conceive of even the meanest person setting his personal ambitions above the fate of the whole species.'

'Oh, my dear Kingsley, how you fail to understand your fellow men! You know the biblical phrase, "Let not your right hand know what your left hand doeth." Do you realize what that means? It means keeping your ideas in nice little watertight compartments, never letting them interact and contradict each other. It means that you can go to church one day a week and sin away the other six. Don't imagine that anyone sees these rockets as a potential extinction for humanity. Not on your life. It's rather the other way round, a bold stroke against an invader that has already destroyed whole communities and brought even the strongest nations near to disaster. It is a defiant answer of determined democracies to the threats of a potential tyrant. Oh, I'm not laughing, I'm being quite serious. And don't forget Harry Leicester's "no wife or daughter safe". There's a bit of that in it too.'

'But this is wholly ridiculous!'

'To us, yes. To them, no. It's only too easy to read your own state of mind into what other people say.'

'Frankly, Parkinson, I think this business must have shaken you out of all good sense. It can't be as bad as you think. There's one point that proves it. How did you come to hear about these rockets? From London, didn't you say?'

'It was from London.'

'Then obviously there's some decency there.'

'I'm sorry to disappoint you, Kingsley. It's true that I can't wholly prove my point, but I suggest that this information would never have reached us if the British Government had been in a position to join the U.S. and the Soviets. You see, we have no rockets to launch. Perhaps you realize that this country is less likely to suffer than others from your presumed rise to world domination. Whatever we like to pretend, Britain is sliding steadily and rapidly down the ladder of world power. Perhaps it wouldn't be an altogether bad thing for the British Government if they saw the U.S., the Soviets, China, Germany, and the rest being made to toe the line by a group of men domiciled in Britain. Perhaps they feel that they will shine more strongly in your – or, if you prefer, *our* – reflected glory than they shine at present. Perhaps indeed when it comes to administrative matters they believe that they can hoodwink you into leaving the effective control in their hands.'

'Strange as it may seem, Parkinson, there have been times when I've persuaded myself that I am over-cynical.'

Parkinson grinned.

'For once in your life, Kingsley, my dear fellow, I'll speak to you with a brutal frankness that should have been exercised on you many years ago. As a cynic you're a dud, a wash-out, a mere playboy. At root, and I mean it quite seriously, you're a starry-eyed idealist.'

Marlowe's voice cut in.

'When you've finished analysing yourselves, don't you think we ought to give some consideration to what we ought to do?'

'Like dam' Chekhov play,' grunted Alexandrov.

'But interesting, and not a little shrewd,' said McNeil.

'Oh, there's no difficulty about what we ought to do, Geoff. We've got to call the Cloud and tell it. That's the only thing to do from every point of view.'

'You're quite satisfied about that are you, Chris?'

'Surely there can't be any possible doubt? I'll put the more selfish reason first. We can probably avoid the danger of being wiped out, because the Cloud isn't likely to be wholly outraged if we warn it. But in spite of what Parkinson has been saying I still believe that I would do the same thing even if this motive didn't exist. Although it sounds queer and the word doesn't express what I really mean, I believe that it's the *humane* thing to do. But to be practical, this seems to me something that we ought to decide by agreement, or if we don't agree, then by a majority vote. We could probably talk about it for hours, but I imagine we've all been milling it over in our minds during the last hour. Suppose we take a snap vote just for the hell of it. Leicester?'

'I'm on.'

'Alexandrov?'

'Warn bastard. Will get throats cut all same.'

'Marlowe?'

'Agreed.'

'McNeil?'

'Yes.'

'Parkinson?'

'Agreed.'

'As a matter of interest, Parkinson, and in spite of a little more Chekhov, will you tell us why you agree? From the first day we met until this morning I got the impression that we were looking at each other from different sides of the fence.'

'We were, because I had a job to do, and I did it as loyally as I could. Today, as I see it, I was released from that old loyalty, which was overwritten by a larger, deeper loyalty. Perhaps I'm opening the way for the charge of starry-eyed idealist myself, but I happen to agree with all you said and implied about our duty to the human species. And I agree with what you said about the humane course of action.'

'So it's agreed that we call up the Cloud and acquaint it with the existence of these rockets?'

'Ought we to consult some of the others, do you think?' Marlowe asked.

Kingsley answered:

'It may sound very dictator-like to say no, Geoff, but I would be against any widening of this discussion. For one thing I believe that if we consulted everybody and a contrary decision was reached I would not accept it – there's the dictator for you all right. But there's also the point that Alexis mentioned, that we could only too easily end by getting our throats cut. So far, we've flouted all the recognized authorities, but we've done it in a half humorous fashion. Any attempt to charge us with some legal offence would surely be laughed out of court. But this business is a very different kettle of fish. If we pass what I might call military information to the Cloud we're taking an obviously grave responsibility, and I'm against too many people being called on to share that responsibility. I wouldn't like Ann to have any part in it, for instance.'

'What do you think, Parkinson?' asked Marlowe.

'I agree with Kingsley. Remember that in point of fact we have no power at all. There's really nothing to stop the police coming and arresting us when they please. It is of course true that the Cloud might wish to support us, especially after this episode. But then again it might not, perhaps it may cease communication with the Earth altogether. We run the risk of being left with nothing but our bluff. As bluff goes it's an extremely good one and it's not surprising that it's been swallowed so far. But we can't go on bluffing for the rest of our lives. Furthermore, even if we can enlist the Cloud as ally, there's still a vital flaw in our position. It sounds all very well to say "I can wipe out the continent of America", but you know perfectly well that you never would. So in any case we're reduced to bluffing.'

This view had a somewhat chilling influence on the company.

'Then it's pretty obvious that we must keep this business of warning the Cloud as secret as we can. Obviously it oughtn't to go outside this meeting,' remarked Leicester.

'Secrecy isn't as easy as you imagine.'

'What d'you mean?'

'You're forgetting the information given me by London. It will be taken for granted in London that we're going to inform the Cloud. That's all right so long as the bluff holds, but if it doesn't ...'

'Then if it's taken for granted, let's get on with it. We might as well commit the crime if we're certain to receive the punishment,' remarked McNeil.

'Yes, let's get on with it. We've done enough talking,' said Kingsley. 'Harry, you'd better prepare a recorded explanation of the whole affair. Then keep broadcasting it continuously. You needn't have any fear of it being picked up by anybody but the Cloud.'

'Well, Chris, I'd sooner you did the recording. You're better at talking than I am.'

'Oh, all right. Let's get started.'

After fifteen hours of transmission a reply was received from the Cloud. Kingsley was sought out by Leicester.

'It wants to know why we've allowed this to happen. It's not pleased about it.'

Kingsley went along to the transmitting lab, picked up a microphone, and dictated the following reply:

'This attack has nothing to do with us. I should have thought my previous message would have made that clear. You are aware of the essential facts concerning the organization of human society, that it is split into a number of self-governing communities, that no one group controls the activities of the others. You cannot therefore suppose that your arrival in the solar system is viewed by other groups in the same way that we view it. It might interest you to know that in sending our warning we are gravely risking our own safety, and perhaps even our lives.'

'Jesu! You don't have to make it worse, do you, Chris? You're not going to improve his temper with that sort of talk.'

'I don't see why not. In any case if we're in for reprisals we might as well have the luxury of some plain speaking.'

Marlowe and Parkinson came in.

'You'll be glad to know that Chris has just been chalking the Cloud off,' Leicester remarked.

'My God, does he have to wade in with the Ajax-treatment?'

Parkinson gave Marlowe a long glance.

'You know in a way this is remarkably like some of the ideas of the Greeks. They thought of Jupiter as travelling in a black cloud and hurling thunderbolts. Really that's pretty much what we've got.'

'It is a bit odd, isn't it? As long as it doesn't end in a Greek tragedy for us.'

The tragedy was nearer than anyone supposed, however.

The reply to Kingsley came in:

'Message and arguments acknowledged. From what you say it is presumed that these rockets have not been launched from near your part of the Earth. Unless I hear from you to the contrary during the next few minutes I shall act on the decision I have reached. It may interest you to hear that I have decided to reverse the motions of the rockets relative to the Earth. In each case the direction of motion will be inverted, but the speed will be kept unchanged. This will be done at times when each rocket has been in flight for an exact number of days. Lastly, when this has been done, some slight perturbation will be added to the motions.'

When the Cloud had finished, Kingsley let out a thin whistle.

'My God, what a decision,' whispered Marlowe.

'Sorry. I don't understand,' admitted Parkinson.

'Well, the reversing of the directions of motion means that the rockets will go back along their paths – all this relative to the Earth, you noticed.'

'You mean they'll hit the Earth!'

'Of course, but that isn't the end of it. If they're turned round after an exact number of days, they'll take an exact number of days to re-traverse their paths, so when they hit the Earth they'll hit the exact points they started out from.'

'Why is that precisely?'

'Because after an exact number of days the Earth will be at the same stage of its rotation.'

'And what was the point of the "relative to the Earth" business?'

'That makes sure that the Earth's motion around the Sun is allowed for,' said Leicester.

'And the Sun's motion around the Galaxy,' added Marlowe.

'So it means that those who sent the rockets will get 'em back again. Ye gods, it's the judgement of Solomon.'

Kingsley had listened to the conversation. Now he said:

'There's one final little tit-bit for you, Parkinson: that point about slight perturbations being added, which means that we don't know *exactly* where they'll land. We only know approximately within a few hundred miles, or perhaps within a thousand miles. I'm sorry about this, Geoff.'

Marlowe looked older than Kingsley ever remembered him.

'It might have been worse; we can console ourselves with that, I suppose. Thank God America is a big country.'

'Well, it's the end of our idea of secrecy,' remarked Kingsley. 'I've never believed in secrecy and now I've got it thrown back in my face. That's another judgement of Solomon.'

'What d'you mean about it being the end of secrecy?'

'Well, Harry, we must warn Washington. If a hundred hydrogen bombs are going to fall on the U.S. in the next couple of days, at least they'll be able to disperse the people in the big cities.'

'But if we do that we'll have the whole world about our ears!'

'I know that. Even so, we must take the risk. What do you think, Parkinson?'

'I think you're right, Kingsley. We must warn them. But don't make any mistake, our position will be desperate in the extreme. We'll have to work that bluff or else ...'

'It's no good worrying about the mess until we get into it. The first thing to do is to get through to Washington. I suppose we can depend on them to pass the information to the Russians.'

Kingsley switched on the ten-centimetre transmitter. Marlowe came resolutely across to him.

'This isn't going to be easy, Chris. If you don't mind I'd rather do it. And I'd rather do it by myself. It may get a bit undignified.'

'It'll probably be tough, Geoff, but if you feel you want to, then go ahead. We'll leave you to it, but remember we won't be far off if you need any help.'

Kingsley, Parkinson, and Leicester left Marlowe alone to pass the message, a message containing an admission of the highest treason, as any terrestrial court would interpret treason.

Marlowe was white and shaken when three-quarters of an hour later he rejoined the others.

'They certainly weren't pleased about it,' was all he would say.

The American and Russian Governments were even less pleased when two days later a hydrogen bomb wiped out the town of El Paso, and others landed, one in south-east Chicago, and another on the outskirts of Kiev. Although hurried attempts had been made in the U.S. to disperse all congested populations, dispersal was of necessity incomplete, and more than a quarter of a million people lost their lives. The Russian Government did not make any attempt to warn its people, with the consequence that casualties in the one Russian city exceeded the combined total in the two American cities.

Lives lost through an 'act of God' are regretted, perhaps deeply regretted, but they do not arouse our wildest passions. It is otherwise with lives that are forfeited through deliberate human agency. The word 'deliberate' is important here. One deliberate murder can produce a sharper reaction than ten thousand deaths on the roads. It will therefore be understood why the half million fatalities caused by the hydrogen rockets impressed themselves more deeply on world Governments than the far vaster disasters that had occurred in the period of great heat, and in the following period of great cold. These latter had been thought of as 'acts of God'. But in the eyes particularly of the United States Government the hydrogen deaths were murder, murder on a gigantic scale, perpetrated by a small group of desperate men, who to gratify insatiable ambitions had allied themselves with the thing in the sky, men who were guilty of treason against the entire human species. From then onwards the principals at Nortonstowe were marked men.

Chapter Twelve

NEWS OF DEPARTURE

PARADOXICALLY, although the episode of the hydrogen rockets had created a host of bitter and implacable enemies, in the short term the position of Kingsley and his friends was greatly strengthened thereby. The reversing of the rockets had given terrible proof of the power of the Cloud. No one outside Nortonstowe now doubted that the Cloud would wreak terrible destruction if called upon to do so by the group at Nortonstowe. It was pointed out in Washington that even if there had been some doubt originally about the Cloud's willingness to take Kingsley's part, there could surely be none now, not if the Cloud had any conception of a *quid pro quo*. The possibility of wiping out Nortonstowe by the use of an intercontinental rocket was considered. Although the likelihood of strong objection by the British Government was discounted, largely because the British Government's own position in the whole business was thought highly suspect, the scheme was soon abandoned. It was considered that the accuracy of delivery of such a rocket was inadequate for the purpose; an abortive bombardment would, it was thought, lead to swift and dreadful retaliation.

Perhaps equally paradoxically, the undoubted strengthening of their bluff did not improve the spirits of the people at Nortonstowe or at least of those who were aware of the facts of the matter. Among these Weichart was now included. He had recovered from a severe attack of influenza that had prostrated him during the critical days. Soon his inquiring mind unearthed the main facts of the case, however. One day he got into an argument with Alexandrov that the others found amusing. This was a rare occurrence. The early comparatively carefree days had gone now. They were never to return.

'It looks to me as if those perturbations of the rockets must have been deliberately engineered,' began Weichart.

'Why do you say that, Dave?' asked Marlowe.

'Well, the probability of three cities being hit by a hundred odd rockets moving at random is obviously very small. Therefore I conclude that the rockets were not perturbed at random. I think they must have been deliberately guided to give direct hits.'

'There's something of an objection to that,' argued McNeil. 'If the rockets were deliberately guided, how is it that only three of 'em found their targets?'

'Maybe only three were guided, or maybe the guiding wasn't all that good. I wouldn't know.'

There was a derisive laugh from Alexandrov.

'Bloody argument,' he asserted.

'What d'you mean "bloody argument"?'

'Invent bloody argument, like this. Golfer hits ball. Ball lands on tuft of grass – so. Probability ball landed on tuft very small, very very small. Million others tufts for ball to land on. Probability very small, very very very small. So golfer did not hit ball, ball deliberately guided on tuft. Is bloody argument. Yes? Like Weichart's argument.'

This was the longest speech that any of them had heard from Alexandrov.

Weichart was not to be budged. When the laugh had subsided he returned to his point.

'It seems clear enough to me. If the things were guided they'd be far more likely to hit their targets than if they moved at random. And since they did hit their targets it seems equally clear that they were more probably guided than that they were not.'

Alexandrov waved in a rhetorical gesture.

'Is bloody, yes?'

'What Alexis means I think,' explained Kingsley, 'is that we are not justified in supposing that there were any particular targets. The fallacy in the argument about the golfer lies in choosing a particular tuft of grass as a target, when obviously the golfer didn't think of it in those terms before he made his shot.'

The Russian nodded.

'Must say what dam' target is before shoot, not after shoot. Put shirt on before, not after event.'

'Because only prediction is important in science?'

'Dam' right. Weichart predict rockets guided. All right, ask Cloud. Only way decide. Cannot be decided by argument.'

This brought their attention to a depressing circumstance. Since the affair of the rockets, all communications from the Cloud had ceased. And nobody had felt sufficiently self-confident to attempt to call it.

'It doesn't look to me as if the Cloud would welcome such a question. It looks as if it's withdrawn in a huff,' remarked Marlowe.

But Marlowe was wrong, as they learned two or three days later. A surprising message was received saying that the Cloud would start moving away from the Sun in about ten days' time.

'It's incredible,' said Leicester to Parkinson and Kingsley. 'Previously the Cloud seems to have been quite certain that it was staying for at least fifty years and perhaps for more than a hundred.' Parkinson was worried.

'I must say it's a grim prospect for us now. Once the Cloud has quit we're finished. There isn't a court of law in the world that would support us. How long can we expect to maintain communication with the Cloud?'

'Oh, so far as the strengths of transmitters are concerned, we could keep in touch for twenty years or more, even if the Cloud accelerates to a pretty high speed. But according to the Cloud's last message we shan't be able to maintain contact at all while it's accelerating. It seems as if electrical conditions will be pretty chaotic in its outer parts. There'll be far too much electrical "noise" for communication to be possible. So we can't expect to get any messages across until the accelerating process stops, and that may take several years.'

'Heavens, Leicester, you mean that we've got ten days more, and then we can do nothing for a number of years?'

'That's right.'

Parkinson groaned.

'Then we're finished. What can we do?'

Kingsley spoke for the first time.

'Nothing much probably. But at least we can find out why the Cloud has decided to push off. It seems to have changed its mind pretty drastically and there must be some strong reason for that. It ought to be worth trying to find out what it is. Let's see what it's got to say.'

'Maybe we won't get any reply at all,' said Leicester gloomily. But they did get a reply:

'The answer to your question is difficult for me to explain since it seems to involve a realm of experience about which neither I nor you know anything. On previous occasions we have not discussed the nature of human religious beliefs. I found these highly illogical, and as I gathered that you did too, there seemed no point in raising the subject. By and large, conventional religion, as many humans accept it, is illogical in its attempt to conceive of entities lying outside the Universe. Since the Universe comprises everything, it is evident that nothing can lie outside it. The idea of a "god" creating the Universe is a mechanistic absurdity clearly derived from the making of machines by men. I take it that we are in agreement about all this.

'Yet many mysterious questions remain. Probably you have wondered whether a larger-scale intelligence than your own exists. Now you know that it does. In a like fashion I ponder on the existence of a larger-scale intelligence than myself. There is none within the Galaxy, and none within other galaxies so far as I am yet aware. Yet there is strong evidence, I feel, that such an intelligence does play an overwhelming part in our existence. Otherwise how is it decided how matter shall behave? How are your laws of physics determined? Why those laws and no others?

'These problems are of outstanding difficulty, so difficult that I have not been able to solve them. What is clear however is that such an intelligence, if it exists, cannot be spatially or temporally limited in any way.

'Although I say these problems are of extreme difficulty there is evidence that they can be solved. Some two thousand million years ago one of us claimed to have reached a solution.

'A transmission was sent out making this claim, but before the solution itself was broadcast the transmission came to an abrupt end. Attempts were made to re-establish contact with the individual concerned, but the attempts were not successful. Nor could any physical trace of the individual be found.

'The same pattern of events occurred again about four hundred million years ago. I remember it well, for it happened soon after my own birth. I remember receiving a triumphant message to say that a solution to the deep problems had been found. I waited with "bated breath", as you would say, for the solutions, but once again none came. Nor again was any trace found of the individual concerned.

'This same sequence of events has just been repeated for a third time. It happens that the one who claimed the great discovery was situated only a little more than two light years from here. I am his nearest neighbour and it is therefore necessary for me to proceed to the scene without delay. This is the reason for my departure.'

Kingsley picked up a microphone.

'What can you hope to discover when you reach the scene of whatever it is that has happened? We take it that you are possessed of an ample reserve of food?'

The reply came:

'Thank you for your concern. I do possess a reserve of food chemicals. It is not ample, but it should be sufficient, provided I travel at maximum speed. I have considered the possibility of delaying my departure for a number of years, but I do not think this justified in the circumstances. As regards what I hope to find, I hope to be able to settle an old controversy. It has been argued, not I think very plausibly, that these singular occurrences arise from an abnormal neurological condition followed by suicide. It is not unknown for a suicide to take the form of a vast nuclear explosion causing an entire disintegration of the individual. If this should have happened, then the failures to discover material traces of the individuals in these strange cases could be explained.

'In the present instance it ought to be possible for me to put this theory to a decisive test, for the incident, whatever it may be, has occurred so near by that I can reach the scene in only two or three hundred years. This is so short a time that the debris from the explosion, if there has been an explosion, should not have entirely dispersed by then.'

At the end of this message Kingsley looked round the lab.

'Now, chaps, this is probably one of our last chances to ask questions. Suppose we make a list of them. Any suggestions?'

'Well, what can have happened to these johnnies, if they

haven't committed suicide? Ask it if it's got any ideas on that,' said Leicester.

'And we'd also like to know whether it's going to leave the solar system in such a way as not to harm the Earth,' remarked Parkinson.

Marlowe nodded.

'That's right. There seem to be three possible troubles:

1. That we get a blast from one of those gas bullets when the Cloud starts to accelerate.
2. That we get mixed up with the Cloud and get our atmosphere ripped off.
3. That we get roasted by too much heat, either from too much reflection of sunlight from the surface of the Cloud, as we had in the great heat, or from the energy liberated in the acceleration process.'

'Right-ho then. Let's put these questions.'

The Cloud's reply was more reassuring over Marlowe's questions than they had expected.

'I have these points actively in mind,' it said. 'I am intending to provide a screen to protect the Earth during the early stages of the acceleration, which will be a great deal more violent than the deceleration that occurred when I came in. Without this screen you would be so severely scorched that all life on the Earth would undoubtedly be destroyed. It will, however, be necessary for the screening material to move across the Sun, the light from which will be cut off for perhaps a fortnight; but this, I imagine, will not cause any permanent harm. In the later stages of my retreat there will be a certain amount of reflected sunlight, but this extra heat will not be so great as it must have been at the time of my arrival.

'It is difficult to give an answer to your other question that would be intelligible to you in the present state of your science. Crudely expressed, it seems as if there may be inherent limitations of a physical nature to the type of information that can be exchanged between intelligences. The suspicion is that an absolute bar exists to the communication of information relating to the deep problems. It seems as if any intelligence that attempts to pass on such information gets itself swallowed up in space, that is, space closes about it in such a fashion that no communication of any sort with other individuals of a similar hierarchy is possible.'

'Do you understand that, Chris?' said Leicester.

'No, I don't. But there's another question that I want to ask.' Kingsley then asked his question:

'You will have noticed that we have made no attempt to ask for information concerning physical theories and facts that are not known to us. This omission was not due to any lack of interest, but because we felt ample opportunities would present themselves at a later stage. Now it appears that the opportunities will not present themselves. Have you any suggestions as to how we may occupy what little time remains to the best advantage?'

The answer came:

'This is a matter to which I have also given some attention. There is a crucial difficulty here. Our discussions have been carried out in your language. We have therefore been limited to ideas that can be understood in terms of your language, which is to say that we have been essentially limited to the things you know already. No rapid communication of radically new knowledge is possible unless you learn something of my language.

'This raises two points, one of practice and the other the vital issue of whether the human brain possesses an adequate neurological capacity. To the latter question I know no certain answer, but there seems to be some evidence that justifies a measure of optimism. The explanations that are usually offered to explain the incidence of men of outstanding genius seem certainly wrong. Genius is not a biological phenomenon. A child does not possess genius at birth: genius is learned. Biologists who maintain otherwise ignore the facts of their own science, namely that the human species has not been selected for genius, nor is there evidence that genius is transmitted between parent and child.

'The infrequency of genius is to be explained in simple probabilities. A child must learn a great deal before it reaches adult life. Processes such as the multiplying of numbers can be learned in a variety of ways. This is to say, the brain can develop in a number of ways, all enabling it to multiply numbers, but not all with by any means the same facility. Those who develop in a favourable way are said to be "good" at arithmetic, while those

who develop inefficient ways are said to be "bad" or "slow".
Now what decides how a particular person develops? The answer
is – chance. And chance accounts for the difference between the
genius and the dullard. The genius is one who has been lucky in
all his processes of learning. The dullard is the reverse, and the
ordinary person is one who has neither been particularly lucky
nor particularly unlucky.'

'I'm afraid I'm far too much of a dullard to understand what
it's talking about. Can anybody explain?' remarked Parkinson
during a pause in the message.

'Well, granted that learning can occur in a number of ways,
some better than others, I suppose it does reduce to a matter of
chance,' answered Kingsley. 'To take an analogy, it's rather like
a football pool. If the brain is to develop in the most efficient
manner, not only in one learning process but in a dozen or
more, well, it's like getting every match right in a penny points
pool.'

'I see. And that explains why the genius is such a rare bird, I
suppose,' exclaimed Parkinson.

'Yes, it's as rare or rarer than winners of a big pool. It also
explains why a genius can't pass his faculties to his children. Luck
isn't a commodity with a strong inheritance.'

The Cloud resumed its message:

'All this suggests that the human brain is inherently capable of
a far improved performance, provided learning is always induced
in the best way. And this is what I would propose to do. I propose
that one or more of you should attempt to learn my method of
thinking and that this be induced as profitably as possible. Quite
evidently the learning process must lie outside your language, so
that communication will have to proceed in a very different
fashion. Of your sense organs, the best suited to the receiving of
complex information is your eyes. It is true that you scarcely use
the eyes in ordinary language, but it is mainly through the eyes
that a child builds up his picture of the intricate world around
him. And it is through the eyes that I intend to open up a new
world to you.

'My requirements will be comparatively simple. I will now
describe them.'

Then followed technical details that were carefully noted by Leicester. When the Cloud had finished Leicester remarked:

'Well, this isn't going to be too difficult. A number of filter circuits and a whole bank of cathode ray tubes.'

'But how are we to get the information?' asked Marlowe.

'Well, of course primarily by radio, then through the discriminating circuits which filter different bits of the messages to the various tubes.'

'There are codes for the various filters.'

'That's right. So some sort of an ordered pattern can be put on the tubes, although it beats me as to what we shall be able to make of it.'

'We'd better get on with it. We've got little enough time,' said Kingsley.

*

During the next twenty-four hours there was a sharp improvement of morale at Nortonstowe. It was a comparatively light-hearted expectant company that assembled before the newly-built equipment on the following evening.

'Beginning to snow,' remarked Barnett.

'It looks to me as if we're in for a devil of a winter, quite apart from another fortnight of arctic night,' said Weichart.

'Any idea what this pantomime is about?'

'None at all. I can't see what we can hope to pick up by staring at these tubes.'

'Nor I.'

The Cloud's first message caused some confusion:

'It will be convenient if only one person is concerned, at any rate to begin with. Later on it may be possible for me to instruct others.'

'But I thought we were all to get a grandstand seat,' someone remarked.

'No, it's fair enough,' said Leicester. 'If you look carefully you can see that the tubes are specially orientated to suit someone sitting in this particular chair, here. We had special instructions about the seating arrangements. I don't know what it all means, but I hope we've got everything right.'

'Well, it looks as though we'll have to call for a volunteer,' Marlowe exclaimed. 'Who is for the first sitting?'

There was a long pause that almost grew into an embarrassed silence. At length Weichart moved forward.

'If everybody else is too bashful, I guess I'm willing to be first guinea pig.'

McNeil gave him a long look.

'There's just one point, Weichart. You realize that this business may carry with it an element of danger? You're quite clear on that, I suppose?'

Weichart laughed.

'Don't worry about that. This won't be the first time I've spent a few hours watching cathode ray tubes.'

'Very well, then. If you're willing to try, by all means take the chair.'

'Be careful about the chair, Dave. Maybe Harry's wired it up specially for you,' grinned Marlowe.

Shortly after this, lights began to flash on the tubes.

'Joe's starting up,' said Leicester.

Whether there was any pattern associated with the lights was difficult to tell.

'What's he saying, Dave? Getting the message?' asked Barnett.

'Nothing I can understand,' remarked Weichart, throwing a leg over his chair. 'Looks a pretty random unintelligible jumble. Still I'll keep on trying to make some sense out of it.'

Time dragged on in a desultory way. Most of the company lost interest in the flickering lights. Multi-way conversations broke out and Weichart was left to a lonely vigil. At length Marlowe asked him.

'How's it going, Dave?'

No answer.

'Hey, Dave, what's going on?'

Still no answer.

'Dave!'

Marlowe and McNeil came one to each side of Weichart's chair.

'Dave, why don't you answer?'

McNeil touched him on the shoulder, but there was still no response. They watched his eyes, fixed on first one group of tubes, then flicking quickly to another.

'What is it, John?' asked Kingsley.

'I think he's in some hypnotic state. He doesn't seem to be noticing any sense data except from the eyes, and they seem to be directed only at the tubes.'

'How could it have happened?'

'A hypnotic condition induced by visual means is not by any means unknown.'

'You think it was deliberately induced?'

'It seems more than likely. I can scarcely believe it could have happened by accident. And watch the eyes. See how they move. This is not a chance business. It looks purposive, very purposive.'

'I wouldn't have said Weichart was a likely subject for a hypnotist.'

'Nor would I. It looks extremely formidable, and very singular.'

'What do you mean?' asked Marlowe.

'Well, although an ordinary human hypnotist might use some visual method for inducing a hypnotic state, he'd never use a purely visual medium for conveying information. A hypnotist talks to a subject, he conveys meaning with words. But there are no words here. That's why it is damn strange.'

'It's funny you should have warned Dave. Had you any idea this would happen, McNeil?'

'No, not in detail, of course. But recent developments in neurophysiology have shown up some extremely queer effects when lights are flashed in the eyes at rates that match closely with scanning speeds in the brain. And then it was obvious that the Cloud couldn't do what it said it would do unless something pretty remarkable happened.'

Kingsley came up to the chair.

'Do you think we ought to do something? Pull him away, perhaps. We could easily do that.'

'I wouldn't advise it, Chris. He'd probably struggle violently and it might be dangerous. Best on the whole to leave him. He went into it with his eyes open, literally and figuratively. I'll stay with him of course. The rest of you ought to clear out, though. Leave somebody who can carry a message – Stoddard will do – and then I can call you if anything crops up.'

'All right. We'll be ready in case you need us,' agreed Kingsley.

Nobody really wanted to leave the lab, but it was realized that McNeil's suggestion had much to recommend it.

'Wouldn't do to have the whole party hypnotized,' remarked Barnett. 'I only hope old Dave will be all right,' he added anxiously.

'We could, I suppose, have switched the gear off. But McNeil seemed to think that might cause trouble. Shock, I suppose.' This from Leicester.

'It beats me as to what information Dave can be getting,' said Marlowe.

'Well, we shall know soon enough, I expect. I don't suppose the Cloud will go on for many hours. It's never done so in the past,' observed Parkinson.

But the transmission turned out to be a long one. As the hours advanced the members of the company retired severally to bed.

Marlowe expressed the general opinion:

'Well, we're not doing Dave any good, and we're missing sleep. I think I shall try to snatch an hour or two.'

Kingsley was woken by Stoddard.

'Doctor wants you, Dr Kingsley.'

Kingsley found that Stoddard and McNeil had managed to move Weichart to one of the bedrooms, so evidently the business was finished, at any rate for the time being.

'What is it, John?' he asked.

'I don't like the position, Chris. His temperature is rising rapidly. There isn't much point in your going in to see him. He's not in a coherent state, and not like to be with a temperature at 104°.'

'Have you any idea what's wrong?'

'I obviously can't be sure, because I've never encountered a case like this before. But if I didn't know what had happened, I'd have said Weichart was suffering from an inflammation of brain tissue.'

'That's very serious, isn't it?'

'Extremely so. There's very little that any of us can do for him, but I thought you'd like to know.'

'Yes, of course. Have you any idea what may have caused it?'

'Well, I'd say too high a rate of working, too great a demand of the neurological system on all the supporting tissues. But again it's only an opinion.'

Weichart's temperature continued to rise during the day, and in the late afternoon he died.

For professional reasons McNeil would have liked to perform an autopsy, but out of consideration for the feelings of the others he decided against it. He kept his own company, thinking gloomily that somehow he ought to have foreseen the tragedy and taken steps to prevent it. But he had not foreseen it, nor did he foresee the events that were to follow. The first warning came from Ann Halsey. She was in a hysterical condition when she accosted McNeil.

'John, you must do something. It's Chris. He's going to kill himself.'

'What!'

'He's going to do the same as Dave Weichart. I've been trying for hours to persuade him not to, but he won't take any notice of me. He says he's going to tell the Thing to go slower, that it was the speed that killed Dave. Is that true?'

'It might be. I don't know for sure, but it's quite possible.'

'Tell me frankly, John, is there any chance?'

'There might be. I just don't know enough to offer any definite opinion.'

'Then you must stop him!'

'I'll try. I'll go along and talk to him straight away. Where is he?'

'In the labs. Talking's no use. He'll have to be stopped by force. It's the only way.'

McNeil made straight for the transmitting lab. The door was locked, so he hammered hard on it. Kingsley's voice came faintly.

'Who is it?'

'It's McNeil. Let me in, will you?'

The door opened and McNeil saw as he stepped inside the room that the equipment was switched on.

'Ann has just been and told me, Chris. Don't you think it's just a little crazy, especially within a few hours of Weichart's death?'

'You don't suppose I like this idea, do you, John? I can assure you that I find life just as pleasant as anyone else. But it's got to be done and it's got to be done now. The chance will have gone in not much more than a week, and it's a chance that we humans simply can't afford to miss. After poor Weichart's experience it wasn't likely that anyone else would come forward, so I've got to do it myself. I'm not one of those courageous fellows who can contemplate danger placidly. If I've got a sticky job to do I prefer to get on with it straight away – saves thinking about it.'

'This is all very well, Chris, but you're not going to do anybody any good by killing yourself.'

'That's absurd, and you know it. The stakes in this business are very high, they're so high as to be worth playing for, even if the chance of winning isn't very great. That's point number one. Point number two is that maybe I stand a pretty fair chance. I've already been on to the Cloud, telling it to go much slower. It has agreed to do so. You yourself said that might avoid the worst of the trouble.'

'It might. Then again it might not. Also, if you avoid Weichart's trouble, there may be other dangers that we know nothing about.'

'Then you'll know about them from my case, which will make it easier for someone else, just as it is a little easier for me than it was for Weichart. It's no good, John. I'm quite resolved, and I'm going to start in a few more minutes.'

McNeil saw that Kingsley was beyond persuasion.

'Well, anyway,' he said, 'I take it you'll have no objection to my staying here. It took about ten hours with Weichart. With you it's going to take longer. You'll need food in order to keep a proper blood supply to your brain.'

'But I can't stop off to eat, man! Do you realize what this means? It means learning a whole new field of knowledge, learning in just one lesson!'

'I'm not suggesting that you stop off for a meal. I'm suggesting that I give you injections from time to time. Judging by Weichart's condition, you won't feel it.'

'Oh, I am not worried about that. Inject away if it makes you happy. But sorry, John, I must get down to this business.'

It is unnecessary to repeat the following events in detail, since they followed much the same pattern in Kingsley's case as they had with Weichart. The hypnotic condition lasted longer however, nearly two days. At the end he was carried to bed under McNeil's direction. During the next few hours symptoms developed that were alarmingly similar to those of Weichart. Kingsley's temperature rose to 102°...103°...104°. But then it steadied, stopped, and, as hour followed hour, fell slowly. And as it fell, the hopes rose of those round his bed, notably McNeil and Ann Halsey who never left him, and Marlowe, Parkinson, and Alexandrov.

Consciousness returned about thirty-six hours after the end of the Cloud's transmission. For some minutes an uncanny series of expressions flitted across Kingsley's face: some were well known to the watchers, others were wholly alien. The full horror of Kingsley's condition developed suddenly. It began with an uncontrolled twitching of the face, and with incoherent muttering. This quickly developed into shouting and then into wild screams.

'My God, he's in some sort of fit,' exclaimed Marlowe.

At length the attack subsided under an injection from McNeil, who thereupon insisted on being left alone with the demented man. Throughout the day the others from time to time heard muffled cries which then died away under repeated injections.

Marlowe managed to persuade Ann Halsey to take a walk with him in the afternoon. It was the most difficult walk in his experience.

In the evening he was sitting in his room gloomily when McNeil walked in, a McNeil gaunt and hollow-eyed.

'He's gone,' announced the Irishman.

'My God, what a dreadful tragedy, an unnecessary tragedy.'

'Aye, man, a bigger tragedy than you realize.'

'What d'you mean?'

'I mean it was touch and go whether he saved himself. In the afternoon he was sane for nearly an hour. He told me what the trouble was. He fought it down and as the minutes passed I thought he was going to win out. But it wasn't to be. He got into another attack and it killed him.'

'But what was it?'

'Something obvious, that we ought to have foreseen. What we

didn't allow for was the tremendous quantity of new material which the Cloud seems able to impress on the brain. This of course means that there must be widespread changes of the structure of a mass of electrical circuits in the brain, changes of synaptic resistances on a big scale, and so on.'

'You mean it was a sort of gigantic brain-washing?'

'No, it wasn't. That's just the point. There was no washing. The old methods of operation of the brain were not washed out. They were left unimpaired. The new was established alongside the old, so that both were capable of working simultaneously.'

'You mean that it was as if my knowledge of science were suddenly added to the brain of an ancient Greek.'

'Yes, but perhaps in a more extreme form. Can you imagine the fierce contradictions that would arise in the brain of your poor Greek, accustomed to such notions as the Earth being the centre of the Universe and a hundred and one other such anachronisms, suddenly becoming exposed to the blast of your superior knowledge?'

'I suppose it would be pretty bad. After all we get quite seriously upset if just one of our cherished scientific ideas turns out wrong.'

'Yes, think of a religious person who suddenly loses faith, which means of course that he becomes aware of a contradiction between his religious and his non-religious beliefs. Such a person often experiences a severe nervous crisis. And Kingsley's case was a thousand times worse. He was killed by the sheer violence of his nervous activity, in a popular phrase by a series of unimaginably fierce brain-storms.'

'But you said he nearly got over it.'

'That's right, he did. He realized what the trouble was and evolved some sort of plan for dealing with it. Probably he decided to accept as rule that the new should always supersede the old whenever there was trouble between them. I watched him for a whole hour systematically going through his ideas along some such lines. As the minutes ticked on I thought the battle was won. Then it happened. Perhaps it was some unexpected conjunction of thought patterns that took him unaware. At first the disturbance seemed small, but then it began to grow. He tried desperately to fight it down. But evidently it gained the upper hand –

and that was the end. He died under the sedative I was forced to give him. I think it was a kind of chain reaction in his thoughts that got out of control.'

'Will you have a whisky? I ought to have asked before.'

'Aye, I think now I will, thank you.'

As Marlowe handed over a glass, he said:

'Don't you think Kingsley was a bad choice for this business? Wouldn't someone of a far slighter intellectual calibre have really been more suitable? If it was contradictions between the old knowledge and the new that destroyed him, then surely someone with very little old knowledge would have done better?'

McNeil looked over his glass.

'It's funny, it's funny you should say that. During one of his later sane spells Kingsley remarked – I'll try to remember his exact words – "The height of irony," he said, "is that I should experience this singular disaster, while someone like Joe Stoddard would have been quite all right." '

CONCLUSION

'AND now, my dear Blythe, I can again adopt a more personal style. Since your mother was born in the year 1966 and since the name of your maternal grandmother was Halsey, it will be clear that I have had reasons other than your interest in the Black Cloud for arranging that these documents be sent to you on the occasion of my death.

'Little more remains to be told. The Sun reappeared in the early spring of 1966, which was bitterly cold. But as the Cloud moved outwards from the Sun it took up such a shape as to reflect in the Earth's direction a small proportion of the solar energy incident on it. This gave warm summer weather early in the month of May, which everyone found exceedingly welcome after the biting winter and spring. So the Cloud departed from the solar system. And so the episode of the Black Cloud, as it was ordinarily understood, came to an end.

'After Kingsley's death, and after the departure of the Cloud, it would have been unrealistic for those of us who remained at Nortonstowe to have attempted to follow our former tactics. Instead Parkinson went to London and claimed that the retreat of the Cloud was in a large measure due to our good offices. This was not at all difficult to maintain, because the real reason for the Cloud's departure never occurred to anyone outside Nortonstowe. I have always deplored that Parkinson saw fit to malign poor Kingsley most reprehensibly, by representing him as a hothead who had at last been deposed by force. This also was believed, since for some reason Kingsley was regarded in London and elsewhere as a thoroughly malevolent person. Kingsley's death added further colour to this story. In short, Parkinson was able to persuade the British Government to take no action against its own nationals and to resist deportation orders for the others. Repeated attempts at deportation were in fact made, but as national affairs stabilized themselves and as Parkinson gained increasing influence in Government circles it became progressively easier to resist them.

'Marlowe, Alexandrov, and the rest, except Leicester, all

stayed on in Britain. Their names may be found in the learned journals, especially that of Alexandrov who achieved great distinction in scientific circles, although his career in other directions was, I believe, a somewhat stormy one. Leicester, as I say, did not remain. Against Parkinson's advice he insisted on returning to his native Australia. He never reached Australia, being reported missing at sea. Marlowe remained on terms of close friendship with both Parkinson and myself until his death in 1981.

'All this is fifty odd years in the past. A new generation now holds the stage. My own generation has already slipped into the shadows of this pageant we call "life". Yet I can still see them all so clearly: Weichart, young, clever, with a character scarcely formed; the gentle Marlowe for ever puffing away at his execrable tobacco; Leicester, droll and gay; Kingsley, brilliant, unconventional, full of words; Alexandrov with his shock of hair, brilliant too and with hardly any words. It was an uncertain generation, not quite knowing where it was going. In a sense it was an heroic generation, linked imperishably in my mind with the opening chords of the great sonata that your grandmother played on that memorable night when Kingsley first divined the real nature of the Black Cloud.

'And so I reach an end, apparently in anticlimax, but not really so. I have one surprise left. The code! Originally only Kingsley and Leicester had access to the code whereby communication with the Cloud could be established. Marlowe and Parkinson believed that the code died with Kingsley and Leicester, but it did not. I acquired it from Kingsley during his last spell of sanity. I have kept it by me all these years, never knowing whether I should reveal its existence or not. This problem I am now handing on to you.

> I send you my best wishes,
>> For the last time,
>>> JOHN McNEIL'

EPILOGUE

I<small>T</small> was a cold day with driving rain, much the same sort of January day that Kingsley had experienced so many years ago, when I first read McNeil's astonishing account of the Black Cloud. All afternoon and evening I sat before an open fire in my rooms in Queens' College. After the conclusion, a conclusion reached in sadness, for McNeil had left us a few days earlier with the irrevocable permanency that only death can bring, I unsealed the last remaining packet. Inside was a small metal box that contained a roll of paper tape, yellowed by age. Punched in the paper were ten thousand or more tiny holes of the sort used by old-fashioned photo-electric readers. This was the code! With a flick I could have sent the paper into the fire, and in a brief second all possibility of any further communication with the Cloud would have been gone for ever.

But this is not what I did. Instead I have had a thousand odd copies of the code made up. Should I distribute them throughout the world, in which event nothing can prevent someone, somewhere, sooner or later, getting into touch with the Cloud again? Do we want to remain big people in a tiny world or to become a little people in a vaster world? This is the ultimate climax towards which I have directed my narrative.

J. B.
17 January 2021

MORE ABOUT PENGUINS

Penguinews, which appears every month, contains details of all the new books issued by Penguins as they are published. From time to time it is supplemented by *Penguins in Print*, which is a complete list of all books published by Penguins which are in print. (There are well over three thousand of these.)

A specimen copy of *Penguinews* will be sent to you free on request, and you can become a subscriber for the price of the postage – 30p for a year's issues (including the complete lists) if you live in the United Kingdom, or 60p if you live elsewhere. Just write to Dept EP, Penguin Books Ltd, Harmondsworth, Middlesex, enclosing a cheque or postal order, and your name will be added to the mailing list.

Some other books by Fred Hoyle in Penguins are described on the following pages.

Note: *Penguinews* and *Penguins in Print* are not available in the U.S.A. or Canada

OCTOBER THE FIRST IS TOO LATE

Fred Hoyle

'There's one thing quite certain in this business: the idea of time as a steady progression from past to future is wrong.' Once you accept that, you can accommodate the thought that, in 1966, the First World War is still being waged. You can see it's possible to meet the ancient Greeks. With Fred Hoyle pushing behind you, you can climb centuries in the future.

For that's the way of Mr Hoyle's world, where a man can be young and old at the same time. Where, in Britain, it's 1966, in America it's 1750, in France it's 1917. Where a man given the time of his life must settle, at last, for life in his time.

Also available:

FIFTH PLANET
by Fred and Geoffrey Hoyle

NOT FOR SALE IN THE U.S.A.

THE NATURE OF THE UNIVERSE

Fred Hoyle

Moving into the foothills of space travel, we naturally ask if it will really be possible to visit other planets. And can life, as we know it, exist elsewhere in the universe? Or again is Earth, in the face of such monstrosities as the hydrogen bomb, a good risk?

In this revised series of broadcast lectures a Professor of Astronomy at Cambridge gives a lucid outline of our present knowledge about heaven and earth. In doing so he not only answers many anxious questions: he also constructs from observable facts a sober and credible image of an expanding universe which, with its continuous creation of endless wheeling systems, makes the most inspired speculations of poetry and mysticism look pallid.

'No one has expounded the physical cosmos so well since Jeans and Eddington' – *Sunday Times*

'Swift, vigorous and original in matter and in manner' – J. Bronowski in the *Observer*